MODERN IRISH LOVE STORIES

MODERN IRISH LOVE STORIES

edited by

DAVID MARCUS

A PAN ORIGINAL

PAN BOOKS LTD : LONDON

This collection first published 1974 by Pan Books Ltd,
33 Tothill Street, London SW1

ISBN 0 330 23895 7

Made and printed in Great Britain by
Cox & Wyman Ltd, London, Reading and Fakenham

Acknowledgements

For permission to reprint stories in this anthology the following acknowledgements are due:

To the Bodley Head for 'The Ballroom of Romance' from the collection of that name by William Trevor.

To Faber and Faber Ltd, for 'My Love, My Umbrella' from *Nightlines* by John McGahern and for 'A Pot of Soothing Herbs' from *We Might See Sights* by Julia O'Faolain.

To Methuen & Co Ltd, for 'Ten Pretty Girls' from *A Journey to the Seven Streams* by Benedict Kiely.

To MacGibbon & Kee Ltd, for 'Interlude' from *All Looks Yellow to the Jaundiced Eye* by Patrick Boyle.

To the Executors of the James Joyce Estate, for 'The Boarding House' from *Dubliners* by James Joyce (Jonathan Cape Ltd).

To A. D. Peters & Co, for 'The Eagles and the Trumpets' from *The Trusting and the Maimed* (Hutchinson) by James Plunkett; for 'Don Juan's Temptation' from *The Stories of Frank O'Connor* (Hamish Hamilton); and for 'The Sinner' from *The Short Stories of Liam O'Flaherty* (Jonathan Cape Ltd).

To Macmillan & Co Ltd, for 'The Cat and the Cornfield' from *The Red Petticoat and Other Stories* by Bryan MacMahon.

To Jonathan Cape Ltd, and Atlantic-Little, Brown & Co, for 'A Dead Cert' from *The Talking Trees* by Sean O'Faolain © 1968 by Sean O'Faolain.

To Constable & Co Ltd, for 'In a Café' from *The Stories of Mary Lavin*.

To *Threshold* for 'The White Flower' by Hugh Bredin.

To *The Irish Press* for 'Henry Died' by Kate Cruise-O'Brien, 'Virginibus Puerisque' by Ita Daly, and 'Faretheewell' by Fred Johnston from their 'New Irish Writing' series where these stories first appeared.

Contents

Introduction

It is typically Irish that the best-known work of Gaelic literature should be a poem which is all about love yet is not a love-poem. *The Midnight Court*, written in the eighteenth century, is an extended (over 1,000 lines) jeremiad castigating the men of Ireland for their stubborn reluctance to enter the matrimonial state. Such a theme might suggest that *The Midnight Court* was not really about love at all so much as about some current lack of libido or character-defect in the Irish male. But libido and passion were never (except in legend) significant characteristics of Irish love-life which was generally a grey and sparkless affair arranged as a deal by the matchmaker and concluded in an indissoluble contract by the priest. This was understandable enough in a predominantly rural and Catholic society but it left precious little chance for pre-marital love (i.e. romance), and – as the sacramental nature of the marriage bond was universally respected – even less chance for extra-marital love. All that remained was post-marital love, and the prevailing view of woman as a work-horse, cook, and procreative punch-bag took care of that. The Latins have been tagged as lousy lovers – but at least they display an amorousness that, up to recently anyway, would have frozen the average Irishman with fear or embarrassment – or both.

Thus it was that before the 1960's the majority of the short stories dealing with love in the Irish context concerned themselves with the broadly social obstacles and prohibitions that loomed largest – poverty, the frustrations and harsh discouragements of a rural environment and the strictures and scarifications of religion and the clergy. Since then, however, with the spread of the so-called 'permissive age' and the relaxation of both the Irish Censorship Laws and Irish censoriousness, the short-story writers have been able to explore their theme on a more intimate, dilemmatic level, treating love as a special experience beset by general difficulties rather than as a general experience beset by special difficulties. This does not mean that today's writers no longer respond to or evoke response from the sort of situation that was typical of the years preceding and following the Second World War – indeed William Trevor's 'The Ballroom of Romance' is a definitive study of Irish love in that empty era; but since the awkwardnesses of love that increasingly inform their work are constitutional rather than institutional, the modern Irish love story has taken on a new freshness and immediacy along with a welcome measure of subtlety.

All of its virtues – early and late – are, I hope, reflected in this anthology which ranges from the work of James Joyce to that of writers still in their early twenties.

David Marcus

James Joyce

THE BOARDING HOUSE

Mrs Mooney was a butcher's daughter. She was a woman who was quite able to keep things to herself: a determined woman. She had married her father's foreman, and opened a butcher's shop near Spring Gardens. But as soon as his father-in-law was dead Mr Mooney began to go to the devil. He drank, plundered the till, ran headlong into debt. It was no use making him take the pledge: he was sure to break out again a few days after. By fighting his wife in the presence of customers and by buying bad meat he ruined his business. One night he went for his wife with the cleaver, and she had to sleep in a neighbour's house.

After that they lived apart. She went to the priest and got a separation from him, with care of the children. She would give him neither money nor food nor house-room; and so he was obliged to enlist himself as a sheriff's man. He was a shabby stooped little drunkard with a white face and a white moustache and white eyebrows, pencilled above his little eyes, which were pink-veined and raw; and all day long he sat in the bailiff's room, waiting to be put on a job. Mrs Mooney, who had taken what remained of her money out of the butcher business and set up a boarding house in Hardwicke Street, was a big imposing woman. Her house had a floating population made up of tourists from Liverpool and the Isle of Man and, occasionally, *artistes* from the music halls. Its resident population was made up of clerks from the city. She governed the house cunningly and firmly, knew when to give credit, when to be stern and when to let things pass. All the resident young men spoke of her as *The Madam.*

Mrs Mooney's young men paid fifteen shillings a week for board and lodgings (beer or stout at dinner excluded). They shared in common tastes and occupations and for this reason they were very chummy with one another. They discussed with one another the chances of favourites and outsiders. Jack Mooney, the Madam's son, who was clerk to a commission agent in Fleet Street, had the reputation of being a hard case. He was fond of using soldiers' obscenities: usually he came home in the small hours. When he met his friends he had always a good one to tell them, and he was always sure to be on to a good thing – that is to say, a likely horse or a likely *artiste*. He was also handy with the mits and sang comic songs. On Sunday nights there would often be a reunion in Mrs Mooney's front drawing-room. The music-hall *artistes* would oblige; and Sheridan played waltzes and polkas and vamped accompaniments. Polly Mooney, the Madam's daughter, would also sing. She sang:

I'm a ... naughty girl
You needn't sham:
You know I am.

Polly was a slim girl of nineteen; she had light soft hair and a small full mouth. Her eyes, which were grey with a shade of green through them, had a habit of glancing upwards when she spoke with anyone, which made her look like a little perverse madonna. Mrs Mooney had first sent her daughter to be a typist in a corn-factor's office, but as a disreputable sheriff's man used to come every other day to the office, asking to be allowed to say a word to his daughter, she had taken her daughter home again and set her to do housework. As Polly was very lively, the intention was to give her the run of the young men. Besides, young men like to feel that there is a young woman not very far away. Polly, of course, flirted with the young men, but Mrs Mooney, who was a shrewd judge, knew that the young men were only passing the time away: none of them meant business. Things went on so for a long time, and Mrs Mooney began to think of sending Polly back to typewriting, when she noticed that something was going on between Polly and one of the young men. She watched the pair and kept her own counsel.

Polly knew that she was being watched, but still her mother's persistent silence could not be misunderstood. There had been no open complicity between mother and daughter, no open understanding, but though people in the house began to talk of the affair, still Mrs Mooney did not intervene. Polly began to grow a little strange in her manner, and the young man was evidently perturbed. At last, when she judged it to be the right moment, Mrs Mooney intervened. She dealt with moral problems as a cleaver deals with meat: and in this case she had made up her mind.

It was a bright Sunday morning of early summer, promising heat, but with a fresh breeze blowing. All the windows of the boarding house were open and the lace curtains ballooned gently towards the street beneath the raised sashes. The belfry of George's Church sent out constant peals, and worshippers, singly or in groups, traversed the little circus before the church, revealing their purpose by their self-contained demeanour no less than by the little volumes in their gloved hands. Breakfast was over in the boarding house, and the table of the breakfast-room was covered with plates on which lay yellow streaks of eggs with morsels of bacon-fat and bacon-rind. Mrs Mooney sat in the straw arm-chair and watched the servant Mary remove the breakfast things. She made Mary collect the crusts and pieces of broken bread to help to make Tuesday's bread-pudding. When the table was cleared, the broken bread collected, the sugar and butter safe under lock and key, she began to reconstruct the interview which she had had the night before with Polly. Things were as she had suspected: she had been frank in her questions and Polly had been frank in her answers. Both had been somewhat awkward, of course. She had been made awkward by her not wishing to receive the news in too cavalier a fashion or to seem to have connived, and Polly had been made awkward not merely because allusions of that kind always made her awkward, but also because she did not wish it to be thought that in her wise innocence she had divined the intention behind her mother's tolerance.

Mrs Mooney glanced instinctively at the little gilt clock on the mantelpiece as soon as she had become aware through her reverie that the bells of George's Church had stopped ringing. It was seventeen minutes past eleven: she would have lots of time to have the matter out with Mr Doran and then catch short twelve at Marlborough Street. She was sure she would win. To begin with, she had all the weight of social opinion on her side: she was an outraged mother. She had allowed him to live beneath her roof, assuming that he was a man of honour, and he had simply abused her hospitality. He was thirty-four or thirty-five years of age, so that youth could not be pleaded as his excuse; nor could ignorance be his excuse, since he was a man who had seen something of the world. He had simply taken advantage of Polly's youth and inexperience: that was evident. The question was: What reparation would he make?

There must be reparation made in such a case. It is all very well for the man: he can go his ways as if nothing had happened, having had his moment of pleasure, but the girl has to bear the brunt. Some mothers would be content to patch up such an affair for a sum of money: she had known cases of it. But she would not do so. For her only one reparation could make up for the loss of her daughter's honour: marriage.

She counted all her cards again before sending Mary up to Mr Doran's room to say that she wished to speak with him. She felt sure she would win. He was a serious young man, not rakish or loud-voiced like the others. If it had been Mr Sheridan or Mr Meade or Bantam Lyons, her task would have been much harder. She did not think he would face publicity. All the lodgers in the house knew something of the affair; details had been invented by some. Besides, he had been employed for thirteen years in a great Catholic wine-merchant's office, and publicity would mean for him, perhaps, the loss of his job. Whereas if he agreed all might be well. She knew he had a good screw for one thing, and she suspected he had a bit of stuff put by.

Nearly the half-hour! She stood up and surveyed herself in the pier-glass. The decisive expression of her great florid face satisfied her, and she thought of some mothers she knew who could not get their daughters off their hands.

Mr Doran was very anxious indeed this Sunday morning. He had made two attempts to shave, but his hand had been so unsteady that he had been obliged to desist. Three days' reddish beard fringed his jaws, and every two or three minutes a mist gathered on his glasses so that he had to take them off and polish them with his pocket-handkerchief. The recollection of his confession of the night before was a cause of acute pain to him; the priest had drawn out every ridiculous detail of the affair, and in the end had so magnified his sin that he was almost thankful at being afforded a loophole of reparation. The harm was done. What could he do now but marry her or run away? He could not brazen it out. The affair would be sure to be talked of, and his employer would be certain to hear of it. Dublin is such a small city: everyone knows everyone else's business. He felt his heart leap warmly in his throat as he heard in his excited imagination old Mr Leonard calling out in his rasping voice: 'Send Mr Doran here, please.'

All his long years of service gone for nothing! All his industry and diligence thrown away! As a young man he had sown his wild oats, of course; he had boasted of his freethinking and denied the existence of God to his companions in public-houses. But that was all passed and done with . . . nearly. He still bought a copy of *Reynolds Newspaper* every week, but he attended to his religious duties, and for nine-tenths of the year lived a regular life. He had money enough to settle down on; it was not that. But the family would look down on her. First of all there was her disreputable father, and then her mother's boarding house was beginning to get a certain fame. He had a notion that he was being had. He could imagine his friends talking of the affair and laughing. She *was* a little vulgar; sometimes she said 'I seen' and 'If I had've known.' But what would grammar matter if he really loved her? He could not make up his mind whether to like her or despise her for what she had done. Of course he had done it too. His instinct urged him to remain free, not to marry. Once you are married you are done for, it said.

While he was sitting helplessly on the side of the bed in shirt and trousers, she tapped lightly at his door and entered. She told him all, that she had made a clean breast of it to her mother and that her mother would speak with him that morning. She cried and threw her arms round his neck, saying:

'O Bob! Bob! What am I to do? What am I to do at all?'

She would put an end to herself, she said.

He comforted her feebly, telling her not to cry, that it would be all right, never fear. He felt against his shirt the agitation of her bosom.

It was not altogether his fault that it had happened. He remembered well, with the curious patient memory of the celibate, the first casual caresses her dress, her breath, her fingers had given him. Then late one night as he was undressing for bed she had tapped at his door, timidly. She wanted to relight her candle at his, for hers had been blown out by a gust. It was her bath night. She wore a loose open combing-jacket of printed flannel. Her white instep shone in the opening of her furry slippers and the blood glowed warmly behind her perfumed skin. From her hands and wrists too as she lit and steadied her candle a faint perfume arose.

On nights when he came in very late it was she who warmed up his dinner. He scarcely knew what he was eating, feeling her beside him alone, at night, in the sleeping house. And her thoughtfulness! If the night was anyway cold or wet or windy there was sure to be a little tumbler of punch ready for him. Perhaps they could be happy together...

They used to go upstairs together on tiptoe, each with a candle, and on the third landing exchange reluctant good nights. They used to kiss. He remembered well her eyes, the touch of her hand and his delirium...

But delirium passes. He echoed her phrase, applying it to himself: *'What am I to do?'* The instinct of the celibate warned him to hold back. But the sin was there; even his sense of honour told him that reparation must be made for such a sin.

While he was sitting with her on the side of the bed Mary came to the door and said that the missus wanted to see him in the parlour. He stood up to put on his coat and waistcoat, more helpless than ever. When he was dressed he went over to her to comfort her. It would be all right, never fear. He left her crying on the bed and moaning softly: *'O my God!'*

Going down the stairs his glasses became so dimmed with moisture that he had to take them off and polish them. He longed to ascend through the roof and fly away to another country where he would never hear again of his trouble, and yet a force pushed him downstairs step by step. The implacable faces of his employer and of the Madam stared upon his discomfiture. On the last flight of stairs he passed Jack Mooney, who was coming up from the pantry nursing two bottles of *Bass.* They saluted coldly; and the lover's eyes rested for a second or two on a thick bulldog face and a pair of thick short arms. When he reached the foot of the staircase he glanced up and saw Jack regarding him from the door of the return-room.

Suddenly he remembered the night when one of the music-hall *artistes,* a little blond Londoner, had made a rather free allusion to Polly. The reunion had been almost broken up on account of Jack's violence. Everyone tried to quiet him. The music-hall *artiste,* a little paler than usual, kept smiling and saying that there was no harm meant; but Jack kept shouting at him that if any fellow tried that sort of a game on with his sister he'd bloody well put his teeth down his throat: so he would.

Polly sat for a little time on the side of the bed, crying. Then she dried her eyes and went over to the looking-glass. She dipped the end of the towel in the water-jug and refreshed her eyes with the cool water. She looked at herself in profile and readjusted a hairpin above her ear. Then she went back to the bed again and sat at the foot. She regarded the pillows for a long time, and the sight of them awakened in her mind secret, amiable memories. She rested the nape of her neck against the cool iron bedrail and fell into a reverie. There was no longer any perturbation visible on her face.

She waited on patiently, almost cheerfully, without alarm, her memories gradually giving place to hopes and visions of the future. Her hopes and visions were so intricate that she no longer saw the white pillows on which her gaze was fixed, or remembered that she was waiting for anything.

At last she heard her mother calling. She started to her feet and ran to the banisters.

'Polly! Polly!'

'Yes, mamma?'

'Come down, dear. Mr Doran wants to speak to you.'

Then she remembered what she had been waiting for.

Liam O'Flaherty

THE SINNER

Julia Rogers lay in bed waiting for her husband to come home. It was long past midnight. The candle at her bedside had guttered out. In the cup of the candlestick the black wick still floated in the warm melted tallow and from the brim of the cup long congealed strings were hanging like stalactites. Books were strewn on the bed. She had been trying to read novels. Now she was propped against the pillows, nervously toying with the figure of a little dove that was wrought in lace on the bosom of her nightgown.

She had a little round face, quite plump, with a slightly darkened upper lip, which gave the impression of a faint moustache. It was, however, devoid of hair. The lip curved upwards and the nose was rather broad at the tip, thus darkening the intervening space, which was unusually short by reason of the lady's excellent breeding. This short, dark, deep, space between mouth and nose gave a peculiar charm to her face in the eyes of a person of taste. Her black eyes and her closely cropped black hair, which had begun to have a greyish tint above the ears, added to this charm. And had her expression been passionate, aggressive and sensual, her face was one that would excite any man to an excess of emotion. But her expression was that of an exceedingly refined woman, thoughtful, reserved and gentle.

Alone in bed, however, the most refined woman exposes her charms in such a manner that the greatest severity of mind is not proof against a suggestion of amorousness. The plump shoulders, covered merely by a slight band, the voluptuous shapes of the white breasts heaving against the laced rim of the nightgown at each soft breath and the plump curves of the body half concealed by the disordered bedclothes gave her a disturbing attractiveness which was increased, not diminished, by the nunnish modesty of her expression.

She was thinking of her husband, with a desire of which she felt ashamed and which alarmed her. She had been married six months to him, but as yet they were almost entirely unknown to one another. She was twenty-eight when she married him, a virgin and entirely ignorant of even the most harmless flirtation. The daughter of an eminent scholar, she had been reared in that curious intellectual environment which, in Dublin, is even more remote from actual life than in other University towns. Brought into contact with minds that treated almost every idea and fact with the most calm intellectual complacency, her body had never felt any inclination towards those pleasures of the senses, which women with puritanical training feel with such force. With an almost unmoral mind she developed the physical instincts of a nun. When her father died and she was free to marry, she deliberately chose this hulking fellow Harry Rogers, known as Buster Rogers among his boon companions. He was a famous footballer, an athlete, and a splendid animal. She chose him for that reason, from among the others who offered themselves for the sake of the fortune which she inherited. This choice was due to the cult now in vogue, presumably as the result of our realist literature; the worship of raw nature.

They had never kissed before they married; except one timorous kiss she gave him on the night he proposed to her. They married and she felt an extraordinary revulsion when confronted with the necessity of abandoning herself to him. He appeared so crude, so like an animal. He was a passionate fellow and the reality of passion appeared brutal to her. He, on the other hand, having married her for her money and the social position of her family, pursued her no further after the failure of his first few clumsy approaches. He returned to his other women and to his boon companions. He did not understand her delicacy and he was not subtle enough to awaken the woman in her. He found her insipid.

Women of her acquaintance, as is customary in Dublin, began to bring her tales of Buster's immoderate conduct. In order to save herself from the contempt of her friends, she persuaded her husband to leave the flat in town and take a bungalow in the mountains. Here matters were even worse. Buster had some sort of a Government position; one of those sinecures that are found for stupid and famous athletes by their admirers. Every morning he left home in his car and returned very late. On Saturday night there was always a celebration and Buster returned home very drunk, usually in a maudlin state. Being a fervent Catholic, he became morbidly repentant in that state. If he had started some fresh amorous adventure or grown tired of an old one, there was always a terrible reaction on these occasions. He cursed, threw things about, called on God to strike him dead for his sins and ended up, sometimes, by rolling over and over on the sitting-room floor, in a state of violent hysteria.

Julia grew desperately lonely. The local doctor, an educated and refined man, was her only consolation. By means of the doctor she tried to make her husband jealous. It was no use. He remained good humoured and inattentive. Every night he peeped into her room, through the door which she always left slightly ajar, said goodnight in a laughing voice and then retired to his own room. On Saturday nights he slept on the couch in the sitting-room, snoring loudly and muttering in his sleep.

It was very desolating. And Julia had begun to feel that horrible desire for him. How she hated those women! Even the doctor, with his little moustache and his Russian manner of bowing, was of no avail against the extraordinary sensation of being close to this brute of an athlete; possessing him and yet not knowing him.

All this she thought as she lay in bed. And she thought of something else too; something that terrified her even more than her longing for her husband. She was not *quite* sure, but if anything really *did* happen it would be *too* awful.

God! It was impossible to sleep or to lie still. She tossed nervously on her bed, casting off her clothes.

It was a warm June night. The large window was thrown open, admitting the sensuous fragrance of the night through the slightly swaying net curtains. Of an orange colour the curtains cast the inflowing moonlight in fairy patterns of many hues on the furniture, on the gaily clothed bed, on Julia's seductively disordered figure. Through the pores of the curtains, the starry blue sky and the mountains seemed to look upon her, longing for her in silence; watching her. The slight breeze was like a whisper beckoning her to some mysterious amorous embrace. The soft warmth of the night and the voluptuous contours of the moonlit heights suggested to her mind the idea of passionate young fairies being out there, thousands of loving fairy couples, lying close together on a bed of moss or heather, lifting their fairy love songs to the moon.

She became terribly ashamed at this and covered her face with her hands. Her cheeks were burning. Then she became afraid. She looked at her watch. It was one o'clock. She became more and more nervous, listened for every sound and started violently when a dog barked in the distance.

At last she jumped out of bed and rang the bell for her servant, rang it violently, before she realized what she had done. A moment later she would have given a fortune not to have rung it. She returned to her bed and pulled the clothes over her head. She waited, panting, hoping the servant was sound asleep. What seemed a long time passed and then she heard a door open. Somebody came shuffling along. It was the servant. There was a knock at the door.

'Come in, Sally,' she said.

A stout woman of middle age came into the room, wearing a night-cap and a voluminous night-dress, which, however, did not altogether conceal her figure. She had a rosy face, heavy jaws and merry blue eyes. Her mouth hung open, after the manner of strong-bodied, strong-willed people; people who feel there is no necessity for them to add to the stern power of their jaws by presenting a tight and often deceptive lip to the world. An enormous woman, in fact.

'Oh! Sally,' said Julia, 'I'm awfully sorry. I had a sort of nightmare. I had rung my bell before I knew what I was doing.'

Sally put her candle on the bedside table slowly.

'A nightmare, is it?' she grumbled, still sour on account of her disturbed sleep. 'I was just droppin' off. A book I was readin'.' She shrugged herself. 'A nightmare, did ye say?'

'Do go back to bed, Sally,' said Julia, tapping the woman on the arm gently. 'Forgive me. There's a dear. It's nothing at all. I'm awfully sorry. Go to bed again.'

'A nightmare, did ye say?' said Sally again, sitting on a chair and folding her arms. 'What was it about?'

Julia flushed. Sally was wide awake now and looking at her mistress in the peculiarly bold and cunning manner of an old servant looking at a young mistress of whom she is fond, when there is 'something wrong' in the house.

Julia made no answer. Instead she lost her dignity and pouted:

'I wish you'd go to bed, Sally.'

'Himself not home yet?' said Sally.

'No.'

Sally made a sound as if she were tasting something.

'That's a nice way to be,' she grumbled. 'I was twenty years with yer mother, so I was, Lord have mercy on her. That was a happy home, so it was.'

Julia suddenly burst into tears.

'Yer not feelin' well?' said Sally.

There was no reply.

'Will I send word to Dr Richards in the morning?'

'No, don't. I don't want a doctor. I just feel lonely.'

'No wonder then. He's no great shakes anyway. I don't like that young man at all. So I don't. They don't forget what they hear and what they don't hear they make up. When my old man was alive, God rest his soul, the divil a one he'd let ...'

'What are you talking about?' said Julia sternly.

'And what would you be losing your temper with me for?'

said Sally champing her jaws. 'Prut! Wasn't I twenty years with yer mother? "Look after her, Sally," says she to me on her dying bed. God rest your father, he was a learned man, but soft, very soft.'

'Oh! Don't talk about these things,' said Julia.

Then she broke down again and said,

'Oh! Sally, I feel so miserable.'

'Ha! Ha!' said Sally, fondling her fat arms. 'It's a long time now since I said to meself, "I must step in here an' say a few words." But they say that a wise daughter gets her teeth slowly and a wise woman takes long thought before she speaks. Not that I didn't notice things as they were. This penny boy of a doctor comin' an' goin', leavin' his umbrella in the hall, with little gadgets on it. More a woman than a man. Then himself playin' the rake. It's clear, says I to meself. But there's no use speakin' before it's time. I had a man meself so I had, Lord have mercy on his immortal soul.'

'But what am I to do?' sobbed Julia. 'I've done my best.'

'Prut!' said Sally. 'Anybody could see through that penny boy. He's not going to get jealous of HIM.'

Julia got very tired. Then a cunning look came into her eyes. The eyes of the two women met. Nothing could be more subtle than that meeting of two pair of feminine eyes. Julia's eyes hated the other eyes. Then the older woman sighed and dropped her eyes. Julia's dark upper lip trembled and she looked exceedingly pretty, just like a cat that is purring, not with pleasure, but in order to hide her spleen.

'You must beat him', whispered Sally. 'That's all there's to it.'

Julia's eyes glistened.

'Yes, beat him', continued Sally. 'I used to beat my old man, nearly every week. He was a gay one too. But he didn't roll on the floor. The crockery he went after. I beat him regular till he died, Lord have mercy on him. Yes, beat him. He's that kind of a man. They respect ye for it. Catch him on the hop and lay on to him. Give it to him as hard as ye can. Wallop him till he cries. He'll cry like a child. I'll stand by ye. And if that doesn't settle him take him into the courts. Otherwise that penny boy of a doctor 'll be the ruination of ye.'

Julia said nothing. She had a look in her eyes, as a cornered cat, beset by dogs, throws her claws into the air and spits. A gentle, purring, pussy cat.

Sally got excited and described in minute detail the proper method of beating a husband. She made minute plans and silenced every attempt at resistance from Julia by stamping her foot and saying 'Prut!' with her fat lips.

They were still talking when Buster drove up to the door in his car.

'Now for it', said Sally. 'Put on yer dressing-gown and wait here.'

She forced Julia out of bed and into her dressing-gown. They listened. They heard Buster put the car into the garage. Then the hall door opened and they heard Buster stagger into the hall.

'Holy Moses', he kept saying in a hoarse voice, 'where am I?'

He went into the sitting-room and pushed things about for some time. He cracked several matches. Then he kicked something with his foot violently. Then he became very still. Then he began to talk, first in a low voice that gradually became a growl and finally became a series of protracted roars.

'Leave me alone', he began. 'I'll sink with the ship. I'm a sinner. I'm damned. A damned sinner. It ain't my fault. I push my weight. But ... but ... They won't let me alone. They won't let me alone. I've done it again. Again and again and again. Away with it, boys. Away away, away.'

'Now's yer time', said Sally pushing Julia out into the hallway.

Julia allowed herself to be pushed to the hall-stand. She accepted the ashplant that was thrust into her hand.

'It's not strong', whispered Sally, 'but if ye break it, I'll be behind ye with this brassie. This should finish him if he offers to hit back. But ye must do it yerself. Otherwise ... Go ahead now. He's in the tantrums all right.'

Sally had picked up a brassie from Julia's golf bag that hung on a peg of the hall mirror, when Buster fell to the floor with a loud thud that slightly shook the wooden bungalow. Then his heels tapped on the carpet like the drumsticks of a drummer boy beating a drum.

'Now's the time,' whispered Sally, pushing Julia in front of her. 'Don't hit him on the head though unless he gets vicious. Don't disfigure him. Aim for his back. They hate it most. Makes 'em feel like children.'

They entered the sitting-room through the open door. There was Buster sprawling on the floor, still kicking, clawing the carpet and roaring something that was entirely unintelligible.

He had failed to light the lamp, but he had taken off the shade and flung it on the floor where it remained, smashed into bits. The room, however, was quite light, as a brilliant moonlight streamed in through the two large windows. Buster was wearing evening dress. The moonlight played on his golden curly hair, making it sparkle. The moonlight also gleamed along his back, turning the black a slightly greenish colour. He was quite long in body, but so well built that he appeared plump and round. He had a splendid figure, very masculine and suggestive of great power, a man like a rock, solid, vigorous, as vital as a young stallion.

When he heard the women enter the room, he let go the head of a tiger he had been gripping with his teeth. He turned his face towards them. It was a stupid face, but exciting physically. It was the kind of face that makes women shiver and say to themselves, 'What a brute!' But when approached by the brute they feel a curious lassitude that causes their faces to become wreathed with smiles and their hearts to beat more rapidly. The languor of their bodies belies the angry denial of their words and they fall, half in ecstasy, half in hatred.

Buster raised his head and looked at his wife stupidly. His mouth was wide open and his eyes were almost closed. He looked very funny. Her appearance merely seemed to increase his extraordinary melancholy, for he cried out in a loud voice, 'Jesus of Nazareth', and struck the floor violently with his head.

'Now, now', muttered Sally excitedly, pushing Julia.

Julia stiffened. She dropped her little hands to her sides, letting her dressing gown hang loosely about her, exposing her bosom. She walked slowly forward, thrusting out her little white feet in their pink high-heeled slippers through the shuffling folds of her dressing-gown. Then she gingerly raised the stick when she was quite close to her husband. She stopped dead.

'Prut!' said Sally, standing near the door.

Julia shuddered and took another little pace forward. Buster groaned and gathered himself together in preparation for another monstrous yell. Julia suddenly stepped forward and tipped him ever so gently on the back with the ashplant. Buster immediately became still.

'Prut!' said Sally.

Julia gripped her bosom with her free hand, gasped and struck her husband a fairly smart blow on the same spot, on the small of the back. Buster slowly raised his head, turned his body slightly and looked at his wife. He looked amazed. He wrinkled his brows, as if he were trying to recognize her. He looked exactly like a loutish rustic, come into town for the first time, standing outside a theatre and gaping at a half-clothed lady of fashion, who is stepping out of her car.

Julia glanced at him. Her expression rapidly changed until her eyes gleamed brilliantly, her teeth showed, her cheeks became pale and the veins in her neck stood out. She looked wild ferocious and as maddeningly alluring as only a woman can be, when she is on fire with passion.

'Julia', murmured Buster in a soft voice.

It was a caress. He had never spoken like that to her. It was the voice of a man seeing a beautiful woman for the first time and completely carried away by a transport of passion.

As soon as she heard him utter her name, a wild excitement took possession of her. Hissing through her teeth, she rained blows on his back. At first she struck with one hand. Then she seized the stick with both hands and struck with all her power, swaying like a peasant woman beetling clothes at a well.

He began to cry out, calling on her to desist. She beat him still more furiously. He uttered a loud yell and turned over on his back. She continued to beat him on the stomach. Then he rolled over again and she beat him on the back once more. At last he began to howl like a dog, making a ludicrous sound. She paused for breath. He gathered himself together and holding up his hands and feet, he cried out:

'Julia, Julia, don't beat me.'

He burst into tears. Gritting her teeth, she swung the stick around her head and struck at him. The stick met his right boot and broke in two pieces with a loud crack.

Julia dropped the broken stick and rubbed her hands. Buster, still weeping rolled over and over on the floor, endeavouring to get out of her reach. She took a pace forward in pursuit. Then she stopped and sucked her thumb.

'Here's the brassie', whispered Sally, coming up behind her.

Julia turned on the servant in a furious rage.

'Clear out', she cried. 'Get back to bed. What are you doing here?'

She grabbed the brassie and pushed the servant out of the room. Sally remonstrated but in a respectful, apologetic manner. There was no trifling with Julia in her present temper. The devil had taken possession of her. Sally shuffled into Julia's bedroom, took her candle and then shuffled off to her own room, holding up her nightdress and muttering under her breath. Julia entered the bedroom, locked the door and then leaned against it, exhausted. Her head fell forward on her shoulders. Her knees were trembling and her throat was dry. But she felt wildly exhilarated. With great joy she listened to the beating of her heart. What had she done? She didn't care. She felt reckless and abandoned and she kept thinking:

'Never again. Never. I'll never suffer again. I'm free.'

The tears began to flow down her cheeks. She staggered into bed and almost immediately she became terribly afraid. She put the bedclothes over her head and drew up her knees, lying on her side. At any moment she felt the clothes might be pulled off her and something dreadful would happen. Hardly daring to breathe, she listened.

Now there was perfect silence in the house. Not a sound was heard. Soon this silence irritated her. She uncovered her head and thought:

'He's fallen asleep. How perfectly ridiculous!'

This thought deeply mortified her. Now instead of being afraid that something dreadful would happen as the result of her beating him, she became disgusted.

Just as she was again on the point of bursting into tears she heard a sound. It was Buster walking slowly along the corridor and breathing heavily, groaning. She drew in a deep breath and clenched her hands. It seemed to her that in the next few moments her fate would be decided. Would he pass her door?

He stopped. She heard the door handle turned carefully. She smiled in a curious manner. There was a pause. Then she heard:

'Damn it. It's locked. Hey, Julia'.

She didn't reply.

'Say, Julia. Are you asleep?'

She didn't speak, but tossed on her bed, making the bed creak, in order to let him know that she was awake.

'Why don't you answer me, Julia?' he muttered in an offended, exhausted tone. 'I know you are not asleep. Open the door, can't you, Julia? I . . . I want to explain everything. I can't talk out here, though. Julia. I'm not a dog. I'm a sinner, but I'm not a dog. Julia, I'll go down on my two knees and confess my sins. Give me ONE chance.'

Julia did not speak. She grew excited. He raised his voice a little higher.

'I . . . I wanted to play the game, but I . . . I thought you were fed up with me . . . sorry you married me. I'll go off now, only let me kneel down and confess my sins. Open the door and let me in. I've got my pride. Open the door, I say. Can't you speak to a fellow?'

He waited and received no answer. Julia was sorely tempted to get up and open the door, but she restrained herself with an effort. Buster began to knock on the door, first with his hands and then with his feet. This exertion, and very possibly the sound that he made, had the effect of dissipating his penitent mood. He shouted.

'You're not going to lock me out. I have my rights. I'll break down the door. Down it comes.'

Stepping back, he put his shoulder to the door with all his force. The lock was burst. The door swung open, torn from the top hinge. It hung sideways and Buster fell in a heap on the bedroom floor. Julia became so terrified that she closed her eyes and clutched the bedclothes on her bosom. Groaning, Buster got to his knees and put his hands on the side of the bed. He looked at her.

'Julia', he whispered, touching her shoulder.

When he touched her, she opened her eyes and looked at him. Their eyes met. His hand tightened its grip on her shoulder. His mouth approached hers. Suddenly he seized her in his arms and embraced her with great violence. Neither spoke.

Soon he was lying beside her, asleep, with his curly golden head resting on her shoulder. She gazed at the head and fondled the hair gently with her palms. Her eyes glowed with tears. They were tears of joy.

The same thought kept running through her head for hours as she lay awake fondling his hair and touching it with her lips:

'Now he will never know that I too am a sinner. He will never know.'

She shuddered in ecstasy at the realization of ALL the happiness which life is capable of giving a woman.

Benedict Kiely

TEN PRETTY GIRLS

Andrew Fox still talks about that visit to Belfast. Listening to his recitals, now one fragment of the story and now another, hearing him repeat himself, reassert himself, occasionally contradict himself, the sequence of events has become more part of me than it ever was of Andrew Fox.

He had a running greyhound, a mouse-coloured bitch called Ballyclogher Comet. She won all before her at the Saturday night dog-track in Ballyclogher where, Jack MacGowan once said, you could see the best dog-racing in Ireland when the machine that moved the hare was working and the poteen and adrenaline convenient for gingering the dogs. But Andrew, to be unusual, ran the mouse-coloured bitch as honest as daylight, won every prize he or she could win, looked around him like Alexander and saw beyond Ballyclogher the distant dog-tracks of Belfast. He set off one morning early, sitting in a dusty box-carriage, with Ballyclogher Comet as comfortable as a queen in a corner of the guard's van.

At Portadown he changed into the fast train that runs between Dublin and Belfast, found himself a seat in the corner of a crowded compartment. Sitting directly opposite him, apologizing when in moving she accidentally kicked his foot, looking up to smile at him out of grey quiet eyes, was the first girl. By her side sat a pert little red-faced woman with a black coat, a black skirt, a high cornucopia of a hat, knitting needles that knitted rapidly at something green, and a tongue that, talking at the girl, chattered ten times as rapidly. When the girl had a chance she made a remark, always sensible, always with a suggestion of that grey smile, and with a voice quiet like her eyes with the quiet of the sea on a calm evening singing the shore to sleep.

'He was once only a special constable,' the little woman said. 'But now he's high and mighty as a full-blown member of the Royal Ulster Constabulary.'

With a nod of her busy fantastically-crowned head she indicated a black-uniformed policeman who sat a few yards away.

'I mind the time,' she said, 'he was smuggling sugar across the border with the best smuggler of the lot of them. He was never out of our wee shop. It's three miles south of the border, you know. We did a roaring trade in sugar.'

She was a friendly little woman. She readily took it for granted that everybody knew the exact, advantageous location of her little shop. She was solidly convinced that the centre of the world wasn't very far from the door of that shop. She gathered the whole compartment into her conversation. She would have gathered the nations of the earth to her in the same way if they had all understood English with a Monaghan accent, if they had all been within comfortable hearing distance. Now and again the girl looked across at Andrew and Andrew was seldom looking at anybody else but the girl. Even when her face was thin and set and serious her eyes were quietly smiling. Her hair was somewhere between the colour of ripe hazel-nuts and the colour of good straw. Her hands were slender and delicate and beautifully made. Her voice was rich, easy and even, the accent of Munster when it ceases to be eccentricity and becomes the loveliest sound on God's earth. Once when an accidental movement brought one shapely knee into contact with Andrew's leg he knew in his soul that the train no longer ran evenly on iron rails between the two prosaic linen towns of Lisburn and Lurgan. It was flying high in the blue air with the soaring, swooping speed and grace of a swallow.

She smiled at Andrew, encouraged the little woman, replied graciously to her questions. It seems she was a native of Cork city and a member of the British ATS. It seems that at Dundalk the customs officer had made her take off her shoes until he examined them. He had suspected her of smuggling new shoes across the border. Remembering that minor indignity she was half-angry and half-amused. But Andrew was on fire with fury, seeing all customs officers as infamous excrescences on God's green Ireland, seeing one particular customs officer as a degraded, decadent creature whose every word was blasphemy, whose most casual action was a symptom of unnatural vice.

At the station in Belfast he carried her heavy case out to the bus-stop on the rattling street. He wanted to take a taxi to have her driven off to her billet in high state. But then he remembered Ballyclogher Comet, her sleek supple limbs, her nervous feet, waiting patiently in the guard's van. He couldn't see the girl, the greyhound, the big suitcase and himself all together in one taxi. He didn't want to lose the girl. He couldn't afford to abandon the greyhound. The rattle of the street confused him. The complications of the situation left him tongue-tied. Before he could sort out ideas or words the bus was moving away from him, the girl standing and waving, her face lonely and no smile to be seen. He didn't know her name. He didn't know where she lived in Cork or where she lodged in Belfast. And she was possibly the only girl Andrew Fox had ever loved.

Jack MacGowan always says you can't mix girls and greyhounds.

When the racing was over, with Ballyclogher Comet a good first in her own class, Andrew strolled, taking the air, around by the City Hall and up Royal Avenue. It was Charity day with the students of Queen's University. At Castle Junction the weirdly-dressed, half-dressed, fantastically-painted boys and girls had blocked the whole central city traffic. The pavements were black with people. The trams stood in long, immovable, unmanoeuvrable lines. A tall young man, his face painted black, clad in a black bathing suit and a pair of wellington boots, climbed to the roof of one tram and danced a hornpipe. A policeman climbed up to dislodge him. The dancer jumped to the roof of another tramcar. The crowd jeered the policeman. Under the circumstances, Andrew thought, it was a good hornpipe.

Then somewhere in the crowd a student threw into the air a roll of toilet paper. As it went up it unwound to drape itself around a trolley cable. In two minutes the air was thick with soaring and unwinding and descending rolls of toilet paper, the streets rustled like a beechwood, black Belfast roared with laughter at the indecorous scheme of municipal decoration. The trams moved with a heave and a great effort. The moving trolleys set the paper burning and falling. Andrew laughed along with Belfast.

Behind him in the crowd a girl said, 'Andrew Fox, you're a disgrace to Ballyclogher. Laughing at the like of that.'

She was a brown-haired girl linked arm-in-arm to her brown-haired sister who was, in turn, linked to a taller dark-haired girl. Andrew knew the three of them. They were all girls from our part of the country and they had steady teaching jobs in Belfast. They were handsome girls. They were smiling, friendly girls. It was good to meet them in the middle of that daft, shouting, laughing crowd. It was good to meet them on the streets of that hard, stony city.

All together they edged their way out to a quiet side-street, chattering in a way that dissolved into nothing the trams, the high houses, buses, lorries and automobiles, and showed Andrew as plain as the nose on his face the little town he came from, the old, humpy roofs, the two or three spires, and all around the blue circle of quiet hills.

'You'll all be coming home soon for the holidays,' he said.

The dark-haired girl said, 'We won't be going to Ballyclogher at all this summer.'

'At most we'll only be stopping there for a few days on our way through to the new Gaelic college in Donegal,' said the elder of the brown-haired sisters.

The younger one said, 'Come with us, Andrew.'

'Is it me? Learn Irish? For a holiday? That's a joke and a half.'

'But it's a lovely holiday. Perhaps it is a wee bit more strict than the other colleges. You get up and go to mass every morning. There's compulsory drill. The tricolour is hoisted every morning and we all salute the flag and sing in Irish one verse and the chorus of The Soldier's Song.'

'It's a fine stirring song,' said Andrew. 'It's a beautiful bright flag. Still, I think I'll go to the ocean waves at Bundoran where they stay in bed in the morning. Or go west to Galway for the races where they don't go to bed at all.'

They talked about scores of things as he walked with them up the steep Falls Road to the house where they lodged. They were friendly girls. They were modest girls. In the lapels of their neat costume jackets they wore shining gold rings to show that they spoke Irish as well as they spoke English.

He said goodbye to them at a street corner. Their steep street went up like a stairway under the shadow of Cave Hill. Above the high dark hill the sky was red with the falling sun.

A bumping bus carried him back to the centre of the city. The streets were cleared of crowds and trailing paper. The traffic was moving normally up and down Royal Avenue, around and around the monstrous Victorian City Hall. He moved aimlessly with the traffic, up and down and around and around, looking into shop windows, looking at the people on the pavements. The darkness came quietly. Suddenly around him windows and street lamps were golden. He liked looking at people and looking into windows. He was also hoping that somewhere in the anonymous crowd he would see again that thin, sensitive face, those grey eyes. Then he would speak to her and she would answer him and the noisy street would be a splendid orchestra around the melody of her voice. Every time he saw a girl in uniform he stared hard. A certain number stared back, some haughtily, some curious, some inviting. The majority didn't even notice his stare.

He walked down Royal Avenue for the twentieth time, crossed the tram-tracks at Castle Junction, saw the tram lumbering up above him and stepped back hurriedly to safety, dragging with him a girl who had walked herself into a similar predicament. The tram sailed past. The conductor looked back wrathfully. The girl waved a hand and called, 'Cheerio, granda, mind your eye.'

Then she looked at Andrew and Andrew looked at her and they laughed.

He said, 'I thought you were gone that time.'

She said, 'Not so easy to kill a bad thing.'

They crossed to the safety of the pavement, fell into step and walked together towards the City Hall. She was well-dressed: a green skirt showed under a sort of fur coat. Dark hair piled up in shiny, complicated coils on the crown of her head. Her face was pretty in a plump good-humoured way, with lips artificially widened into expansive and inviting redness. He could guess at soft, generous curves under the loose coat, keeping the beauty of things soft and generous until between her knees and the ground she thickened into unattractive calves and ankles.

'Do you live here?' Andrew asked.

'Born and bred here.'

'Do you like it?'

'Like it? Hell. I like it so little I'm getting out to Australia. As far as I can go. As soon as I can get away.'

'Did you marry an Australian?'

'Did I marry a dingo dog?' she said.

She looked sideways at him. The outsize crimson mouth twisted in a good-humoured, pitying smile.

'You're telling me,' she said 'Did I marry an aborigine or a bushranger? Did I marry a kangeroo?'

Her voice was soft. The words, like the curves of her body were rounded elegantly, a little too elegantly, a little too obviously refined by imitation of English accents and American accents, any accents native to people who were not poor and didn't belong to Belfast.

'Not me,' she said. 'I'd marry no man from the other end of the earth. Some of the girls thought every American soldier was a millionaire or a movie-star. They thought his people back home lived in a palace. Were they cheesed when they found out.'

They passed the City Hall. The curves, the soft voice, the red, friendly mouth comforted Andrew and drove the loneliness from streets of strangers where his eyes might search for ever but never see the thin girl from the south with an accent that belonged to her as liquid song belonged to the skylark.

'Come and have supper with me,' he said.

'I'd only be wasting your time. I had a date. The girl-friend and myself. Her boy was there. I was stood-up. I'm going home now. It's too late to go anywhere.'

'It's not too late to eat.'

'All right, stranger. But don't say I didn't warn you.'

They passed two cinemas and a railway station and found a bright noisy restaurant, smelling of fish, warm and smoky and comfortable. Andrew thought how pretty she was when she was sitting with those fat legs hidden under the table, how pleasant, friendly and confidential she was once she was assured that he wasn't a wolf on the prowl for succulent innocence. She was a factory girl. Her friend was another factory girl. She knew a boy in Bangor was the living image of Andrew Fox. She and the girl-friend were going to Australia together. They didn't intend to remain factory girls. Somebody had told her the boarding-house business was good in Melbourne. So Andrew gave her the home address of his brother who had gone to his uncle in Melbourne when he was a boy.

He was proud of her ambition to be something more in Melbourne than she had been in Belfast. Australia was a big country, a new world, a new life.

When a group of half-drunken soldiers and three ATS girls took possession of the neighbouring three tables Andrew paid his bill and they left the restaurant. At the risk of provoking a brawl he had a quick look at the three girls. But she wasn't there. He hadn't really expected to find her in that company.

He left the girl with the fat legs as far as her bus-stop. She was gone from his mind almost as soon as the bus was out of sight. Once again the crowded streets were painful with loneliness. Friendliness was all very well as far as it went. But there was the wide world of difference between grey, quiet beauty, sensitive shapely hands, a voice that spoke softly and naturally, and a round friendly girl with a dozen false accents who was pretty only when her legs were hidden under a table.

The crowds bursting out from cinemas swept around him like a flood. Buses packed with people set off with strain and effort, pulling up the bumpy slopes that led out of the city. Faces swept past him, white patches against darker backgrounds. The nightmare that can overtake men in the middle of unknown, uncaring crowds made him weak and dizzy, showed him the hopelessness of walking up and down and around looking for a face that he would never see again. Leaning against a street-corner he watched the heedless people hammering past, the crowds decreasing, the traffic thinning and growing quiet. Somewhere above the buildings a clock struck midnight. Three women came slowly out of a dark side-street, eyed him speculatively, stopped in a group a few yards away.

The youngest of the three looked at him steadily until she caught his eye. Then she said: 'Who are you looking at?'

He didn't in the least mind being accosted. But he didn't like the way the girl did it. He didn't like the look of the young brat. She was pretty. Her face was shiny and brazen. Her wandering eyes showed no indication of either brains or good feeling. He didn't like the way her stockings wrinkled. He didn't like the way she tightened the belt of her brown coat or the way her flaxen hair hung untidily about her head. He stared at her stonily, then looked away up the street to show her he had seen nothing worth looking at a second time. She muttered something to the other couple, then walked away by herself along the pavement.

'Don't mind her, mister,' said the elder of the two. 'She has no more manners than a pig.'

'Five months up from the country,' said the other, 'and all the polis in the place are after her for the way she carries on in the street.'

They had a high sense of decorum and dignity, a precise knowledge of the way a possible friend or patron should be spoken to. They were outraged by the uncouth, ill-mannered approach of the flaxen-haired hussy. Andrew struck a match to light a cigarette for the elder woman. She was stout and not unhandsome, her hair grey in middle-age. The younger woman didn't smoke. She was bony, wistfully pretty, pregnant, red-headed, friendly and exceedingly coarse-tongued. They studied the slow, stately progress of two helmeted policemen on the far side of the street.

'They're not after us anyway,' said the red-headed girl. 'They're out to get Blonde Margaret. Big Joe the taximan nearly lost his licence over her when a cop halted his taxi on the Antrim Road. Only the cop was a fella Joe knew, Margaret woulda been in the clink. But Joe threw herself and the Yankee sailor was with her out on the road. Said he'd pull the white hair outa her head if she ever came near his taxi again.'

'She's as bold as brass.'

'She's as ignorant as sin.'

'She oughta get jail.'

'Jail's too good for her. I'm only out myself and, honest to God, I liked it. I get along all right in there.'

'You would, Mary,' said the red-head. 'You're the contented, motherly type. But I did my fourteen days an' God it was awful. They'd take the skin off Margaret in there.'

Andrew smoked his cigarette and listened. They had accepted him as part of their company. Common dislike of the uneasiness created by Margaret's rudeness drew them together. He was a friend. They didn't seem to think of him as a possible customer. They may have sensed that he was searching for something they couldn't offer. The contented motherly woman sucked her cigarette, puffed out smoke in the direction of the two policemen.

'They're not so bad, the cops,' she said. 'That big fellow

over there helped me home one night I was down on Royal Avenue too drunk to put one foot past the other.'

Margaret came back along the pavement with three rough, dirty, cap-wearing, scarf-wearing young fellows. They pushed each other about and shouted and laughed, and used every dirty and doubtful word under the moon. Margaret, in one scuffle, lost an ear-ring and groped for it on the stone setts of the street while her companions, hands in pockets, looked at her and chatted to her derisively.

'She has her own sort there,' Mary said.

'Not much money between them,' said the red-head.

The noisy group, abandoning the ear-ring, moved on down the street. On the opposite pavement the two policemen strode impassively in the same direction.

'What did I tell you,' said Mary.

'They'll get her yet,' said the red-head.

'She lost another ear-ring the other night round at the City Hall.'

'She must have a big stock of ear-rings,' said Andrew.

'When I got three months,' Mary said, 'it was with a fellow like you. He was younger, even. The cop that caught us said: What are you at there, mister? Having a pee, constable, he said. A quare pee, said the constable, hitting him down like that; a sore blow. He got off with forty shillings on account of he wasn't married, and was respectable.'

Respectability, Andrew thought, can be at times useful and at times both embarrassing and perilously precarious.

He offered Mary a cigarette, lighted it for her. He bade the pair of them farewell and walked away. Margaret was standing at another street corner. Her entourage had swollen to a dozen or more, all loud and shouting, and in the middle of them Margaret as proud as a princess in a circle of courtiers. Across the street the two policemen had patiently taken up their position.

Beyond the City Hall the streets were completely deserted. He walked on without any particular objective, with no definable hope. Even if she had been in the city at a picture or a play or a concert or a dance she would have gone back by this time to her lodging or her barracks or her billet or wherever in heaven she slept at night. The thought that some other man might have left her at the doorstep or the barrack gate gave him momentary pain. But he soothed it with a great effort of deliberate hope. He walked on slowly, expecting, who knows, the dead streets to reawaken, the little comical two-legged symbols of life to go hurrying up and down the pavements and in and out among hooting, ridiculous traffic. Then he would find her, not hurrying comically, but moving with graceful deliberation, not a symbol or a fragment of life but the whole fullness thereof, the essence and meaning of all the living.

An hour later when his feet were tired and the streets had grown cold, and he had smoked his last cigarette, he knew that hope was folly and hope was a dream. He leaned for rest against the parapet of a railway bridge and a girl came walking up from the centre of the city. She stopped and asked him for a cigarette. He fumbled through all his pockets.

'Smoked my last,' he said.

But he wasn't anxious to lose the comfort of her company.

He said, 'You're late out tonight.'

She was a plain girl, nothing notable in figure, feature or dress. She was a decent girl. But she was lonely and inclined to be trusting and innocently confidential. Her name was Minnie. She worked in the kitchen in a big city restaurant. She lived in Bangor. Her boy-friend was a soldier. She came up on the train every morning to her work. It wasn't easy being in time. Once a week she went down to a military camp on the outskirts of the city to see her boy-friend. Usually after that weekly assignation, she got the last train back to Bangor. Tonight, when she had separated herself from her boy-friend and returned to the city, she was just in time to see the tail-end of the last train to Bangor vanishing out of the station. There was a fix to find yourself in. She had to get a night's sleep somewhere so as to be able to work in the morning. Her father in Bangor was as cross as hell.

In sympathy for the plain girl without a bed to lie on or a roof over her head Andrew for a moment forgot his own despair.

'Do you know nobody in Belfast?'

'My sister's in digs up this way. If I could get her to let me in quietly. But her bitch of a landlady would write to my father about me being out at this time of the night.'

'On our way,' said Andrew.

They walked for a mile along hard pavements, through narrow streets lined with small kitchen-houses. To Andrew who loved running dogs and sport on windy uplands it was all a nightmare of men, women and children sweating away the night in rooms as small as coffins, sweating away the day in factories and mills as big as palaces, as comfortable as prisons and as noisy as nine bedlams. He waited at the corner of one narrow street while she walked fifty yards ahead and surveyed the house her sister lodged in. There was only one lighted window in the whole street, one small room where people were still alive in this city of death. The rest of the city, the rest of the world was dead. Andrew Fox and the homeless girl called Minnie were two people forgotten and left to exist through all eternity on the back of an abandoned desolate globe. Perhaps the light was shining in that room only because somebody was sick there, coughing up blood, dying in pain. When death would go into the room the window would be as dark as all the other windows in the street. Outside in the withering, chilly night there would be homeless Minnie and Andrew Fox looking hopelessly for something he would never find.

There would also be the policemen, as black as the devil and six feet high, looking suspiciously at Andrew Fox.

The policeman said, 'Are you waiting on somebody?'

No policeman in Belfast or in the world could have appreciated exactly what he was waiting for and hoping for.

'For that girl,' he said.

The policeman peered up the street. He said, 'What in the name of God is she doing?'

Andrew explained. He explained with the extravagant

good humour, the exaggerated, detailed politeness of the civilized, sensible, law-abiding man caught in a position that savours even ever so slightly of law-breaking. The policeman was partially convinced. He continued to peer up the street. The light in the one window was suddenly extinguished. The policeman said, 'Why doesn't she knock?'

Andrew explained further. He explained about the landlady and the cross father. He was beginning to feel annoyed with the policeman's curiosity. After all he wasn't a thief. He wasn't an IRA man. He was Andrew Fox, the owner of Ballyclogher Comet who had seen for a moment a thin girl from Cork and lost his heart, his peace of mind and his night's rest.

Minnie came back down the street. The people of the house were in bed. Her sister was in bed. For the benefit of the policeman Minnie commenced her own explanation. The policeman was completely convinced. He was even anxious to help. He would knock on the door himself and waken the people. If they wouldn't heed a girl then they would heed a member of the force. Minnie's honest, pimpled face went grey with unaffected horror. Suppose her da in Bangor heard she had turned up at two in the morning escorted by a policeman. Her da, mind you, had been a policeman himself. There was nothing he didn't know.

'Get me a taxi,' said Andrew. 'I'll take you to the house of a friend of mine in Ballyhackamore.'

He didn't have a friend in Ballyhackamore. But for his own sake and for the sake of the terrified girl he wanted to see the end of that hellish, helpful constable. He led the way to a telephone kiosk, rang a taxi rank, chattered amicably until the car arrived, pushed Minnie in ahead of him, thanked the policeman with high, firm politeness, and was driven off to no particular destination. Somewhere in a select, fashionable suburb he dismissed the taxi, having first bought a packet of cigarettes from the driver, and sitting on a seat between the respectable road and a row of shadowy tennis-courts, Minnie and himself chain-smoked the cigarettes. No policeman passed to molest them. They were miles away from the rough, narrow places where the poor lived. They were high above the terrible pavements where the abandoned sold their bodies. In the sky above the streets there was the reflection of light. But there was no sound, absolutely no sound.

Down there, Andrew thought, she is resting her head on a pillow and sleep has closed the grey eyes and she will not smile again until morning. Or, possibly, she smiles in her sleep, seeing the bright curves of Patrick Street in Cork and hearing the soft voices of her Southern people. Or does she lie awake and restless wondering why the fool of a fellow who sat facing her in the train didn't ask her to meet him again? Or, perhaps, she hears the voice and sees the face of somebody who wasn't so slow nor so foolish, who hadn't a valuable greyhound bitch waiting for him in the guard's van.

When the last cigarette was smoked he telephoned another taxi, paid the fare in advance and sent simple Minnie careering proudly back to the house where her sister lodged. The policeman would certainly be gone. She could knock quietly at her sister's window.

Then he walked slowly down to his hotel. It was that strange time, about four or five on a summer morning, when you realize that suburban gardens are alive with loudly singing birds.

Stretching himself on his bed he thought that, if it was a story in the pictures, he would be awakened by a heavy knock on his door, there would be two policemen to arrest him and tell him that Minnie had been found murdered and horribly mutilated in a back alley. But the knocking on the door that did awaken him was merely the night porter hammering loudly to arouse him for the early train. He wasn't sure whether he was glad or sorry. Notoriety could have its uses and, anyway, he would be innocent and she might be standing there to welcome him out of the court, smiling at him out of quiet grey eyes.

When Ballyclogher Comet was safe in the guard's van he found himself a seat. Sitting across from him was a fat, heavily-breathing man with a red face and black moustache.

* * *

When the last houses of Belfast melted into the flat green fields he went up to the dining-car and ordered breakfast. He ate slowly, ruminating, reading the paper casually, and when he folded up the paper and laid it aside he saw the girl in uniform facing him across the table. Her face was thin and sun-tanned and for half a minute he tried to bludgeon himself into believing that this was the girl he had spoken to twenty-four hours previously, the girl whose features were already fading and becoming vague in his memory. Cold with fear he realized that if in days to come he did meet her somewhere, on the street or in a train or coming out of a cinema, he mightn't even recognize her, might confuse her with any one of a thousand uniformed girls.

The girl across the table looked at him over the rim of her raised cup. The letters on the shoulder of her jacket told him, as he returned to a sensible acceptance of reality, that she came not from Cork but Canada. When she spoke her voice was quiet enough but it drawled lazily and easily with accent, intonation and pronunciation known neither in Cork nor Ballyclogher. She had been on a holiday in Dublin and a friend had advised her to go north and see Belfast. She had seen Belfast and was very glad to be returning to Dublin. Her father and mother were English and somewhere in her blood there was a trace of Pennsylvania Dutch. But Ireland was the country of her choice. The people were so friendly. Almost everybody had a relative somewhere in Canada or the USA, and they expected you to be fairly well acquainted with their relatives even though you lived thousands of miles away from the places mentioned. She found that very amusing. The men in Ireland, she said, were handsomer than the men in most other countries; an opinion that gratified Andrew. And there weren't many wolves about. Leastways, she hadn't met them. The men didn't seem to want to push you around.

She talked with the easy assurance of a girl who had travelled and been around and seen things. She judged people easily and humorously, with a charity as wide as the wide plains of Canada. Andrew found it easy to talk to her, easy to be friends with her, to forget that she had come over vast distances and would return again for ever to distant places.

When the train pulled into Portadown they shook hands like old friends. She said, 'You're not a bad scout, Andrew Fox. It's been nice knowing you.'

She leaned from the window and waved as he went racing up the platform to the guard's van and the greyhound bitch. He had her name and address written down on the back of an envelope.

There's the poem about the fellow who, using a berry as a bait, fished in a stream and caught a little silver trout. Then when he was greasing the pan and kindling the fire the trout changed into a lovely girl who ran from him, calling his name. He followed her through hollows and over hills, growing old in the chase, keeping his aged limbs supple with hope for the day when he would find her and kiss her and live with her in an enchanted land.

We all know the poem. We learned it at school, those of us who learn anything at school. Our greatest poet wrote it. It's a lovely poem. We should be proud of it. We are – those of us who know enough to be proud of anything.

Then there are ninety-nine poems, good, bad and indifferent, about poets pursuing ideal and evasive beauty.

I wonder do they ever find it. I wonder did that old fellow keep up the pursuit as long as he said, searching over hills and through hollows for the girl that had once been a silver trout. Perhaps he grew tired, kissed somebody with a real father and mother and with money in the bank: somebody with fat legs, somebody as trite as three school-teachers learning languages, as stupid as a pimply girl missing her train and living in mortal terror of a father who had been a policeman. Perhaps he went down into the dark night of mercenary misery and forgot his vision. Or could it be that men can realize their visions in the strangest ways and places?

Andrew Fox still writes letters to that Canadian girl. He signs them, 'Your sincere friend, Andrew Fox, Canonhill

Road, Ballyclogher.' He shows them to me. They're mostly about the dogs he's breeding and the books he's reading. He reads a lot and he's lucky with dogs. He doesn't show her letters to me but the whole town knows that they arrive regularly. He tells me he's not in love with her, yet something may come of it. If anything does it will be the sensation of Ballyclogher, for Andrew is generally regarded as a prosaic person unlikely to rush out to far horizons. The girls in Ballyclogher would be annoyed. So, for all I know, would the boys be in a little town somewhere in Ontario.

All I do know for certain is that when he got into the train in Belfast, Andrew was determined to go to Cork as soon as possible, to walk around the streets and make inquiries of the friendly, talkative people. He was determined, too, that every time he went to Belfast he would ask every ATS girl he met if she knew a girl from Cork who looked this way and talked that way, and so on.

But when he had left the Canadian girl at Portadown and changed into the Ballyclogher train he went down to the guard's van, sat chatting with the guard and admiring his own greyhound: the quivering thin nose, the strong legs, the nervous electric feet.

He has never gone to Cork. He doesn't talk to ATS girls any more than to any other girls.

Hugh Bredin

THE WHITE FLOWER

A young man, fair-haired and thin-lipped, went through the swing glass door, letting it slam behind him with a flat, opaque sound. He was a first year student. He went up the stairs to the left, bunching his new soutane in front to avoid tripping. He was going to confession. It was a miserably wet day, and the bannister was sticky. The walls were cream, peeling to reveal pink plaster underneath. At the top of the stairs was a corridor with a shiny, slippery wooden floor. His shoes squeaked as he walked along to a bench which ran down the wall from the Spiritual Director's door, almost filled with first year students waiting to go in. He sat down, and stared out through a window, into the Square.

The main quadrangle in St Augustine's is hemmed in on three sides by long grey three-storey buildings, joined at the corners, each with the single door and rows of blank symmetrical windows that mark institutional edifices. The fourth side, detached from the other three, is a tall semi-Gothic structure of grey stone, with impressionistic turrets in the Pugin style, its tall windows inset with tiny, unglinting panes. It is not felt by the authorities to need the addition of a parisitic creeper to its bleak exterior, whereas the other more modern buildings, do. On rainy days the Square looks indescribably empty, as if forsaken by the last man on earth and consigned to an eternal watery, windswept doom. The rain lies in vast shallow puddles on the paved walks and on the cropped weedy triangles and squares of lawn. Miniature moats circumscribe the edges of the flowerbeds, the shrubs wave stockily back and forth, and the parasitic creeper ripples damply on the walls.

David prepared his sin.

He distilled it from his experience – dropping pebbles from the bridge into the river trickling thinly between its gravel banks. Tiny plops. Grey dust mottling the grass beside the road. Words echoing and bouncing from one hedge to the other, skipping hollowly from the road, slipping away into the empty haze.

'Have you ever kissed a girl, you complacent sod?'

Rebecca did not walk; she strode, like a long-legged bird, with a ferocious glare. He tasted the voluptuous thrill of disobedience, the ecstatic sin of Adam. The sun slanting through the open barn, chickens scrabbling, on his hand and breast. Like an atheist who sees a miracle happening before his eyes. David could, literally, hardly believe his senses.

Saying gloomily, 'I may as well give St Augustine's a try. Too much of a tizzy, you know . . .'

He had got up from his seat in the Church and stared, curiously, impersonally at the tabernacle, and genuflected and hurried out, missal in hand. Splendiloquent sun. In the hollow, gorse-bushes shimmering. Curved grass-blades stirring, ridged backs twined against the sky.

'Catholic bastard,' Rebecca said, twisting his ears painfully.

'*Will* you write to me?' she asked lazily, suspicious.

David occupied the kneeler outside the Spiritual Director's door, eyes exactly on a level with a crucifix nailed to the wall. Around the crucifix were filthy finger-marks. The door-knob rattled, and he got up and went in. It was a shabby room with faded yellow wallpaper, and there were rainspecks on the windows. In the grate was an unlighted fire of shiny turf briquettes. Behind the door the Spiritual Director sat on a plain wooden chair, with another kneeler beside him, and another crucifix nailed to the wall. There was an unpleasant effect of senile austerity.

'In the name of the Father and of the Son and of the Holy Ghost. Amen,' said David kneeling.

'Well now, what Diocese are you from?' the priest asked with dutiful pleasantry.

'Derry.'

'Ah you're from the north ...' He was ill and weary-looking, deep lines round his sunken eyes and cheeks. 'Well I hope you like it down here.'

'Oh I'm sure .. ' The priest's hair was dirty grey. The only darkness on his pallid skin, apart from the deep lines, was a thick greyish beard stubble, as if he shaved carelessly with a blunt electric razor. His soutane was not, David noticed, very clean.

'Well now,' with a faint air of relief, 'will we get down to confession. And remember now that this is your first confession in your life as a cleric, preparing for the priesthood. Your past life is gone and done with. You're starting afresh, as it were. You've committed yourself to a life of study and earnest preparation for a career devoted to God ...' He mumbled with remarkable lucidity, clichés falling from his mouth like the contents of a well-thumbed reference book. As he spoke his pale blue eyes skimmed about over David's face, or glanced at the window or down at his hands resting on his lap.

When a Catholic confesses a transgression of sexual morality, the standard formula is that he has committed a 'sin of impurity', or of 'unchastity', or an 'impure act'. David said pedantically, 'Father, I performed an action which gave me sexual pleasure.'

The Spiritual Director's eyes rested on David's nose. 'Yes?'

'Well, tell me about it. Is that all? Is there anything special.' He spoke quickly, casually, the soul of impersonality, the personification of disinterest. Above all, David felt, be courteous and reasonable. 'No nothing special,' and there was a short pause.

'Oh I thought there might be' – the mumble sharpened a little – 'when you were so careful to say 'performed' and 'action' and 'pleasure'. A sin of impurity, is that what it was?'

'Yes.' Formulae with meanly hidden assumptions. He nursed his weapon vengefully. The priest's authority and power useless before it, his total lack of commitment, hang ing in the balance. The Church existed on faith. Without faith it crumbled, withdrew, frightened.

'Was it alone ...?'

'No, with a girl.'

'Ah, I see.' He was the soul of impersonality. 'Was there actual intercourse?'

'Yes.'

'Just the once, I suppose.'

'No, ten times.'

This seemed to shake him all right, for there was a brief pause and his tongue flickered for a second over his lips. 'Ten times with the same ... ah ... ten times with the same girl, is that it?'

'Well, it must be very worrying for you.' He went on quickly, 'Was this long ago ... just recently, I suppose?'

'All during the four days before coming here.'

'Oh dear! Well, do you feel happy about coming here now that this has happened?'

The question startled David. That he might not be wanted at St Augustine's was – unexpected. 'Happy ...?'

'Well, I mean, do you think this has affected your vocation, perhaps? Had you ever sexual intercourse before this particular ... ah ... girl.'

'No, she was the first.'

'Well, it's a funny time to start lying with girls, just before you enter a Seminary to study for the priesthood.' To David's amazement, he was amused. 'Do you not think so?' Images, conjured up by these unevocative words, juggled irresistibly in David's mind, the images of new life: Chapel in the morning, communal male prayers, clanking male refectory, football, new shiny books, tree-lined walks, rooks jarring. He looked at the priest in his shabby room and smiled. 'It *is* funny,' he said. He thought of Rebecca's ferocious glare, indescribably comical. He laughed, and the Spiritual Director laughed too, saying, 'Yes, you see,' his shoulders shaking sluggishly.

'But at the same time it's very serious,' the Spiritual Director mumbled, looking down at his hands, stretching his fingers. 'I mean we've laughed at it now, and seen a kind of funny side to it, but at the same time it must cause you to think very carefully. When you enter a Seminary for the priesthood you enter a life of dedication, a life in the service of Christ, a life of prayer and sacrifice and meditation, and you must cast all worldly thoughts aside. In the words of St Paul, you must put on the new man ...' David half listened. Did he think in a moment of laughter to gain control, dissolve his difficulties? Or avoiding them, trying to bury, unresolved, the doubts, fears, scepticism, unbelief, anguish? He examined the haggard, mumbling face, guiding hundreds of men in the religious life, tempted to conceal and bury, to soothe with platitudes, with well-tried persuasions, ritual panaceas for ritual difficulties.

'... so you see how you must put away from your mind everything that has gone before. You must turn to this new life, you must give *all*, *all* to the service of Christ.' He looked intently at David. 'Do you follow all this? Wouldn't you say so yourself?'

'It's not as easy as that.'

'Well, what's the trouble?'

'This girl, this sin ... I don't feel it was a sin.'

'Oh nonsense, of course it was a sin. Didn't you have intercourse with her? Maybe you ... did you ... ah ... connect?'

'I know exactly what it means ... I did have intercourse with her. And now, tell me ... *what* is sinful about having sexual intercourse?'

'*What* is sinful?' He seemed amazed. 'Well, it's forbidden' – stating the obvious – 'in the sixth and ninth commandments. Sixth thou shalt not commit adultery, ninth thou shalt not covet ...'

'I know that. I don't want to become technical and talk about the differences between adultery and fornication – but how can God have made such an incredible commandment, assuming He did, which is doubtful. And if He did, are we not justified in feeling a certain scepticism? And how is it possible for an act of ours, a simple human act, to be a sin, an infinite sin. Can we affect God so extravagantly?'

'Ah, I see. Well, of course, this is something you'll learn all about when you come to do your theology, but roughly, simply, to give a very brief kind of sketch ... ah ... you want to know how a finite act can have an infinite value, or rather disvalue, or can be infinitely evil, isn't that it. You want to know how, in a sense, man seems to be raising himself up to the level of God. But you see that's not how it is. It's that God has condescended to come down to us. It's precisely because He has created us and takes an interest in us and has destined us for eternal happiness in union with Him in Heaven that our acts become so important. We're all part of the Mystical Body, and when we commit a sin we offend the infinite God, the infinitely good God, and so it's an infinite evil. And as for the other thing, about the difference between fornication and adultery, it's quite clear from the Scriptures that the commandments involving chastity refer to all kinds of impure acts. It's quite clear from the Scriptures, which we believe are inspired by God Himself. The meaning of His commandments is made clear for us in them ... Is that all right? That's only a rough sketch, of course, but is it clear enough now?' His face was open, frank with expectancy, waiting for agreement. David was furious. He remembered his watchword of courtesy and said, with tremendous irony, 'It's clear, but it's very hard to believe.'

Immediately he knew he had said the wrong thing. The priest's face widened in understanding and relief. 'Of course it is,' he said. 'Of course it's hard to believe, on the intellectual level anything is hard to believe. But this is why the Church relies on faith. Everyone has difficulties in faith. The thing is not to get discouraged, but to pray for strength and guidance.'

Seeping poisonous words, power of the innocent. That the penitent had faith was the whole point. If you did not believe you might be missed or regretted, but you were not wanted. Who would demand or enforce it? Not the priest. Not the Church. In a sense there was no Church. It had a kind of idiot simplicity.

And with sickness, with bitterness, David knew that he did not want to get out.

'I suppose you feel I'm rather offhand,' the Spiritual Director continued. 'Perhaps you think I'm just reeling off . . . oh, what's the word . . . platitudes. That I'm not really trying to cope with *your* difficulties? Is that it?'

'Well . . .' the priest waited for his reply, 'something like that.'

'Yes. Well, of course, it's something I can't help. They're *your* difficulties, you see . . . and then there are scruples of course. Only God can help. I can't. I can only indicate how you might set about overcoming your difficulties, but *you* must do it, with God's help, not mine. You see? This is something that your training in the Seminary is for . . . to help you to set up on your own, as it were. After all, if with God's help you do become a priest in the end you'll have to spend many years on the mission, and you'll have to rely on your own resources, and on the spiritual life that you begin to develop here, in St Augustine's. But I can't do it for you. You must strive yourself. Just as you chose to come here in the first place, and must choose either to stay or to leave, whichever with God's guidance you find is meant for you. It's not easy, but then life in the service of God isn't meant to be easy . . .'

David listened apathetically. The challenge he had carefully rehearsed, the articulate problems, tumbled about his ears. They led to an abyss. 'A terrible Catholic', Rebecca called him – menaced by the drabness, the unendingness, the tenacity of existence, stretching into an empty future drearily the same and unpredictable, rooted in the faceless mists of the past. All his questions swirling glibly on the surface, luring him down to shadowy problems of faith and meaning and purpose formlessly dispersed. That he wanted to believe in God anonymous in the multitude. Was there one single stable thing for him to hold, to seize greedily like a drowning man at a straw?

'Well now, is there anything else?' said the Spiritual Director. After talking so much there was a lot of saliva in his mouth, which he now disposed of with a slight sucking sound.

'No ... well, I must admit it's still hard for me to feel I've committed a sin, to feel sorry ...'

'Well then, in so far as you have offended God you're sorry. All right?'

'Yes, all right.'

'Good. For your penance say the Rosary once. Now make a good act of contrition.'

The words of absolution were pronounced. 'And God bless you,' the Spiritual Director finished, 'and say a prayer for me.'

As David arose he said quickly, 'The girl cried.'

'Pardon?' The priest stared at him inquiringly. He really hadn't heard. David could not follow it up with any thought whatsoever. The words seemed, astoundingly, to have come by accident to his lips. 'I didn't say anything,' he replied politely, and let himself out.

An odd thing to say, he thought as he squeaked along the shiny corridor. Why had Rebecca, disdaining, cried? Why for that matter should anyone ever shed tears, on any conceivable occasion? Especially if, he thought grimly, they knew – as he knew, now ...

Out of the corner of his eye, he saw something white down in the Square. He stopped at one of the windows and peered. The rain had temporarily stopped, though the wind still crimpled the pale, shallow puddles, that reflected the watery white light of the sky. Ah, there it was. In one of the shrubs, waving fitfully with violent thrashings in the gusts – it must be a flower of some kind, a white flower, only one, like a piece of white cloth caught flying out of the air, ensnared by the stubbly branches. How curious that there should be just the one flower, gleaming pallidly in the dripping wilderness of the Square, all alone in the wet, bleak desert of green and grey.

Bryan MacMahon

THE CAT AND THE CORNFIELD

In Ireland, all you need to make a story is two men with completed characters – say, a parish priest and his sexton. There at once you have conflict. When, as a foil for the sexton, you throw in a mature tinker girl, wild and lissom, love interest is added to conflict. And when, finally, you supply a snow-white cat, a cornfield, and a shrewish woman who asks three questions, the parts if properly put together should at least provide a moderate tale.

The scene is laid in a village asleep on a summer hill: the hour of the day is mid-morning. The village is made up of a church that lacks a steeple, a pair of pubs – one thatched and the other slated – with maybe a dozen higgledy-piggledy houses divided equally as between thatch and slate. The gaps between the houses yield glimpses of well-foliaged trees beyond which the countryside falls away into loamy fields.

On the morning of our story, the sexton, a small grumpy fellow of middle age with irregular red features, by name Denny Furey, had just finished sweeping out the brown flagstones of the church porch. He then took up the wire mat at the door and tried irritably but vainly to shake three pebbles out of it.

At the sound of the rattling pebbles, the sexton's white cat which was sitting on the sunny wall of the church beside his master's cabin, looked up and mewed soundlessly.

Denny glanced sourly at the cat. 'Pangur Bán,' he said, 'if you didn't sleep in my breeches and so have 'em warm before my shanks on frosty mornings, I'd have you drowned long 'go!' The cat – he had pale green eyes and a blotch on his nose – silently mewed his misunderstanding.

Suddenly there came a sound of harness bells. A tinker's spring-cart, painted bright green and blue, with a shaggy piebald cob between the shafts, drew slowly past the church gate. Sitting on the near wing of the cart was a tinker girl wearing a tartan dress and a bright shoulder-shawl. Eighteen, perhaps; more likely, nineteen. She had wild fair hair and a nut-brown complexion. Spying the sexton struggling with the mat, her eyes gleamed with puckish pleasure.

Meeting her gaze, Denny grimaced ill-temperedly and then half-turned his back on her. As on a thought, he swung around to scowl her a reminder of her duty. Slowly the girl cut the Sign of the Cross on herself.

Just beyond the church gateway, the cob's lazy motion came to a halt. The girl continued to stare at the sexton. Angrily Denny dropped the mat. Swiftly he raised his right hand as if he had been taken with a desire to shout: 'Shoo! Be off with yourself at once!' The words refused to come.

Pangur Bán raised himself on shuddering legs, arched his back and sent a gracious but soundless mew of welcome in the girl's direction.

'That you may be lucky, master!' the tinker girl said. Then: 'Your wife – have she e'er an old pair of shoes?'

'Wife! Wife! I've no wife!' Denny turned sharply away and snatched up his brush.

The girl watched as the sexton's movements of sweeping became indefinably jaunty. Then her smiling eyes roved and rested for a moment on the thatched cabin at the left of the church gate.

Without turning round, Denny shouted: 'Nothing for you today!'

The girl was slow in replying. Her eyes still fast on the cabin, she said: 'I know you've nothin' for me, master!' She did not draw upon the reins.

Denny stopped brushing. His stance indicated that again he was struggling to say: 'Be off!' Instead of speaking, he set his brush against the church wall, turned his head without moving his shoulders and looked fully at the girl. She answered his eyes with frankness. They kept looking at one another for a long time. At last, his altering gaze still locked in hers, Denny turned his body around.

As if caught in drowse, Denny set aside his brush. He donned his hat, then walked slowly towards the church gate. Lost rosaries clinked as the white-painted iron yielded to his fingers. Denny looked to left and to right. Up to this their eyes had been bound fast to one another.

The sunlit village was asleep. Pangur Bán lay curled and still on the warm wall.

A strange tenderness glossed Denny's voice. 'Where are you headin' for?' he asked. The gate latched shut behind him.

'Wherever the cob carries me!'

Again the girl's gaze swivelled to the cabin. 'Is that your house?' she asked, and then, as she glanced again at the wall: 'Is that your cat?'

'Ay . . . Ay!'

For a long while the girl kept looking at the little house with its small deeply-recessed windows. She noted well the dark-green half-door above which shone a latch of polished brass.

'Do you never tire of the road?' Denny asked.

'Do you never tire of being fettered?' the girl flashed. She had turned to look at him directly.

Both sighed fully and deeply. Under the black hat Denny's eyes had begun to smoulder.

Secretly the girl dragged on the rein. As the cob shifted from one leg to another, she uttered a small exclamation of annoyance. Her red and green skirt made a wheel as she leaped from the vehicle and advanced to make an obscure adjustment to the harness. This done she prepared to lead her animal away.

Denny glanced desperately around. Uproad stood a hissing gander with his flock of geese serried behind him.

'I'll convey you apass the gander!' he blurted.

The tinker girl glanced at the gander; her mouth corners twitched in a smile. She made a great to-do about gathering up the reins and adjusting her shawl. As she led the animal away, Denny moved to the far side of the road and kept pace with her as she went. Walking thus, apart yet together, they left the village and stepped downhill. Once the sexton glanced fearfully over his shoulder; the village was not so much asleep as stone dead.

As the white road twisted, the village on the hillock was unseen. The cob – a hairy, bony animal – moved swiftly on the declivity so that Denny had to hurry to keep up with the girl and her animal. . .

The splendour of the summer accompanied them. The gauds of the harness were winking in the bright light. The countryside was a silver shield inclining to gold. Their footfalls were muted in the limestone road dust. Muted also were the noise of the horse's unshod hooves and the ringing of the harness bells. At last they came to the foot of the hillock. Here the road ran between level fields. Denny looked over his shoulder and saw Pangur Bán fifty yards behind him walking stealthily on the road margin.

'Be off!' the sexton shouted.

Pangur Bán paused to utter his soundless mew.

The girl smiled. They walked on for a space. Again Denny turned. 'Be off, you Judas!' he shouted. He snatched up a stone and flung it at the cat.

The instant the stone left the sexton's hand, Pangur judged that it was going to miss him. He remained utterly without movement. When the stone had gone singing away into stillness, the cat went over and smelled at a piece of road metal the bounding stone had disturbed. Pangur mewed his mystification into the sky; then spurted faithfully on.

The road again twisted. Now it was commanded by the entrance to the village on the hillock.

Here in a cornfield at the left-hand side of the road, the ripening corn was on the swing from green to gold. The field was a house of brightness open to the southern sky. Directly beside their boots a gap offered descent to the sown ground. The cob stopped dead and began to crop the roadside grass.

'Let us sit in the sun,' the sexton ventured. He indicated the remote corner of the cornfield.

The girl smiled in dreamy agreement. With slow movements she tied her cob to the butt of a whitethorn bush. The pair walked along by the edge of the corn and sat down on the grassy edge of the farthest headland. Here the corn screened them from the view of a person passing on the road. The fierceness and lushness of growth in this sun-trap had made the hedge behind them impenetrable. Denny set his hat back on his poll. Then he took the girl's hand in his and began to fondle it. Points of sweat appeared on his agitated face.

Twice already, from the top of the grassy fence, Pangur Bán had stretched out a paw in an attempt to descend into the cornfield. On each occasion thistles and thorns tipping his pads had dissuaded him from leaping. Through slim upended ovals of dark pupil the cat ruefully eyed the cropping horse, then turned to mew his upbraiding in the direction of his master. Tiring of this, he settled himself patiently to wait.

Pangur Bán sat with his tail curled around his front paws. His eyes were reluctant to open in the sunlight. His ears began to sift the natural sounds of the day.

Reading his Office, the huge old priest walked the village. Glancing up from his breviary, he noticed the brush idle against the church wall: he also spied the wire mat that lay almost concealed on the lawn grass. The impudence of the gander the priest punished with a wave of his blackthorn stick. Standing on the road in front of the sexton's cabin, he sang out: 'Denny! Denny Furey!' There was no reply.

The priest shuffled to the church door and in a lowered voice again called for his sexton. At last, with an angry shrug of his shoulders, he again turned his attention to his breviary. Still reading, he sauntered downhill and out into the open country.

After a while he raised his eyes. First he saw the brown

and white pony, then he spied the flame that was the cat burning white beside the olive cornfield.

The old man's face crinkled. He grunted. Imprisoning his stick in his left armpit, he began to slouch in the direction of Pangur Bán. From time to time his eyes strayed over the gilt edging and the coloured markers of his book.

Denny glanced up from his sober love-making.

'Divine God!' he exclaimed.

The girl was leaning back on the grass: her doing so had tautened a swath of green hay to silver. She was smiling up at the sky as she spaced her clean teeth along a grass stem.

Reaching the cat, the priest halted. 'Pangur Bán,' he wheedled in a low voice. His eyes were roving over the cornfield. The cat tilted his back against the lower may leaves, set his four paws together and drooped as if for a bout of languid gaiety.

For a moment or two the priest tricked with the cat. Then he threw back his shoulders. 'To think that I don't see you, Denny Furey!' he clarioned.

Denny and the girl were silent and without movement. About them the minute living world asserted itself in the snip of grasshoppers.

Again the priest thundered: 'Nice example for a sexton!'

The sweat beaded above Denny's eyebrows. His legs began to shiver in the breeches his white cat slept in. The girl peered at the priest through the altering lattice of the corn-heads. Her expression was quizzical as she glanced at Denny.

From the roadway came again the dreaded voice: 'If it's the last thing I do, Denny Furey, I'll strip you of your black coat!'

At this moment a shrewish woman, wearing a black and green shawl, thrust around the bend of the road. She was resolutely headed for the village.

Seeing the woman approach, the priest quickly turned his face away from the cornfield and resumed his pacing along the road. His lips grew busy with the Latin psalms. Peeping out and recognizing the newcomer, Denny Furey at first swore softly, then he began to moan. 'The parish will be ringin' with the news before dark!' he sniffled.

The woman blessed the priest so as to break him from his Office: then in a tone of voice that expressed thin concern: 'Did I hear your voice raised, Father?'

The priest lowered his shaggy eyebrows. 'Sermons don't sprout on bushes, my good woman!'

'Ah! Practisin' you were!'

Her crafty eyes alighted on the white cat. 'Would it be bird-chasin' the sexton's cat is?'

'It could be, now that you mention it!'

There was a pause. The conversation of the wheat spars was only one step above silence. Flicking the cornfield and the cart with a single glance, the woman said, in a half-whisper: 'People say that tinker girls 'd pick the eye out of your head!'

'Did you never hear tell of the virtue of charity, woman?' the priest growled.

The woman made her grumbled excuses. It suited the priest not to accept them. Hurriedly she walked away. Resentment was implicit in the puffs of road-dust that spouted from beneath her toecaps. Before the village swallowed her up, she looked over her shoulder. The priest was standing in mid-road waiting to parry this backward glance.

Again the priest turned his attention to the cornfield. With a sound half-grunt, half-chuckle, he untied the cob, and leading it by the head, turned away in the direction of the village.

The instant the harness bells began to ring, the tinker girl sprang to her feet and raced wildly but surefootedly along the edge of the cornfield. 'Father!' she cried out. 'Father!'

The priest came to a halt. Well out of the range of his stick, the girl stopped: 'So I've drawn you, my vixen!' the priest said.

Breathlessly, the girl bobbed a half-curtsey.

'What're you goin' to do with my animal, Father?'

'Impounding him I am – unless you get that sexton o' mine out of the cornfield at once.'

The girl leaped on to the low fence: 'Come out o' the cornfield,' she shouted. 'I want to recover my cob!'

There was a pause. Then Denny shuffled to his feet. The cat stood up and mewed loyal greetings to his lord.

The priest stood at the horse's head. The angry girl was on the fence: her arms akimbo. Shambling dismally, Denny drew nearer. When he had reached the roadway, the tinker girl cried out: 'I was goin' my road, Father, when he coaxed me into the cornfield!'

Denny opened his mouth, but no words came. He began to blink his moist eyes. His mouth closed fast. He kept his distance from the priest's stick. As Pangur Bán began rubbing himself against the end of the beloved breeches, the sexton gave the cat the side of his long boot and sent him careering into the bushes.

'*A chait,* ou'r that!' he said.

'Aha, you scoundrel!' the priest reproved. 'Can you do no better than abuse a dumb animal?'

Turning to the girl: 'Take your cob! And if I catch you in this village again, by the Holy Man, I'll give you the length and breadth of my blackthorn!'

'He said he'd convey me apass the gander, Father!'

Three times she lunged forward. Three times her buttocks winced away. At last she mustered courage enough to grasp the winkers. Clutching the ring of the mouthpiece, she swung the pony downroad. When she had gained a few yards she leaped lightly on to the broad board on the side of the cart and slashed at the cob's rump with the free dangle of the reins. The animal leaped forward.

The priest, the sexton, the cat. The sunlit, rustling cornfield.

'Come on, me bucko!' the priest said grimly.

He began to lead the way home. The sexton trailed a miserable yard or two behind. Glory was gone out of his life.

The wonderful day seemed to mock him. The future was a known road stretching before his leaden legs. What he had thought would prove a pleasant bauble had turned to a crown of thorns. In the past, whenever he had chafed against the drab nature of his existence, he had consoled himself thus: 'One day, perhaps today, I'll run and buy me a hoop of bright colours.'

Denny began to compare his soul to a pebble trapped in a wire mat of despair.

Gradually the priest became infected with Denny's moroseness. Side by side, the priest and his sexton continued to move homewards. In the faraway, the sound of the harness bells was a recessional song of adventure.

Behind the pair and at a discreet distance, Pangur Bán travelled quietly. Now and again he paused to mew his loyalty into the sunny world.

Frank O'Connor

DON JUAN'S TEMPTATION

Against the Gussie Leonards of the world, we poor whores have no defences. Sons of bitches to a man, we can't like them, we can't even believe them, and still we must listen to them because deep down in every man jack of us there is the feeling that our own experience of life is insufficient. Humanly we understood our wives and girls and daughters; we put up with their tantrums and consider what we imagine are their wishes, but then the moment comes and we realize that that fat sleeky rascal understands them at a level where we can never even meet them, as if they put off their ordinary humanity as they put off their clothes, and went wandering through the world invisible except to the men like Gussie whose eyes are trained only to see them that way. The only consolation we have is that they too have their temptations – or so at least they say. The sons of bitches! Even that much you can't believe from them.

Anyhow, Gussie met this girl at a party in the Green and picked her out at once. She was young, tall, dark, good-looking, but it wasn't so much her looks that appealed to Gussie as the naturalness with which she moved among all those wooden dolls in nightdresses. She was a country-town girl who had never learned to dress up and pose, and however she moved or whatever she said it always seemed to be natural and right.

They left together and she took Gussie's arm with a boyish camaraderie that delighted him. It was a lovely night with the moon nearly at the full. Gussie's flat was in a Georgian house on the street which ran through the Green; she had a room in Pembroke Road, and as they passed the house

Gussie halted and asked her in. She gave a slight start, but Gussie, having a few drinks in, didn't notice that until later.

'For what?' she asked gaily.

'Oh, for the night if you like,' Gussie replied in the same tone and felt like biting off his tongue when he heard it. It sounded so awkward, like a schoolboy the first time he goes with a girl.

'No, thanks,' she said shortly. 'I have a room of my own.'

'Oh, please, Helen, please!' he moaned, taking her hand and squeezing it in the way of an old friend of the family. 'You're not taking offence at my harmless little joke. Now you'll have to come up and have a drink, just to show there's no ill-feeling.'

'Some other night,' she said, 'when it's not so late.'

He let it go at that because he knew that anything further he said would only frighten her more. He knew perfectly well what had happened. The Sheehans, mischief-makers and busybodies, had warned her against him, and he had walked straight into the trap. She still held on to his arm, but that was only not to make a fuss. Inside she was as hurt as anything. Hurt and surprised. In spite of the Sheehans' warnings she had taken him at his face value, not believing him to be that sort at all. Or rather, as Gussie, whose eyes were differently focused from ours, phrased it to himself, knowing damn well he was that sort but hoping that he would reveal it gradually so that she wouldn't be compelled to take notice.

She stopped at the canal bridge and leaned over to look at the view. It was beautiful there in the moonlight with the still water, the trees, the banked houses with odd windows caught in the snowy light, but Gussie knew it was not the moonlight she was thinking of. She was getting over her fright and now it was her pride that was hurt.

'Tell us,' she said, letting on to be very light-hearted and interested in the subject, as it were, only from the psychological standpoint, 'do you ask all the girls you meet the same thing?'

'But my goodness, didn't I tell you it was only a joke?' Gussie asked reproachfully.

She rested her head on her arms and looked back at him over her shoulder, the cloche hat shading her face to the chin. It was a natural, beautiful pose but Gussie knew she wasn't aware of it.

'Now you're not being honest,' she said.

'Are you?' Gussie asked with a faint smile.

'Am I what?' she replied with a start.

'Can't you admit that you were warned against me?' he said.

'As a matter of fact I was,' she replied candidly, 'but I didn't pay much attention. I take people as I find them.'

'Now you're talking sensibly,' said Gussie and thought in a fatherly way: 'The girl is nice. She's a bit shocked but she'll have to learn sooner or later and it would be better for her to learn from someone who knows.' The awkwardness of Irish husbands was a theme-song of Gussie's. The things their wives told you were almost incredible.

'You probably wouldn't believe me if I told you how few women interest me enough for that,' he said.

'But the ones you do ask,' she went on, sticking to her point, though pretending to be quite detached as though she really were only looking for information, 'do they come?'

'Some,' he said, smiling at her innocence. 'Sometimes you meet a difficult girl who makes a hullabaloo and won't even come and have a drink with you afterwards.'

'Married women or girls?' she asked in the tone of an official filling up a form, but the quaver in her voice gave her away.

'Both,' said Gussie. If he had been perfectly honest he would have had to admit that at that time there was only one of the former and not exactly a queue of the latter but he had decided, purely in Helen's own interest, that since she needed to have her mind broadened there was no use doing it by halves. It was better to get it over and be done with it, like having a tooth out. 'Why?'

'Oh, nothing,' she said casually, 'but I'm not surprised you have such a poor opinion of women if you can pick them up as easily as that.'

This view of the matter came as a real surprise to Gussie, who would never have described his conduct in that way.

'But my dear young lady,' he said offering her a cigarette, 'whoever said I have a poor opinion of women? What would I be doing with women if I had? On the contrary, I have a very high opinion of women, and the more I see of them the more I like them.'

'Have you?' she asked, stooping low over the match-flame so that he shouldn't see her face. He guessed that it was very flushed. 'It must be a poor opinion of me so.'

'What an extraordinary idea!' said Gussie, still genuinely trying to fathom it. 'How can you make out that wanting to see more of you means I have a poor opinion of you. Even if I do want to make love to you. As a matter of fact, if it's any news to you, I do.'

'You want it rather easy, don't you?' she asked with a trace of resentment.

'Why?' he asked blandly. 'Do you think it should be made difficult?'

'I thought it was the usual thing to ask a girl to go to the pictures with you first,' she said with a brassy air that wouldn't have taken in a child.

'I wouldn't know,' murmured Gussie in amusement 'Anyway, I suppose I thought you weren't the usual sort of girl.'

'But if you get it as easy as that, how do you know if it's the real thing or not?' she asked.

'How do you know anything is the real thing?' he retorted 'As you say yourself, you have to take things as you find them.'

'Taking them as you find them doesn't mean swallowing them whole,' she said. 'It would be rather late in the day to change your mind about a thing like that.'

'But what difference does it make?' he asked wonderingly 'It happens every day of the week. You do it yourself with boys you go out walking with. You spoon with them till you find they bore you and then you drop them. There's no difference. You don't suddenly change your character. People don't say when they meet you in the street: "How different that girl is looking! You can see she has a man." Of course, if you attach so much importance to the physical side of it—'

'I do,' she said quickly. By this time Gussie noticed to his surprise that she was almost laughing. She had got over her fright and hurt and felt that in argument she was more than a match for him. 'Isn't it awful?' she added brightly. 'But I'm very queer like that.'

'Oh, there's nothing queer about it,' Gussie said, determined on keeping control of the situation and not letting her away with anything. 'It's just ordinary schoolgirl romanticism.'

'Is that all?' she asked lightly, and though she pretended not to care he saw she was stung. 'You have an answer for everything, haven't you?'

'If you call that everything, my dear child,' he replied paternally patting her on the shoulder. 'I call it growing-pains. I don't know, with that romantic nature of yours, whether you've noticed that there's a nasty wind coming up the canal.'

'No,' she said archly, 'I hadn't,' and then turned to face him, resting her elbows on the coping of the bridge. 'Anyhow, I like it. Go on with what you were saying. Being romantic is thinking you ought to stick to someone you're fond of, isn't that it?'

Gussie was amused again. The girl was so transparent. It was clear now that she was in love with some young fellow who couldn't afford to marry her and that they were scarifying one another in the usual adolescent rough-and-tumble without knowing what ailed them.

'No, my dear, it isn't,' said Gussie. 'Being romantic is thinking you're very fond of someone you really don't give a damn about, and imagining on that account that you're never going to care for anyone else. It goes with your age. Come on now, or you'll be catching something worse.'

'You don't mean you were ever like that?' she asked, taking his arm again as they went on down Pembroke Road. Even her tone revealed her mingled fascination and loathing. It didn't worry Gussie. He was used to it.

'Oh,' he said sentimentally, 'we all go through it.'

There were a lot of contradictions in Gussie. Despising youth and its illusions, he could scarcely ever think of his own youth without self-pity. He had been lonely enough; sometimes he felt no one had ever been so lonely. He had woken up from a nice, well-ordered, intelligible world to find eternity stretching all round him and no one, priest or scientist, who could explain it to him. And with that awakening had gone the longing for companionship and love which he had not known how to satisfy, and often he had walked for hours, looking up at the stars and thinking that if only he could meet an understanding girl it would all explain itself naturally. The picture of Gussie's youth seemed to amuse Helen.

'Go on!' she said gaily, her face turned to his, screwed up with mischief. 'I could have sworn you must have been born like that. How did you get sense so young?'

'Quite naturally,' Gussie said with a grave priestly air. 'I saw I was only making trouble for myself, as you're doing now, and as there seemed to be quite enough trouble in the world without that, I gave it up.'

'And lived happy ever after?' she said mockingly. 'And the women you knock round with? Aren't they romantic either?'

'Not since they were your age,' he said mockingly.

'You needn't rub it in about the age,' she said without taking umbrage. 'It'll cure itself soon enough. Tell us more about your girls – the married ones, for instance.'

'That's easy,' he said. 'There's only one at the moment.'

'And her husband? Does he know?'

'I never asked him,' Gussie said slyly. 'But I dare say he finds it more convenient not to.'

'Obliging sort of chap,' she said. 'I could do with a man like that myself.'

Gussie stopped dead. As I say there were contradictions in Gussie, and for some reason her scorn of Francie's husband filled him with indignation. It was so uncalled-for, so unjust!

'Now you are talking like a schoolgirl,' he said reproachfully.

'Am I?' she asked doubtfully, noticing the change in him. 'How?'

'What business have you talking in that tone about a man you never even met?' Gussie went on, growing quite heated. 'He isn't a thief or a blackguard. He's a decent, good-natured man. It's not his fault if after seventeen or eighteen years of living together his wife and himself can't bear the living sight of one another. That's a thing that happens to everybody. He only does what he thinks is the best thing for his family. You think, I suppose, that he should take out a gun to defend his wife's honour?'

'I wasn't thinking of her honour,' she protested quietly.

'His own then?' Gussie cried mockingly. 'At the expense of his wife and children? He's to drag her name in the mud all because some silly schoolgirl might think his position undignified. Ah, for goodness' sake, child, have sense! His wife would have something to say to that. Beside, don't you see that at his age it would be a very serious thing is she was to leave him?'

'More serious than letting her go to your flat – how often did you say?'

'Now you're talking like a little cat,' he snapped, and went on. He really was furious. 'But as a matter of fact it would,' he went on in a more reasonable tone. 'Where she goes in the evenings is nobody's business. Whether the meals are ready is another matter. They have two daughters at school – one nearly the one age with yourself.'

'I wonder if he lets them out at night,' she said dryly. 'And what sort of woman is their mother?'

'You wouldn't believe me if I told you,' said Gussie, 'but she's a great sort; a woman who'd give you her heart out.'

'I wonder what she'd say if she heard you asking another

girl in to spend the night,' she added in the same casual tone. Gussie was beginning to conceive a considerable respect for her tongue.

'Ah,' he said without conviction, 'I don't suppose she has many illusions left,' but the girl had scored and she knew it. The trouble with Francie was that she had far too many illusions left, even about Gussie. And the greatest illusion of all was that if only she had married a man whose intelligence she respected as she respected his, she could have been faithful to him.

'She can't have,' said Helen, 'but I still have a few.'

'Oh, you!' Gussie said with a jolly laugh which had got him out of many tight corners. 'You're walking with them.'

'They must be in the family,' she said. 'Daddy died five years ago and Mum still thinks he was the one really great man that walked the world.'

'I dare say,' Gussie said wearily. 'And they were probably often sick to death of one another.'

'They were,' she agreed. 'They used to fight like mad and not talk for a week, and then Dad would go on the booze and Mum would take it out of me. Cripes, I used to go up to him with my bottom so sore I could hardly sit down and there he'd be sprawled in his big chair with his arms hanging down, looking into the grate as if 'twas the end of the world, and he'd just beckon me to come on his knee. We'd stop like that for hours without opening our gobs, just thinking what a bitch of hell Mum was ... But the thing is, young man they stuck it out, and when 'tis her turn to go, she won't regret it because she's certain the Boss will be waiting for her. She goes to Mass every morning but that's only not to give God any excuse for making distinctions. Do you think he will?'

'Who will?' asked Gussie. In a curious way the story had gripped him. A woman could bawl her heart out on Gussie and he'd only think her a nuisance, but he was exceedingly vulnerable to indirect sentiment.

'The Boss,' she explained. 'Meet her, I mean?'

'Well,' Gussie said feebly, 'there's nothing like optimism.' At the same time he knew he was not being altogether truthful, because orthodoxy was one of Gussie's strongest lines.

'I know,' the girl said quickly. 'That's the lousy part of it. But I suppose she's lucky even to be able to kid herself about it. Death doesn't frighten her the way it frightens me . . . But that's what I mean by love, Mr L.,' she added, light-heartedly.

'I hope you get it, Miss C.,' replied Gussie in the same tone.

'I don't suppose I'm likely to,' she said with resignation. 'There doesn't seem to be much of it round. I suppose it's the shortage of optimists.'

When they reached her flat, she leaned against the railings with her legs crossed and her hands behind her back – again a boyish attitude which attracted Gussie.

'Well, good night, Miss Romantic,' he said ceremoniously, taking her hand and kissing it.

'Good night, Don Juan,' she replied to Gussie's infinite delight. Nobody had even called Gussie that before.

'When do I see you again?'

'Are you sure you want to see me?' she asked with light mockery. 'An old-fashioned girl like me!'

'I still have hopes of converting you,' said Gussie.

'That's marvellous,' she said. 'I love being converted. I was nearly converted by a parson once. Give us a ring-up sometime.'

'I will to be sure,' said Gussie, and it was not until he reached the canal bridge that he realized he had really meant: 'What a fool you think I am!' He felt sore all over. 'The trouble with me is that I'm getting things too easy,' he thought. He felt exactly like that man with a thousand a year whom somebody wanted to push back into the thirty-shillings-a-week class. Thirty shillings a week was all right when you had never been accustomed to anything else, but to Gussie it meant only one thing – destitution. He knew exactly what he would be letting himself in for if he took the girl on her own terms; the same thing that some poor devil of a boy was enduring with her now; park benches and canal banks with a sixty-mile-an-hour gale blowing round the corner, and finally she would be detained at the office – by a good-looking chap in uniform. 'What a fool I am!' he thought mockingly.

But even to find himself summing up the odds like this was a new experience for Gussie. He was attracted by the girl; he couldn't deny that. Instead of crossing the bridge he turned up the moonlit walk by the canal. This was another new thing and he commented ironically on it to himself. 'Now this, Gussie,' he said, 'is what you'll be letting yourself in for if you're not careful.' He suddenly realized what it was that attracted him. It was her resemblance to Joan, a girl who had crossed for a moment his lonely boyhood. He had haunted the roads at night, trying to catch even a glimpse of her as she passed. She was a tall, thin, reedy girl, and, though Gussie did not know it, already far gone with the disease which killed her. On the night before she left for the sanatorium he had met her coming from town, and as they came up the hill she had suddenly slipped her hand into his. So she too, it seemed, had been lonely. He had been too shy to look for more; he hadn't even wished to ask for more. Perfectly happy, he had held her hand the whole way home and neither had spoken a word. It had been something complete and perfect, for in six months' time she was dead. He still dreamt of her sometimes. Once he dreamt that she came into the room where he was sitting with Francie, and sat on the other side of him and spoke to Francie in French, but Francie was too indignant to reply.

And now, here he was fifteen years later feeling the same sort of thing about another girl who merely reminded him of her, and though he knew Helen was talking rubbish he understood perfectly what she wanted; what Joan had wanted that night before she went to the sanatorium; something bigger than life that would last beyond death. He felt himself a brute for trying to deprive her of her illusions. Perhaps people couldn't do without illusions. Walking by

'I really wanted Miss O'Halloran. It's a room for a gentleman tonight.' She hesitated. Then reluctantly she added, 'Mr Sweeney.' As she had expected, Cissy betrayed immediate curiosity.

'Not Mr Sweeney that stayed here last autumn?'

'Yes. He hopes to get in on the afternoon bus.'

Cissy said she would ask Miss O'Halloran. When she had gone to inquire, the girl turned her back on the traveller and pretended interest in an advertisement for whiskey which featured two dogs, one with a pheasant in its mouth. The voice from behind her asked:

'Boy friend?'

She had expected something like that. Without turning she said, 'You're very curious.'

'Sorry. I didn't mean that. I don't give a damn. Do you drink?'

'No, thank you.'

'I was going to offer you something better than a drink. Good advice.' The girl stiffened. She was the town librarian, not a chambermaid. Then she relaxed and almost smiled.

'If you ever do,' the voice added sadly, 'don't mix the grain with the grape. That's what happened to me last night.'

Cissy returned and said Mr Sweeney could have room seven. Miss O'Halloran was delighted. Mr Sweeney had been such a nice young man. Her eyes caught the traveller and she frowned.

'Mr Cassidy,' she said pertly, 'Miss O'Halloran says your breakfast's ready.'

The traveller looked at her with distaste. He finished his whiskey and indicated with a nod of his head the glass of Bass which he had taken in his hand.

'Tell Miss O'Halloran I'm having my breakfast,' he said. But Cissy was admiring the new dress.

'You certainly look pretty,' she said enviously.

'Prettiest girl in town,' the traveller added for emphasis.

The girl flushed. Cissy winked and said, 'Last night he told me I was.'

'Did I,' the traveller said, finishing his Bass with a grimace of disgust. 'I must have been drunk.'

On the first Friday of every month, precisely at eleven-forty-five, the chief clerk put on his bowler hat, hung his umbrella on his arm and left to spend the rest of the day inspecting the firm's branch office. It was one of the few habits of the chief clerk which the office staff approved. It meant that for the rest of the day they could do more or less as they pleased. Sweeney, who had been watching the monthly ceremony from the public counter with unusual interest, turned around to find Higgins at his elbow.

'You're wanted,' he was told.

'Who?'

'Our mutual musketeer – Ellis. He's in his office.'

That was a joke. It meant Ellis was in the storeroom at the top of the building. Part of the duties assigned to Ellis was the filing away of forms and documents. The firm kept them for twenty-five years, after which they were burned. Ellis spent interminable periods in the storeroom, away from supervision and interference. It was a much-coveted position. Sweeney, disturbed in his day-dreaming, frowned at Higgins and said:

'Why the hell can't he come down and see me?' It was his habit to grumble. He hated the stairs up to the storeroom and he hated the storeroom. He disliked most of the staff, especially the few who were attending night school classes for accountancy and secretarial management in order to get on in the job. Put into the firm at nineteen years of age because it was a good, safe, comfortable job, with a pension scheme and adequate indemnity against absences due to ill-health, he realized now at twenty-six that there was no indemnity against the boredom, no contributory scheme which would save his manhood from rotting silently inside him among the ledgers and the comptometer machines. From nine to five he decayed among the serried desks with their paper baskets and their telephones, and from five onwards there was the picture house, occasional women, and drink when there was money for it.

The storeroom was a sort of paper tomb, with tiers of forms and documents in dusty bundles, which exhaled a musty odour. He found Ellis making tea. A paper-covered book had been flung to one side. On the cover he could make out the words *Selected Poems,* but not whose they were. He was handed a cup with a chocolate biscuit in the saucer.

'Sit down,' Ellis commanded.

Sweeney, surprised at the luxury of the chocolate biscuit, held it up and inspected it with raised eyebrows.

Ellis offered milk and sugar.

'I pinched them out of Miss Bouncing's drawers,' he said deliberately.

Sweeney, secure in the knowledge that the chief clerk was already on his way across town, munched the biscuit contentedly and looked down into the street. It was filled with sunshine. Almost level with his eyes, the coloured flags on the roof of a cinema lay limp and unmoving, while down below three charwomen were scrubbing the entrance steps. He took another biscuit and heard Ellis saying conversationally, 'I suppose you're looking forward to your weekend in the country.'

The question dovetailed unnoticed in Sweeney's thought.

'I've been wanting to get back there since last autumn. I told you there was a girl . . .'

'With curly eyes and bright blue hair.'

'Never mind her eyes and her hair. I've tried to get down to see her twice but it didn't come off. The first time you and I drank the money – the time Dacey got married. The second, I didn't get it saved in time. But I'm going today. I've just drawn the six quid out of Miss Bouncing's holiday club.'

'What bus are you getting?'

'The half past two. His nibs has gone off so I can slip out.'

'I see,' Ellis said pensively.

'I want you to sign me out at five.'

They had done things like that for one another before. Turning to face him, Ellis said, 'Is there a later bus?'

'Yes. At half past eight. But why?'

'It's . . . well, it's a favour,' Ellis said uncertainly. With sinking heart Sweeney guessed at what was coming.

'Go on,' he invited reluctantly.

'I'm in trouble,' Ellis said. 'The old man was away this past two weeks and I hocked his typewriter. Now the sister's 'phoned me to tip me off he's coming home at half past two. They only got word after breakfast. If I don't slip out and redeem it there'll be stinking murder. You know the set-up at home.'

Sweeney did. He was aware that the Ellis household had its complications.

'I can give it back to you at six o'clock,' Ellis prompted.

'Did you try Higgins?' Sweeney suggested hopefully.

'He hasn't got it. He told me not to ask you but I'm desperate. There's none of the others I can ask.'

'How much do you need?'

'Four quid would do me – I have two.'

Sweeney took the four pound notes from his wallet and handed them over. They were fresh and stiff. Miss Bouncing had been to the bank. Ellis took them and said:

'You'll get this back. Honest. Byrne of the Prudential is to meet me in Slattery's at six. He owes me a fiver.'

Still looking at the limp flags on the opposite roof Sweeney suggested, 'Supposing he doesn't turn up.'

'Don't worry,' Ellis answered him. 'He will. He promised me on his bended knees.'

After a pause he diffidently added, 'I'm eternally grateful . . .'

Sweeney saw the weekend he had been aching for receding like most of his other dreams into a realm of tantalising uncertainty:

'Forget it,' he said.

II

Sweeney, who was standing at the public counter, looked up at the clock and found it was half past two. Behind him many of the desks were empty. Some were at lunch, others were taking advantage of the chief clerk's absence. It only meant that telephones were left to ring longer than usual. To his right, defying the grime and the odd angles of the windows, a streak of sunlight slanted across the office and lit up about two square feet of the counter. Sweeney stretched his hand towards it and saw the sandy hairs on the back leap suddenly into gleaming points. He withdrew it shyly, hoping nobody had seen him. Then he forgot the office and thought instead of the country town, the square with its patriotic statue, the trees which lined it, the girl he had met on that autumn day while he was walking along through the woods. Sweeney had very little time for romantic notions about love and women. Seven years knocking about with Ellis and Higgins had convinced him that Romance, like good luck, was on the side of the rich. It preferred to ride around in motor-cars and flourished most where the drinks were short and expensive. But meeting this strange girl among the trees had disturbed him. Groping automatically for the plausible excuse, he had walked towards her with a pleasurable feeling of alertness and wariness.

'This path,' he said to her, 'does it lead me back to the town?' and waited with anxiety for the effect. He saw her assessing him quickly. Then she smiled.

'It does,' she said, 'provided you walk in the right direction.'

He pretended surprise. Then after a moment's hesitation he asked if he might walk back with her. He was staying in the town, he explained, and was still finding his way about. As they walked together he found out she was the town librarian, and later, when they had met two or three times and accepted one another, that she was bored to death with the town. He told her about being dissatisfied too, about the office and its futility, about having too little money. One evening when they were leaning across a bridge some distance from the town, it seemed appropriate to talk rather solemnly about life. The wind ripped the brown water which reflected the fading colours of the sky. He said:

'I think I could be happy here. It's slow and quiet. You don't break your neck getting somewhere and then sit down to read the paper when you've got there. You don't have twenty or thirty people ahead of you every morning and evening – all queuing to sign a clock.'

'You can be happy anywhere or bored anywhere. It depends on knowing what you want.'

'That's it,' he said, 'but how do you find out? I never have. I only know what I don't want.'

'Money – perhaps?'

'Not money really. Although it has its points. It doesn't make life any bigger though, does it? I mean look at most of the people who have it.'

'Dignity?' she suggested quietly.

The word startled him. He looked at her and found she was quite serious. He wondered if one searched hard enough, could something be found to be dignified about. He smiled.

'Do you mean an umbrella and a bowler hat?'

He knew that was not what she meant at all, but he wanted her to say more.

'No,' she said, 'I mean to have a conviction about something. About the work you do or the life you lead.'

'Have you?' he asked.

She was gazing very solemnly at the water, the breeze now and then lifting back the hair from her face.

'No,' she murmured. She said it almost to herself. He slipped his arm about her. When she made no resistance he kissed her.

'I'm wondering why I didn't do that before,' he said when they were finished.

'Do you . . . usually?' she asked.

He said earnestly, 'For a moment I was afraid.'

'Of me?'

'No. Afraid of spoiling everything. Have I?'

She smiled at him and shook her head.

At five they closed their ledgers and pushed in the buttons which locked the filing cabinets. One after the other they signed the clock which automatically stamped the time when they pulled the handle. The street outside was hardly less airless than the office, the pavements threw back the dust-smelling August heat. Sweeney, waiting for Higgins and Ellis at the first corner, felt the sun drawing a circle of sweat about his shirt collar and thought wistfully of green fields and roadside pubs. By now the half past two bus would have finished its journey. The other two joined him and they walked together by the river wall, picking their way through the evening crowds. The tea-hour rush was beginning. Sweeney found the heat and the noise of buses intolerable. A girl in a light cotton frock with long hair and prominent breasts brushed close to them. Higgins whistled and said earnestly: 'Honest to God, chaps. It's not fair. Not on a hot evening.'

'They're rubber,' Ellis offered with contempt.

'Rubber bedamned.'

'It's a fact,' Ellis insisted. 'I know her. She hangs them up on the bedpost at night.'

They talked knowledgeably and argumentatively about falsies until they reached Slattery's lounge. Then, while Ellis began to tell them in detail how he had smuggled the typewriter back into his father's study, Sweeney sat back with relief and tasted his whiskey. A drink was always welcome after a day in the office, even to hold the glass in his hand and lie back against his chair gave him a feeling of escape. Hope was never quite dead if he had money enough for that. But this evening it wasn't quite the same. He had hoped to have his first drink in some city pub on his way to the bus, a quick drink while he changed one of his new pound notes and savoured the adventure of the journey before him, a long ride with money in his pocket along green hedged roads, broken by pleasant half hours in occasional country pubs. When Higgins and Ellis had bought their rounds he called again. Whenever the door of the lounge opened he looked up hopefully. At last he indicated the clock and said to Ellis, 'Your friend should be here.'

'Don't worry,' Ellis assured him, 'he's all right. He'll turn up.' Then he lifted his drink and added, 'Well – here's to the country.'

'The country,' Higgins sighed. 'Tomorrow to fresh fiends and pastors new.'

'I hope so,' Sweeney said. He contrived to say it as though it didn't really matter, but watching Ellis and Higgins he saw they were both getting uneasy. In an effort to keep things moving Higgins asked, 'What sort of a place is it?'

'A square with a statue in it and trees,' Sweeney said. 'A hotel that's fairly reasonable. Free fishing if you get on the right side of the Guards. You wouldn't think much of it.'

'No sea – no nice girls in bathing dresses. No big hotel with its own band?'

'Samuel Higgins,' Ellis commented. 'The man who broke the bank at Monte Carlo.'

'I like a holiday to be a real holiday,' Higgins said stoutly. 'Stay up all night and sleep all day. I like sophistication, nice girls and smart hotels. Soft lights and glamour and sin. Lovely sin. It's worth saving for.'

'We must write it across the doorway of the office,' Sweeney said.

'What?'

'Sin Is Worth Saving For.'

It had occurred to him that it was what half of them did. They cut down on cigarettes and scrounged a few pounds for their Post Office Savings account or Miss Bouncing's Holiday Club so that they could spend a fortnight of the year in search of what they enthusiastically looked upon as sin. For him sin abounded in the dusty places of the office, in his sweat of fear when the morning clock told him he was late again, in the obsequious answer to the official question, in the impulse which reduced him to pawing the hot and willing typist who passed him on the deserted stairs.

'I don't have to save for sin,' he commented finally.

'Oh – I know,' Higgins said, misunderstanding him. 'The tennis club is all right. So are the golf links on Bank Holiday. But it's nicer where you're not known.'

'View Three,' Ellis interjected. 'Higgins the hen butcher.'

'Last year there was a terrific woman who got soft on me because I told her I was a commercial pilot. The rest of the chaps backed me up by calling me Captain Higgins. I could have had anything I wanted.'

'Didn't you?'

'Well,' Higgins said, in a tone which suggested it was a bit early in the night for intimate details. 'More or less.' Then they consulted the clock again.

'It doesn't look as though our friend is coming,' Sweeney said.

'We'll give him 'til seven,' Ellis said. 'Then we'll try for him in Mulligan's or round in the Stag's Head.'

III

The girl watched the arrival of the bus from the entrance to the hotel. As the first passenger stepped off she smiled and moved forward. She hovered uncertainly. Some men went past her into the bar of the Commercial, the conductor took luggage from the top, the driver stepped down from his cabin and lit a cigarette. Towns-people came forward too, some with parcels to be delivered to the next town, some to take parcels sent to them from the city. He was not among the passengers who remained. The girl, aware of her new summer frock, her long white gloves, the unnecessary handbag, stepped back against the wall and bumped into the traveller.

'No boy friend,' he said.

She noticed he had shaved. His eyes were no longer bloodshot. But the sun emphasized the grey colour of his face with its sad wrinkles and its protruding upper lip. As the crowd dispersed he leaned up against the wall beside her.

'I had a sleep,' he said. 'Nothing like sleep. It knits up the ravelled sleeve of care. Who said that, I wonder?'

'Shakespeare,' she said.

'Of course,' he said, 'I might have guessed it was Shakespeare.'

'He said a lot of things.'

'More than his prayers,' the traveller conceded. Then he looked up at the sun and winced.

'God's sunlight,' he said unhappily. 'It hurts me.'

'Why don't you go in out of it?' she suggested coldly.

'I've orders to collect. I'm two days behind. Do you like the sun?'

'It depends.'

'Depends with me too. Depends on the night before. Mostly I like the shade. It's cool and it's easy on the eyes. Sleep and the shade. Did Shakespeare say anything about that, I wonder?'

'Not anything that occurs to me.' She wished to God he would go away.

'He should then,' the traveller insisted. 'What's Shakespeare for, if he didn't say anything about sleep and the shade?'

At another time she might have been sorry for him, for his protruding lip, his ashen face, the remote landscape of sorrow which lay behind his slow eyes. But she had her own disappointment. She wanted to go into some quiet place and weep. The sun was too strong and the noise of the awakened square too unsettling. 'Let's talk about Shakespeare some other time,' she suggested. He smiled sadly at the note of dismissal.

'It's a date,' he said. She saw him shuffling away under the cool trees.

When they left Slattery's they tried Mulligan's and in the Stag's Head Higgins said he could eat a farmer's arse, so they had sandwiches. The others had ham and beef but

Sweeney took egg because it was Friday. There was a dogged streak of religion in him which was scrupulous about things like that. Even in his worst bouts of despair he still could observe the prescribed forms. They were precarious footholds which he hesitated to destroy and by which he might eventually drag himself out of the pit. After the Stag's Head Ellis thought of the Oval.

'It's one of his houses,' he said. 'We should have tried it before. What's the next bus?'

'Half eight.'

'Is it the last?'

'The last and ultimate bus. Aston's Quay at half past eight. Let's forget about it.'

'It's only eight o'clock. We might make it.'

'You're spoiling my drink.'

'You're spoiling mine too,' Higgins said, 'all this fluting around.'

'You see. You're spoiling Higgins' drink too.'

'But I feel a louser about this.'

'Good,' Higgins said pleasantly. 'Ellis discovers the truth about himself.'

'Shut up,' Ellis said.

He dragged them across the city again.

The evening was cooler. Over the western reaches of the Liffey barred clouds made the sky alternate with streaks of blue and gold. Steeples and tall houses staggered upward and caught the glowing colours. There was no sign of Byrne in the Oval. They had a drink while the clock moved round until it was twenty minutes to nine.

'I shouldn't have asked you,' Ellis said with genuine remorse.

'That's what I told you,' Higgins said. 'I told you not to ask him.'

'Byrne is an arch louser,' Ellis said bitterly. 'I never thought he'd let me down.'

'You should know Byrne by now,' Higgins said. 'He has medals for it.'

'But I was in trouble. And you both know the set-up at

home. Christ if the old man found out about the type-writer ...'

'Look,' Sweeney said, 'the bus is gone. If I don't mind, why should you? Go and buy me a drink.' But they found they hadn't enough money left between them, so they went around to the Scotch House where Higgins knew the manager and could borrow a pound.

IV

Near the end of his holiday he had taken her to a big hotel at a seaside resort. It was twenty miles by road from the little town, but a world away in its sophistication. They both cycled. Dinner was late and the management liked to encourage dress. A long drive led up to the imposing entrance. They came to it cool and fresh from the sea, their wet swimming togs knotted about the handlebars. It was growing twilight and he could still remember the rustle of piled leaves under the wheels of their bicycles. A long stone balustrade rose from the gravelled terrace. There was an imposing ponderousness of stone and high turrets.

'Glenawling Castle,' he said admiringly. She let her eyes travel from the large and shiny cars to the flag-mast some hundreds of feet up in the dusky air.

'Comrade Sweeney,' she breathed, 'cast your sweaty night-cap in the air.'

They walked on thick carpet across a foyer which smelled of rich cigar smoke. Dinner was a long, solemn ritual. They had two half bottles of wine, white for her, red for himself. When he had poured she looked at both glasses and said happily:

'Isn't it beautiful? I mean the colours.' He found her more astoundingly beautiful than either the gleaming red or the white.

'You are,' he said. 'Good God, you are.' She laughed happily at his intensity. At tables about them young people were in the minority. Glenawling Castle catered to a notable extent for the more elevated members of the hierarchy, Monsignors and Bishops who took a little time off from the affairs of the Church to play sober games of golf and drink discreet glasses of brandy. There were elderly business men with their wives, occasional and devastatingly bored daughters.

After dinner they walked in the grounds. The light had faded from the sky above them but far out to sea an after-glow remained. From the terrace they heard the sound of breakers on the beach below and could smell the strong, autumn smell of the sea. They listened for some time. He took her hand and said, 'Happy?'

She nodded and squeezed his fingers lightly.

'Are you?'

'For the old Bishops and the Monsignors and the business men with their bridge-playing wives.'

They both laughed. Then she shivered suddenly in the cool breeze and they went inside again to explore further. They investigated a room in which elderly men played billiards in their shirt sleeves, and another in which the elderly women sat at cards. In a large lounge old ladies knitted, while in deep chairs an occasional Bishop read somnolently from a priestly book. Feeling young and a little bit out of place, they went into the bar which adjoined the ballroom. There were younger people here. He called for drinks and asked her why she frowned.

'This is expensive for you,' she said. She took a pound note from her bag and left it on the table.

'Let's spend this on the drinks,' she suggested.

'All of it?'

She nodded gravely. He grinned suddenly and gave it to the attendant.

'Pin that on your chest,' he said, 'and clock up the damage until it's gone.'

The attendant looked hard at the note. His disapproval was silent but unmistakable.

'It's a good one,' Sweeney assured him. 'I made it myself.'

They alternated between the ballroom and the bar. In the bar she laughed a lot at the things he said, but in the ballroom they danced more or less silently. They were dancing when he first acknowledged the thought which had been hovering between them.

'I've only two days left.'

'One, darling.'

'Tomorrow and Saturday.'

'It's tomorrow already,' she said, looking at her watch. Now that it was said it was unavoidably necessary to talk about it.

'It's only about two hours by bus,' he said. 'I can get down to see you sometimes. There'll be weekends.'

'You won't though,' she said sadly.

'Who's going to stop me?'

'You think you will now but you won't. A holiday is a holiday. It comes to an end and you go home and then you forget.'

They walked through the foyer which was deserted now. The elderly ladies had retired to bed, and so had the somnolent churchmen with their priestly books.

'I won't forget,' he said when they were once again on the terrace. 'I want you too much.'

The leaves rustled again under their wheels, the autumn air raced past their faces coldly.

'That's what I mean,' she said simply. 'It's bad wanting anything too much.' Her voice came anonymously from the darkness beside him.

'Why?' he asked.

Their cycle lamps were two bars of light in a vast tunnel of darkness. Sometimes a hedge gleamed green in the light or a tree arched over them with mighty and gesticulating limbs.

'Because you never get it,' she answered solemnly.

V

Sweeney, looking through the smoke from Higgins and Ellis to the heavily built man whom he did not like, frowned and tried to remember what public house he was in. They had been in so many and had drunk so much. He was at that stage of drunkenness where his thoughts required an immense tug of his will to keep them concentrated. Whenever he succumbed to the temptation to close his eyes he saw them wandering and grazing at a remote distance from him, small white sheep in a landscape of black hills and valleys. The evening had been a pursuit of something which he felt now he would never catch up with, a succession of calls on some mysterious person who had always left a minute before. It had been of some importance, whatever he had been chasing, but for the moment he had forgotten why. Taking the heavily built man whom he didn't like as a focal point, he gradually pieced together the surroundings until they assumed first a vague familiarity and then a positive identity. It was the Crystal. He relaxed, but not too much, for fear of the woolly annihilation that might follow, and found Higgins and the heavily built man swopping stories. He remembered that they had been swopping stories for a long time. The heavily built man was a friend of Higgins'. He had an advertising agency and talked about the golf club and poker and his new car. He had two daughters – clever as hell. He knew the Variety Girls and had a fund of smutty stories. He told them several times they must come and meet the boys. 'Let's leave this hole,' he said several times, 'and I'll run you out to the golf club. No bother.' But someone began a new story. And besides, Sweeney didn't want to go. Every time he looked at the man with his neat suit and his moustache, his expensively fancy waistcoat and the pin in his tie, he was tempted to get up and walk away. But for Higgins' sake he remained and listened. Higgins was telling a story about a commercial traveller who married a hotel keeper's daughter in a small country town.

The traveller had a protruding upper lip while the daughter, Higgins said, had a protruding lower lip. Like this, Higgins said. Then he said look here he couldn't tell the story if they wouldn't pay attention to him.

'This'll be good, boys,' the man said, 'this will be rich. I think I know this one. Go on.'

But Higgins said hell no they must look at his face. It was a story and they had to watch his face or they'd miss the point.

'Christ no,' Ellis said, 'not your face.'

Sweeney silently echoed the remark not because he really objected to Higgins' face but because it was difficult to focus it in one piece.

Well, Higgins, they could all sugar off, he was going to tell the story and shag the lot of them.

'Now, now,' the man said, 'we're all friends here. No unpleasantness and no bickering, what?'

'Well,' Higgins continued, 'the father of the bride had a mouth which twisted to the left and the mother's mouth, funny enough, twisted to the right. So on the bridal night the pair went to bed in the hotel which, of course, was a very small place, and when the time came to get down to certain important carry-on, the nature of which would readily suggest itself to the assembled company, no need to elaborate, the commercial traveller tried to blow out the candle. He held it level with his mouth but, of course, on account of the protruding upper lip his breath went down the direction of his chin and the candle remained lit.' Higgins stuck out his lip and demonstrated for their benefit the traveller's peculiar difficulty. ' "Alice," said the traveller to his bride, "I'll have to ask you to do this." So her nibs had a go and, of course, with the protruding lower lip, her breath went up towards her nose, and lo and behold the candle was still lighting.' Again Higgins demonstrated. ' "There's nothing for it, John, but call my father," says she. So the oul' fella is summoned and he has a go. But with his lips twisted to the left the breath goes back over his shoulder and the candle is still lighting away. "Dammit, this has me bet," says the father,

"I'll have to call your mother," and after a passable delay the oul' wan appears on the scene but, of course, same thing happens, her breath goes over her right this time, and there the four of them stand in their nightshirts looking at the candle and wondering what the hell will they do next. So they send out for the schoolmaster, and the schoolmaster comes in and they explain their difficulty and ask him for his assistance and "certainly," he says, "it's a great pleasure." And with that he wets his fingers and thumb and pinches the wick and, of course, the candle goes out.' Higgins wet his finger and thumb and demonstrated on an imaginary candle. 'Then the father looks at the other three and shakes his head. "Begod," says he, "did youse ever see the likes of that, isn't education a wonderful thing?" ' The heavily built man guffawed and asserted immediately that he could cap that. It was a story about a commercial traveller too. But as he was about to start they began to call closing time and he said again that they must all come out to the golf club and meet the boys.

'Really,' he said, 'you'll enjoy the boys. I'll run you out in the car.'

'Who's game?' Higgins asked.

Ellis looked at Sweeney and waited. Sweeney looked at the heavily built man and decided he didn't dislike him after all. He hated him.

'Not me,' he said, 'I don't want any shagging golf clubs.'

'I don't care for your friend's tone,' the man began, his face reddening.

'And I don't like new cars,' Sweeney interrupted, rising to his feet.

'Look here,' the heavily built man said threateningly. Ellis and Higgins asked the stout man not to mind him.

'Especially new cars driven by fat bastards with fancy waistcoats,' Sweeney insisted. He saw Ellis and Higgins moving in between him and the other man. They looked surprised and that annoyed him further. But to hit him he would have had to push his way through them and it would take so much effort that he decided it was hardly worth it after all. So he changed his mind. But he turned around as he went out.

'With fancy pins in their ties,' he concluded. People moved out of his way.

They picked him up twenty minutes later at the corner. He was gazing into the window of a tobacconist shop. He was wondering now why he had behaved like that. He had a desire to lean his forehead against the glass. It looked so cool. There was a lonely ache inside him. He barely looked round at them.

'You got back quick,' Sweeney said.

'Oh, cut it out,' Ellis said, 'you know we wouldn't go without you.'

'I hate fat bastards with fancy pins,' Sweeney explained. But he was beginning to feel it was a bit inadequate.

'After all,' Higgins said, 'he was a friend of mine. You might have thought of that.'

'Sugar you and your friends.'

Higgins flushed and said, 'Thanks, I'll remember that.'

Pain gathered like a ball inside Sweeney and he said with intensity, 'You can remember what you sugaring well like.'

'Look,' Ellis said, 'cut it out – the pair of you.'

'He insulted my friend.'

'View four,' Ellis said, 'Higgins the Imperious.'

'And I'll be obliged if you'll cut out this View two View three View four stuff . . .'

'Come on,' Ellis said wearily, 'kiss and make up. What we all need is another drink.'

It seemed a sensible suggestion. They addressed themselves to the delicate business of figuring out the most likely speak-easy.

VI

The last bus stayed for twenty minutes or so and then chugged out towards remoter hamlets and lonelier roads, leaving the square full of shadows in the August evening, dark under the trees, grey in the open spaces about the statue. The air felt thick and warm, the darkness of the sky was relieved here and there with yellow and green patches. To the girl there was a strange finality about the departure of the bus, as though all the inhabitants had boarded it on some impulse which would leave the square empty for ever. She decided to have coffee, not in the Commercial where Cissy was bound to ask questions, but in the more formal atmosphere of the Imperial. She had hoped to be alone, and frowned when she met the traveller in the hallway. He said:

'Well, well. Now we can have our chat about Shakespeare.' She noticed something she had not observed earlier – a small piece of newspaper stuck on the side of his cheek where he had cut himself shaving. For some reason it made her want to laugh. She could see too that he was quite prepared to be rebuffed and guessed his philosophy about such things. Resignation and defeat were his familiars.

'I see you've changed your location,' she said, in a voice which indicated how little it mattered.

'So have you.'

'I was going to have coffee.'

'We can't talk Shakespeare over coffee,' he invited. 'Have a drink with me instead.'

'I wonder should I. I really don't know you,' she answered coolly.

'If it comes to that,' he said philosophically, 'who does?'

They went into the lounge. The lounge in the Imperial paid attention to contemporary ideas. There were tubular tables and chairs, a half moon of a bar with tube lighting which provided plenty of colour but not enough light. The drink was a little dearer, the beer, on such evenings in

August, a little too warm. He raised his glass to her.

'I'm sorry about the boy friend,' he said. She put down her glass deliberately.

'I'd rather you didn't say things like that,' she said. 'It's not particularly entertaining. I'm not Cissy from the Commercial, you know.'

'Sorry,' he said repentantly, 'I meant no harm. It was just for talk's sake.'

'Then let's talk about you. Did you pick up your two days' orders?'

'No,' he said sadly, 'I'm afraid I didn't. I'm afraid I'm not much of a commercial traveller. I'm really a potter.'

'Potter?'

'Yes. I potter around from this place to that.'

She noticed the heavy upper lip quivering and gathered that he was laughing. Then he said:

'That's a little joke I've used hundreds of times. It amuses me because I made it up myself.'

'Do you often do that?'

'I try, but I'm not much good at it. I thought of that one, God knows how many years ago, when things began to slip and I was in bed in the dark in some little room in some cheap hotel. Do you ever feel frightened in a strange room?'

'I'm not often in strange rooms.'

'I am. All my life I've been. When I put out the light I can never remember where the door is. I suppose that's what makes me a pretty poor specimen of a traveller.'

'So you thought of a joke.'

'Yes.'

'But why?'

'It helps. Sometimes when you feel like that a joke has more comfort than a prayer.'

She saw what he meant and felt some surprise.

'Well,' she prompted. 'Why do you travel?'

'It was my father's profession too. He was one of the old stock. A bit stiff and ceremonious. And respected of course. In those days they didn't have to shoot a line. They had dignity. First they left their umbrella and hat in the hall stand. Then there was some polite conversation. A piece of information from the city. A glass of sherry and a biscuit. Now you've got to talk like hell and drive like hell. I suppose he trained me the wrong way.'

He indicated her glass.

'You'll have another?' he asked.

She looked again at his face and made her decision. She was not quite sure what it would involve, but she knew it was necessary to her to see it out.

'I think I will,' she said.

He asked her if she liked her work but she was not anxious to discuss herself at all. She admitted she was bored. After their third drink he asked her if she would care to drive out with him to Glenawling Castle. There were not likely to be people there who knew them and besides, there would be dancing. She hesitated.

'I know what you're thinking,' he said, 'but you needn't worry. I'm no he-man.' She thought it funny that that was not what had occurred to her at all. Then he smiled and added:

'With this lip of mine I don't get much opportunity to practise.'

They got into the car which took them up the hill from the square and over the stone bridge with its brown stream. The traveller looked around at her.

'You're a pretty girl,' he said warmly, 'prettiest I've met.'

She said coolly, 'Prettier than your wife?'

'My wife is dead.'

She glanced involuntarily at the black tie.

'Yes,' he said, 'a month ago.' He waited. 'Does that shock you?' he asked.

'I'm afraid it does.'

'It needn't,' he said. 'We were married for eighteen years, and for fifteen of that she was in a lunatic asylum. I didn't visit her this past eight or nine years. They said it was better. I haven't danced for years either. Do you think I shouldn't?'

'No,' she said after a pause. 'I think it might do you good. You might get over being afraid of strange rooms.'

'At forty-five?' he asked quietly.

His question kept the girl silent. She looked out at the light racing along the hedges, the gleaming leaves, the arching of trees.

VII

They eventually got into Annie's place. It was one of a row of tall and tottering Georgian houses. Ellis knew the right knock and was regarded with professional affection by the ex-boxer who kept the door. They went in the dark up a rickety stairs to a room which was full of cigarette smoke. They had to drink out of cups, since the girls and not the liquor were the nominal attraction. There was some vague tradition that Annie was entitled to serve meals too, but to ask for one was to run the risk of being thrown out by the ex-boxer. The smell of the whiskey in his cup made Sweeney shiver. He had had whiskey early in the evening and after it plenty of beer. Experience had taught him that taking whiskey at this stage was a grave mistake. But no long drinks were available and one had to drink. Ellis noted his silence.

'How are you feeling?' he asked with friendly solicitude. 'Like the Chinese maiden?' Higgins suggested amiably and tickled the plump girl who was sitting on his knee.

'No,' Sweeney said, 'like the cockle man.'

'I know,' Higgins said. 'Like the cockle man when the tide came in. We all appreciate the position of that most unfortunate gentleman.' He tickled the plump girl again. 'Don't we, Maisie?'

Maisie, who belonged to the establishment, giggled.

'You're a terrible hard root,' she said admiringly.

There were about a dozen customers in the place. One group had unearthed an old-fashioned gramophone complete with sound horn and were trying out the records. They quarrelled about whose turn it was to wind it and laughed uproariously at the thin nasal voices and the age of the records. Sweeney was noted to be morose and again Ellis had an attack of conscience.

'I feel a louser,' Ellis said.

'Look,' Sweeney said, 'I told you to forget it.'

'Only for me you could be down the country by now.'

'Only for me you could be out at the golf club,' Sweeney said, 'drinking with the best spivs in the country. You might even have got in the way of marrying one of their daughters.'

The gramophone was asking a trumpeter what he was sounding now.

'God,' Maisie said, 'my grandfather used to sing that. At a party or when he'd a few jars aboard. I can just see him.'

'My God. Where?' Higgins asked in mock alarm.

'In my head – Smarty,' Maisie said. 'I can see him as if it was yesterday. Trumpet-eer what are yew sounding now – Is it the cawl I'm seeking?'

They looked in amazement at Maisie who had burst so suddenly into song. She stopped just as suddenly and gave a sigh of warm and genuine affection. 'It has hairs on it right enough – that thing,' she commented.

'What thing?' Higgins inquired salaciously and was rewarded with another giggle and a playful slap from Maisie.

'Maisie darling,' Ellis appealed, 'will you take Higgins away to some quiet place?'

'Yes,' Sweeney said. 'Bury his head in your bosom.' Maisie laughed and said to Higgins: 'Come on, sweetheart. I want to ask them to put that thing on the gramophone again.' As they went away the thought struck Sweeney that Mary Magdalene might have looked and talked like that and he remembered something which Ellis had quoted to him earlier in the week. He waited for a lull among the gramophone playing group and leaned forward. He said, groping vaguely:

'Last week you quoted me something, a thing about the baptism of Christ ... I mean a poem about a painting of the baptism of Christ . . . do you remember what I mean?'

'I think I do,' Ellis said. Then quickly and without punctuation he began to rattle off a verse. 'A painter of the Umbrian School Designed upon a gesso ground The nimbus of the baptized God The wilderness is cracked and browned.'

'That's it,' Sweeney said. 'Go on.'

Ellis looked surprised. But when he found Sweeney was not trying to make a fool of him he clasped the cup tightly with both hands and leaned across the table. He moved it rhythmically in a small wet circle and repeated the previous verse. Then he continued with half-closed eyes:

'But through the waters pale and thin
Still shine the unoffending feet . . .'

'The unoffending feet,' Sweeney repeated almost to himself. 'That's what I wanted. Christ – that's beautiful.'

But the gramophone rasped out again and the moment of quietness and awareness inside him was shattered to bits. Higgins came with three cups which he let down with a bang on the table.

'Refreshment,' he said, 'Annie's own. At much personal inconvenience.'

Sweeney looked up at him. He had been on the point of touching something and it had been knocked violently away from him. That always happened. The cups and the dirty tables, the people drunk about the gramophone, the girls and the cigarette smoke and the laughter seemed to twist and tangle themselves into a spinning globe which shot forward and shattered about him. A new record whirled raspingly on the gramophone for a moment before a tinny voice gave out the next song.

'Have you got another girl at home
Like Susie,
Just another little girl upon the family tree?
If you've got another girl at home
Like Susie . . .'

But the voice suddenly lost heartiness and pitch and dwindled into a lugubrious grovelling in the bass.

'Somebody wind the bloody thing,' Ellis screamed. Somebody did so without bothering to lift off the pick-up arm. The voice was propelled into a nerve-jarring ascent from chaos to pitch and brightness. Once again the composite globe spun towards him. Sweeney held his head in his hands and groaned. When he closed his eyes he was locked in a smelling cellar with vermin and excrement on the floor, a cellar in which he groped and slithered. Nausea tautened his stomach and sent the saliva churning in his mouth. He rose unsteadily.

'What is it?' Ellis asked.

'Sick,' he mumbled. 'Filthy sick.'

They left Higgins behind and went down into the street. Tenements with wide open doors yawned a decayed and malodorous breath, and around the corner the river between grimy walls was burdened with the incoming tide. Sweeney leaned over the wall.

'Go ahead,' Ellis said.

'I can't?'

'Stick your fingers down your throat.'

Sweeney did so and puked. He trembled. Another spasm gripped him. Ellis, who was holding him, saw a gull swimming over to investigate this new offering.

'It's an ill wind . . .' he said aloud.

'What's that?' Sweeney asked miserably, his elbows still on the wall, his forehead cupped in his hand.

'Nothing,' Ellis said. He smiled quietly and looked up at the moon.

VIII

'Do you mind if I ask you something?' the girl said. 'It's about your wife.'

'Fire ahead,' the traveller said gently.

They stood on the terrace in front of the hotel. Below

them the sea was calm and motionless, but from behind them where the large and illuminated windows broke the blackened brick of the castle the sounds of the band came thinly.

'You haven't seen her for eight or nine years.'

'Fifteen,' the traveller corrected. 'You needn't count the few visits between.'

The girl formulated her next question carefully.

'When you married her,' the girl asked, 'did you love her?' The traveller's face was still moist after the dancing. She saw the small drops of sweat on his forehead while he frowned at the effort to recall the emotion of eighteen years before.

'I don't know,' he answered finally. 'It's funny. I can't exactly remember.'

The girl looked down at the pebbles. She poked them gently with her shoe.

'I see,' she said softly.

He took her hand. Then they both stood silently and watched the moon.

It rode in brilliance through the August sky. It glinted on the pebbled terrace. It stole through curtain chinks into the bedrooms of the sleeping Monsignors and Bishops, it lay in brilliant barrenness on the pillows of stiff elderly ladies who had no longer anything to dream about. Sweeney, recovering, found Ellis still gazing up at it, and joined him. It was high and radiant in the clear windy spaces of the sky. It was round and pure and white.

'Corpus Domini Nostri,' Sweeney murmured.

Ellis straightened and dropped his cigarette end into the water below.

'Like an aspirin,' he said, 'like a bloody big aspirin.'

Mary Lavin

IN A CAFÉ

The café was in a back street. Mary's ankles ached and she was glad Maudie had not got there before her. She sat down at a table near the door.

It was a place she had only recently found, and she dropped in often, whenever she came up to Dublin. She hated to go anywhere else now. For one thing, she knew that she would be unlikely ever to have set foot in it if Richard were still alive. And this knowledge helped to give her back a semblance of the identity she lost willingly in marriage, but lost doubly, and unwillingly, in widowhood.

Not that Richard would have disliked the café. It was the kind of place they went to when they were students. Too much water had gone under the bridge since those days, though. Say what you liked, there was something faintly snobby about a farm in Meath, and together she and Richard would have been out of place here. But it was a different matter to come here alone. There could be nothing – oh, nothing – snobby about a widow. Just by being one, she fitted into this kind of café. It was an unusual little place. She looked around.

The walls were distempered red above and the lower part was boarded, with the boards painted white. It was probably the boarded walls that gave it the peculiarly functional look you get in the snuggery of a public house or in the confessional of a small and poor parish church. For furniture there were only deal tables and chairs, with black-and-white checked tablecloths that were either unironed or badly ironed. But there was a decided feeling that money was not so much in short supply as dedicated to other purposes – as witness the paintings on the walls, and a notice over the fire-grate to say that there were others on view in a studio overhead, in rather the same way as pictures in an exhibition. The paintings were for the most part experimental in their technique.

The café was run by two students from the Art College. They often went out and left the place quite empty – as now – while they had a cup of coffee in another café – across the street. Regular clients sometimes helped themselves to coffee from the pot on the gas-ring, behind a curtain at the back; or, if they only came in for company and found none, merely warmed themselves at the big fire always blazing in the little black grate that was the original grate when the café was a warehouse office. Today, the fire was banked up with coke. The coffee was spitting on the gas-ring.

Would Maudie like the place? That it might not be exactly the right place to have arranged to meet her, above all under the present circumstances, occurred vaguely to Mary, but there was nothing that could be done about it now. When Maudie got there, if she didn't like it, they could go somewhere else. On the other hand, perhaps she might like it? Or perhaps she would be too upset to take notice of her surroundings? The paintings might interest her. They were certainly stimulating. There were two new ones today, which Mary herself had not seen before: two flower paintings, just inside the door. From where she sat she could read the signature, Johann van Stiegler. Or at least they suggested flowers. They were nameable as roses surely in spite of being a bit angular. She knew what Richard would have said about them. But she and Richard were no longer one. So what would *she* say about them? She would say – she would say—

But what was keeping Maudie? It was all very well to be glad of a few minutes' time in which to gather herself together; it was a different thing altogether to be kept a quarter of an hour.

Mary leaned back against the boarding. She was less tired

than when she came in, but she was still in no way prepared for the encounter in front of her.

What had she to say to a young widow recently bereaved? Why on earth had she arranged to meet her? The incongruity of their both being widowed came forcibly upon her. Would Maudie, too, be in black with touches of white? Two widows! It was like two magpies: one for sorrow, two for joy. The absurdity of it was all at once so great she had an impulse to get up and make off out of the place. She felt herself vibrating all over with resentment at being coupled with anyone, and urgently she began to sever them, seeking out their disparities.

Maudie was only a year married! And her parents had been only too ready to take care of her child, greedily possessing themselves of it. Maudie was as free as a girl. Then – if it mattered – ? – she had a nice little income in her own right too, apart from all Michael had left her. So?

But what was keeping her? Was she not coming at all?

Ah! the little iron bell that was over the door – it too, since the warehouse days – tinkled to tell there was another customer coming into the café.

It wasn't Maudie though. It was a young man – youngish anyway – and Mary would say that he was an artist. Yet his hands at which, when he sat down, he began to stare, were not like the hands of an artist. They were peculiarly plump soft-skinned hands, and there was something touching in the relaxed way in which, lightly clasped one in the other, they rested on the table. Had they a womanish look perhaps? No; that was not the word, but she couldn't for the life of her find the right word to describe them. And her mind was teased by trying to find it. Fascinated, her eyes were drawn to those hands, time and again, no matter how resolutely she tore them away. It was almost as if it was by touch, not sight, that she knew their warm fleshiness.

Even when she closed her eyes – as she did – she could still see them. And so, innocent of where she was being led, she made no real effort to free her thoughts from them, and not until it was too late did she see before her the familiar shape of her recurring nightmare. All at once it was Richard's hands she saw, so different from those others, wiry, supple, thin. There they were for an instant in her mind, limned by love and anguish, before they vanished.

It happened so often. In her mind she would see a part of him, his hand – his arm, his foot perhaps, in the finely worked leather shoes he always wore – and from it, frantically, she would try to build up the whole man. Sometimes she succeeded better than others, built him up from foot to shoulder, seeing his hands, his grey suit, his tie, knotted always in a slightly special way, his neck, even his chin that was rather sharp, a little less attractive than his other features—

--But always at that point she would be defeated. Never once voluntarily since the day he died had she been able to see his face again.

And if she could not remember him, at will, what meaning had time at all? What use was it to have lived the past, if behind us it fell away so sheer?

In the hour of his death, for her it was part of the pain that she knew this would happen. She was standing beside him when, outside the hospital window, a bird called out with a sweet, clear whistle, and hearing it she knew that he was dead, because not for years had she really heard bird-song or bird-call, so loud was the noise of their love in her ears. When she looked down it was a strange face, the look of death itself, that lay on the pillow. And after that brief moment of silence that let in the bird-song for an instant, a new noise started in her head; the noise of a nameless panic that did not always roar, but never altogether died down.

And now – here in the little café – she caught at the table-edge – for the conflagration had started again and her mind was a roaring furnace.

It was just then the man at the end of the table stood up and reached for the menu-card on which, as a matter of fact, she was leaning – breasts and elbows – with her face in her hands. Hastily, apologetically, she pushed it towards him, and at once the roar died down in her mind. She looked at him. Could he have known? Her heart was filled with gratitude, and she saw that his eyes were soft and gentle. But she had to admit that he didn't look as if he were much aware of her. No matter! She still was grateful to him.

'Don't you want this too?' she cried, thankful, warm, as she saw that the small slip of paper with the speciality for the day that had been clipped to the menu card with a paper-pin, had come off and remained under her elbow, caught on the rough sleeve of her jacket. She stood up and leant over the table with it.

'Ah! thank you!' he said, and bowed. She smiled. There was such gallantry in a bow. He was a foreigner, of course. And then, before she sat down again she saw that he had been sketching, making little pencil sketches all over a newspaper on the table, in the margins and in the spaces between the newsprint. Such intricate minutely involuted little figures – she was fascinated, but of course she could not stare.

Yet, when she sat down, she watched him covertly, and every now and then she saw that he made a particular flourish: it was his signature, she felt sure, and she tried to make it out from where she sat. A disproportionate, a ridiculous excitement rushed through her, when she realized it was Johann van Stiegler, the name on the new flower paintings that had preoccupied her when she first came into the place.

But it's impossible, she thought. The sketches were so meticulous; the paintings so—

But the little bell tinkled again.

'Ah! Maudie!'

For all her waiting, taken by surprise in the end, she got to her feet in her embarrassment, like a man.

'Maudie, my dear!' She had to stare fixedly at her in an effort to convey the sympathy, which, tongue-tied, she could express in no other way.

They shook hands, wordlessly.

'I'm deliberately refraining from expressing sympathy –

you know that?' said Mary then, as they sat down at the checkered table.

'Oh, I do!' cried Maudie. And she seemed genuinely appreciative. 'It's so awful trying to think of something to say back! – Isn't it? It has to come right out of yourself, and sometimes what comes is something you can't even say out loud when you do think of it!'

It was so true. Mary looked at her in surprise. Her mind ran back over the things people had said to her, and her replies.

Them: It's a good thing it wasn't one of the children.

Her: I'd give them all for him.

Them: Time is a great healer.

Her: Thief would be more like: taking away even my memory of him.

Them: God's ways are wonderful. Some day you'll see His plan in all this.

Her: Do you mean, some day I'll be glad he's dead?

So Maudie apprehended these subtleties too? Mary looked hard at her. 'I know, I know,' she said. 'In the end you have to say what is expected of you – and you feel so cheapened by it.'

'Worse still, you cheapen the dead!' said Maudie.

Mary looked really hard at her now. Was it possible for a young girl – a simple person at that – to have wrung from one single experience so much bitter knowledge? In spite of herself, she felt she was being drawn into complicity with her. She drew back resolutely.

'Of course, you were more or less expecting it, weren't you?' she said, spitefully.

Unrepulsed, Maudie looked back at her. 'Does that matter?' she asked, and then, unexpectedly, she herself put a rift between them. 'You have the children, of course!' she said, and then, hastily, before Mary could say anything, she rushed on. 'Oh, I know I have my baby, but there seems so little link between him and his father! I just can't believe that it's me, sometimes, wheeling him round the park in his pram: it's like as if he was illegitimate. No! I mean it really.

I'm not just trying to be shocking. It must be so different when there has been time for a relationship to be started between children and their father, like there was in your case.'

'Oh, I don't know that that matters,' said Mary. 'And you'll be glad to have him some day.' This time she spoke with deliberate malice, for she knew so well those same words had lacerated her. She knew what they were meant to say: the children would be better than nothing.

But the poison of her words did not penetrate Maudie. And with another stab she knew why this was so. Maudie was so young; so beautiful. Looking at her, it seemed quite inaccurate to say that she had lost her husband: it was Michael who had lost her, fallen out, as it were, while she perforce went onward. She didn't even look like a widow. There was nothing about her to suggest that she was in any way bereft or maimed.

'You'll marry again, Maudie,' she said, impulsively. 'Don't mind my saying it,' she added quickly, hastily. 'It's not a criticism. It's because I know how you're suffering that I say it. Don't take offence.'

Maudie didn't really look offended though, she only looked on the defensive. Then she relaxed.

'Not coming from you,' she said. 'You know what it's like.' Mary saw she was trying to cover up the fact that she simply could not violently refute the suggestion. 'Not that I think I will,' she added, but weakly, 'After all, you didn't!'

It was Mary who was put upon the defensive now.

'After all, it's only two years – less even,' she said stiffly.

'Oh, it's not altogether a matter of time,' said Maudie, seeing she had erred, but not clear how or where. 'It's the kind of person you are, I think. I admire you so much! It's what I'd want to be like myself if I had the strength. With remarriage it is largely the effect on oneself that matters I think, don't you? I don't think it really matters to – to the dead! Do you? I'm sure Michael would want me to marry again if he were able to express a wish. After all, people say it's a compliment to a man if his widow marries again, did you ever hear that?'

'I did,' said Mary curtly. 'But I wouldn't pay much heed to it. A fat lot the dead care about compliments.'

So Maudie *was* already thinking about marriage? Mary's irritation was succeeded by a vague feeling of envy, and then the irritation returned tenfold.

How easily it was accepted that *she* would not marry again. This girl regards me as too old, of course. And she's right – or she ought to be right! She remembered the way, even two years ago, people had said she 'had' her children. They meant, even then, that it was unlikely, unlooked for, that she'd remarry.

Other things that had been said crowded back into her mind as well. So many people had spoken of the special quality of her marriage – hers and Richard's – their remarkable suitability one for the other, and the uniqueness of the bond between them. She was avid to hear this said at the time.

But suddenly, in this little café, the light that had played over those words, flickered and went out. Did they perhaps mean that if Richard had not appeared when he did, no one else would have been interested in her?

Whereas Maudie – ! If she looked so attractive now, when she must still be suffering from shock, what would she be like a year from now, when she would be 'out of mourning', as it would be put? Why, right now, she was so fresh and – looking at her there was no other word for it – virginal. Of course she was only a year married. A year! You could hardly call it being married at all.

But Maudie knew a thing or two about men for all that. There was no denying it. And in her eyes at that moment there was a strange expression. Seeing it, Mary remembered at once that they were not alone in the café. She wondered urgently how much the man at the other end of the table had heard and could hear of what they were saying. But it was too late to stop Maudie.

'Oh Mary,' cried Maudie, leaning forward, 'it's not what they give us – I've got over wanting things like a child – it's what we have to give them! It's something – ' and she pressed her hands suddenly to her breasts, 'something in here!'

'Maudie!'

Sharply, urgently, Mary tried to make her lower her voice, and with a quick movement of her head she did manage at last to convey some caution to her.

'In case you might say something,' she said, in a low voice.

'Oh, there was no fear,' said Maudie. 'I was aware all the time.' She didn't speak quite so low as Mary, but did lower her voice. 'I was aware of him *all the time,*' she said. 'It was *him* that put it into my mind – about what we have to give.' She pressed her hands to her breasts again. 'He looks so lonely, don't you think? He is a foreigner, isn't he? I always think it's sad for them; they don't have many friends, and even when they do, there is always a barrier, don't you agree?'

But Mary was too embarrassed to let her go on. Almost frantically she made a diversion.

'What are you going to have, Maudie?' she said, loudly. 'Coffee? Tea? And is there no one to take an order?'

Immediately she felt a fool. To whom had she spoken? She looked across at Johann van Stiegler. As if he were waiting to meet her glance, his mild and patient eyes looked into hers.

'There is no one there', he said, nodding at the curtained gas-ring, 'but one can serve oneself. Perhaps you would wish that I—'

'Oh, not at all,' cried Mary. 'Please don't trouble! We're in absolutely no hurry! Please don't trouble yourself,' she said, 'not on our account.'

But she saw at once that he was very much a foreigner, and that he was at a disadvantage, not knowing if he had perhaps made a gaffe. 'I have perhaps intruded?' he said, miserably.

'Oh, not at all,' cried Mary, and he was so serious she had to laugh.

The laugh was another mistake though. His face took on a look of despair that could come upon a foreigner, it seemed, at the slightest provocation, as if suddenly everything was obscure to him – everything.

'Please,' she murmured, and then vaguely, ' – your work,' meaning that she did not wish to interrupt his sketching.

'Ah, you know my work?' he said, brightening immediately, pleased and with a small and quite endearing vanity. 'We have met before? Yes?'

'Oh no, we haven't met,' she said, quickly, and she sat down, but of course after that it was impossible to go on acting as if he were a complete stranger. She turned to see what Maudie would make of the situation. It was then she felt the full force of her irritation with Maudie. She could have given her a slap in the face. Yes: a slap right in the face! For there she sat, remotely, her face indeed partly averted from them.

Maudie was waiting to be introduced! To be *introduced*, as if she, Mary, did not need any conventional preliminaries. As if it was all right that she, Mary, should begin an unprefaced conversation with a strange man in a café because – and of course that was what was so infuriating, that she knew Maudie's unconscious thought – it was all right for a woman of *her* age to strike up a conversation like that, but that it wouldn't have done for a young woman. Yet, on her still partly averted face, Mary could see the quickened look of interest. She had a good mind not to make any gesture to draw her into the conversation at all, but she had the young man to consider. She had to bring them together whether she liked it or not.

'Maudie, this is—' she turned back and smiled at van Stiegler, 'this is—' But she was confused and she had to abandon the introduction altogether. Instead, she broke into a direct question.

'Those are your flower pictures, aren't they?' she asked.

It was enough for Maudie – more than enough you might say.

She turned to the young man, obviously greatly impressed; her lips apart, her eyes shining. My God, how attractive she was!

'Oh no, not really?' she cried. 'How marvellous of you!'

But Johann van Stiegler was looking at Mary.

'You are sure we have not met before?'

'Oh no, but you were scribbling your signature all over that newspaper,' she looked around to show it to him, but it had fallen on to the floor.

'Ah yes,' he said, and – she couldn't be certain, of course – but she thought he was disappointed.

'Ah yes, you saw my signature,' he said, flatly. He looked dejected. Mary felt helpless. She turned to Maudie. It was up to her to say something now.

Just then the little warehouse bell tinkled again, and this time it was one of the proprietors who came in, casually, like a client.

'Ah good!' said van Stiegler. 'Coffee,' he called out. Then he turned to Mary. 'Coffee for you too?'

'Oh yes, coffee for us,' said Mary, but she couldn't help wondering who was going to pay for it, and simultaneously she couldn't help noticing the shabbiness of his jacket. Well – they'd see! Meanwhile, she determined to ignore the plate of cakes that was put down with the coffee. And she hoped Maudie would too. She pushed the plate aside as a kind of hint to her, but Maudie leaned across and took a large bun filled with cream.

'Do you mind my asking you something – about your work—?' said Mary.

But Maudie interrupted.

'You are living in Ireland? I mean, you are not just here on a visit?'

There was intimacy and intimacy, and Mary felt nervous in case the young man might resent this question.

'I teach art in a college here,' he said, and he did seem a little surprised, but Mary could see too, that he was not at all displeased. He seemed to settle more comfortably into the conversation.

'It is very good for a while to go to another country,' he

said, 'and this country is cheap. I have a flat in the next street to here, and it is very private. If I hang myself from the ceiling, it is all right – nobody knows; nobody cares. That is a good way to live when you paint.'

Mary was prepared to ponder. 'Do you think so?'

Maudie was not prepared to ponder. 'How odd,' she said, shortly, and then she looked at her watch. 'I'll have to go,' she said inexplicably.

They had finished the coffee. Immediately Mary's thoughts returned to the problem of who was to pay for it. It was a small affair for which to call up all one's spiritual resources, but she felt enormously courageous and determined when she heard herself ask in a loud voice for her bill.

'My bill, please,' she called out, over the sound of spitting coffee on the gas stove.

Johann van Stiegler made no move to ask for his bill, and yet he was buttoning his jacket and folding his newspaper as if to leave too. Would his coffee go on her bill? Mary wondered.

It was all settled, however, in a second. The bill was for two eight-penny coffees, and one bun, and there was no charge for van Stiegler's coffee. He had some understanding with the owners, she supposed. Or perhaps he was not really going to leave then at all?

As they stood up, however, gloved and ready to depart, the young man bowed.

'Perhaps we go the same way?' They could see he was anxious to be polite.

'Oh, not at all,' they said together, as if he had offered to escort them, and Maudie even laughed openly.

Then there was, of course, another ridiculous situation. Van Stiegler sat down again. Had they been too brusque? Had they hurt his feelings?

Oh, if only he wasn't a foreigner, thought Mary, and she hesitated. Maudie already had her hand on the door.

'I hope I will see some more of your work sometime,' said Mary. It was not a question, merely a compliment.

But van Stiegler sprang to his feet again.

'Tonight after my classes I am bringing another picture to hang here,' he said. 'You would like to see it? I would be here—' he pulled out a large, old-fashioned watch, ' – at ten minutes past nine.'

'Oh, not tonight – I couldn't come back tonight,' said Mary. 'I live in the country, you see,' she said, explaining and excusing herself. 'Another time perhaps? It will be here for how long?'

She wasn't really listening to what he said. She was thinking that he had not asked if Maudie could come. Perhaps it was that, of the two of them, she looked the most likely to buy a picture, whereas Maudie, although in actual fact more likely to do so, looked less so. Or was it that he coupled them so that he thought if one came, both came. Or was it really Maudie he'd like to see again, and that he regarded her as a chaperone? Or was it—?

There was no knowing, however, and so she said goodbye again, and the next minute the little bell had tinkled over the door and they were in the street. In the street they looked at each other.

'Well! if ever there was—' began Maudie, but she didn't get time to finish her sentence. Behind them the little bell tinkled yet again, and their painter was out in the street with them.

'I forgot to give you the address of my flat – it is also my studio,' he said. 'I would be glad to show you my paintings at any time.' He pulled out a notebook and tore out a sheet. 'I will write it down,' he said, concisely. And he did. But when he went to hand it to them, it was Maudie who took it. 'I am nearly always there, except when I am at my classes,' he said. And bowing he turned and went back into the café.

They dared not laugh until they had walked some distance away, until they turned into the next street in fact.

'Well, I never!' said Maudie, and she handed the paper to Mary.

'Chatham Row,' Mary read, 'number 8.'

'Will you go to see them?' asked Maudie.

Mary felt outraged.

'What do you take me for?' she asked. 'I may be a bit unconventional, but can you see me presenting myself at his place? Would *you* go?'

'Oh, it's different for me,' said Maudie, enigmatically. 'And anyway, it was you he asked. But I see your point – it's a pity. Poor fellow! – he must be very lonely. I wish there was something we could do for him – someone to whom we could introduce him.'

Mary looked at her. It had never occurred to her that he might be lonely! How was it that the obvious always escaped her?

They were in Grafton Street by this time.

'Well, I have some shopping to do. I suppose it's the same with you,' said Maudie. 'I am glad I had that talk with you. We must have another chat soon.'

'Oh yes,' said Mary, over-readily, replying to her adieux though, and not to the suggestion of their meeting again! She was anxious all at once to be rid of Maudie.

And yet, as she watched her walk away from her, making her passage quickly and expertly through the crowds in the street, Mary felt a sudden terrible aimlessness descend upon herself like a physical paralysis. She walked along, pausing to look in at the shop windows.

It was the evening hour when everyone in the streets was hurrying home, purposeful and intent. Even those who paused to look into the shop windows did so with direction and aim, darting their bright glances keenly, like birds. Their minds were all intent upon substantives; tangibles, while her mind was straying back to the student café, and the strange flower pictures on the walls; to the young man who was so vulnerable in his vanity: the legitimate vanity of his art.

It was so like Maudie to laugh at him. What did she know of an artist's mind? If Maudie had not been with her, it would have been so different. She might, for one thing, have got him to talk about his work, to explain the discrepancy between the loose style of the pictures on the wall and the exact, small sketches he'd been drawing on the margins of the paper.

She might even have taken up his invitation to go and see his paintings. Why had that seemed so unconventional – so laughable? Because of Maudie, that was why.

How ridiculous their scruples would have seemed to the young man. She could only hope he had not guessed them. She looked up at a clock. Supposing, right now, she were to slip back to the café and suggest that after all she found she would have time for a quick visit to his studio? Or would he have left the café? Better perhaps to call around to the studio? He would surely be back there now!

For a moment she stood debating the arguments for and against going back. Would it seem odd to him? Would he be surprised? But as if it were Maudie who put the questions, she frowned them down and all at once purposeful as anyone in the street, began to go back, headlong, you might say, towards Chatham Street.

At the point where two small streets crossed each other she had to pause, while a team of Guinness's dray horses turned with difficulty in the narrow cube of the intersection. And, while she waited impatiently, she caught sight of herself in the gilded mirror of a public house. For a second, the familiar sight gave her a misgiving of her mission, but as the dray horses moved out of the way, she told herself that her dowdy, lumpish, and unromantic figure vouched for her spiritual integrity. She pulled herself away from the face in the glass and hurried across the street.

Between two lock-up shops, down a short alley – roofed by the second storey of the premises overhead, till it was like a tunnel – was his door. Away at the end of the tunnel the door could clearly be seen even from the middle of the street, for it was painted bright yellow. Odd that she had never seen it in the times she had passed that way. She crossed the street.

Once across the street, she ran down the tunnel, her footsteps echoing loud in her ears. And there on the door, tied to the latchet of the letter-box, was a piece of white cardboard with his name on it. Grabbing the knocker, she gave three clear hammer-strokes on the door.

The little alley was a sort of cul-de-sac; except for the street behind her and the door in front of her, it had no outlet. There was not even a skylight or an aperture of any kind. As for the premises into which the door led, there was no way of telling its size or its extent, or anything at all about it, until the door was opened.

Irresponsibly, she giggled. It was like the mystifying doors in the trunks of trees that beguiled her as a child in fairy tales and fantasies. Did this door, too, like those fairy doors, lead into rooms of impossible amplitude, or would it be a cramped and poky place?

As she pondered upon what was within, seemingly so mysteriously sealed, she saw that – just as in a fairy tale – after all there was an aperture. The letter-box had lost its shutter, or lid, and it gaped open, a vacant hole in the wood, reminding her of a sleeping doll whose eyeballs had been poked in its head, and creating an expression of vacancy and emptiness.

Impulsively, going down on one knee, she peered in through the slit.

At first she could see only segments of the objects within, but by moving her head, she was able to identify things: an unfinished canvas up against the splattered white wainscot, a bicycle-pump flat on the floor, the leg of a table, black iron bed-legs and, to her amusement dangling down by the leg of the table, dripping their moisture in a pool on the floor, a pair of elongated, grey, wool socks. It was, of course, only possible to see the lower portion of the room, but it seemed enough to infer conclusively that this was indeed a little room in a tree, no bigger than the bulk of the outer trunk, leading nowhere, and – sufficient or no – itself its own end.

There was just one break in the wainscot, where a door ran down to the floor, but this was so narrow and made of roughly-jointed boards, that she took it to be the door of a press. And then, as she started moving, she saw something else, an intricate segment of fine wire spokes. It was a second before she realized it was the wheel of a bicycle.

So, a bicycle, too, lived here, in this little room in a tree-trunk!

Oh, poor young man, poor painter: poor foreigner, inept at finding the good lodgings in a strange city. Her heart went out to him.

It was just then that the boarded door – it couldn't have been a press after all – opened into the room, and she found herself staring at two feet. They were large feet, shoved into unlaced shoes, and they were bare to the white ankles. For, of course, she thought wildly, focusing her thoughts, his socks are washed! But her power to think clearly only lasted an instant. She sprang to her feet.

'Who iss that?' asked a voice. 'Did someone knock?'

It was the voice of the man in the café. But where was she to find a voice with which to reply? And who was she to say what she was? Who – to this stranger – was she?

And if he opened the door, what then? All the thoughts and words that had, like a wind, blown her down this tunnel, subsided suddenly, and she stood, appalled, at where they had brought her.

'Who iss that?' came the voice within, troubled.

Staring at those white feet, thrust into the unlaced shoes, she felt that she would die on the spot if they moved an inch. She turned.

Ahead of her, bright, shining and clear, as if it were at the end of a powerful telescope, was the street. Not caring if her feet were heard, volleying and echoing as if she ran through a mighty drain-pipe, she kept running till she reached the street, kept running even then, jostling surprised shoppers, hitting her ankles off the wheel-knobs of push-cars and prams. Only when she came to the junction of the streets again, did she stop, as in the pub mirror she caught sight again of her familiar face. That face steadied her. How absurd to think that anyone would sinisterly follow this middle-aged woman?

But suppose he had been in the outer room when she

knocked! If he had opened the door? What would have happened then? What would she have said? A flush spread over her face. The only true words that she could have uttered were those that had sunk into her mind in the café; put there my Maudie.

'I'm lonely!' That was all she could have said. 'I'm lonely. Are you?'

A deep shame came over her with this admission and, guiltily, she began to walk quickly onward again, towards Grafton Street. If anyone had seen her, there in that dark alleyway! If anyone could have looked into her mind, her heart!

And yet, was it so unnatural? Was it so hard to understand? So unforgiveable?

As she passed the open door of the Carmelite Church she paused. Could she rid herself of her feeling of shame in the dark of the confessional? To the sin-accustomed ears of the wise old fathers her story would be lightweight; a tedious tale of scrupulosity. Was there no one, no one who'd understand?

She had reached Grafton Street once more, and stepped into its crowded thoroughfare. It was only a few minutes since she left it, but in the street the evasion of light had begun. Only the bustle of people, and the activity of traffic, made it seem that it was yet day. Away at the top of the street, in Stephen's Green, to which she turned, although the tops of the trees were still clear, branch for branch, in the last of the light, mist muted the outline of the bushes. If one were to put a hand between the railings now, it would be with a slight shock that the fingers would feel the little branches, like fine bones, under the feathers of mist. And in their secret nests the smaller birds were making faint avowals in the last of the day. It was the time at which she used to meet Richard.

'Oh Richard!' she cried, almost out loud, as she walked along by the railings to where the car was parked. 'Oh Richard! It's you I want.'

And as she cried out, her mind presented him to her, as

she so often saw him, coming towards her: tall, handsome, and with his curious air of apartness from those around him. He had his hat in his hand, down by his side, as on a summer day he might trail a hand in water from the side of a boat. She wanted to preserve that picture of him for ever in an image, and only as she struggled to hold on to it did she realize there was no urgency in the search. She had a sense of having all the time in the world to look and look and look at him. That was the very way he used to come to meet her – indolently trailing the old felt hat, glad to be done with the day; and when they got nearer to each other she used to take such joy in his unsmiling face, with its happiness integral to it in all its features. It was the first time in the two years he'd been gone from her that she'd seen his face.

Not till she had taken out the key of the car, and gone straight around to the driver's side, not stupidly, as so often, to the passenger seat – not till then did she realize what she had achieved. Yet she had no more than got back her rights. No more. It was not a subject for amazement. By what means exactly had she got them back though – in that little café. That was the wonder.

Patrick Boyle

INTERLUDE

It all started – the engagement, I mean – the morning that the landlady's fourteen-year-old daughter came bursting into Molly's bedroom to call her for work, shouting as she opened the door:

'Eight o'clock. Time to get—' Her startled gaze fell on me.

I was sitting on the edge of the bed, nothing on but my jockey briefs, scratching my armpits and yawning.

'Oh hello, Mr Doyle,' she said.

A muffled groan from Molly showed that I was going to get no assistance from *that* quarter. She had rolled the bedclothes over her head and was now coiled up against the wall.

I cupped a hand over each bare knee, cocked my head aslant and gazed at the intruder with, what I hoped was, a quizzical stare.

'Hello, Babs,' I said. 'You're up early this morning.'

She eyed me up and down with bright, black, suspicious eyes.

'You're early yourself,' she said.

I drummed my fingers irritably on my knee caps, very conscious that the rest of my clothes were scattered round the room and that I was in a poor position to carry on a sustained conversation.

'I didn't sleep too well,' I said. 'I had a big feed of fish and chips before I went to bed last night.'

'Which bed?' Babs said, as she turned to go out.

Molly's head shot up from under the bedclothes; her face was scarlet.

'Stop her, Jim,' she begged. 'Don't let her away like that.'

I rushed out into the corridor.

'Babs!' I called.

The small, sturdy figure disappearing down the stairs, halted.

'Yes?'

'Come back up a moment, will you.'

'All right.'

When I got back to the bedroom, Molly was sitting up, wrapped in a bed jacket. Her fair hair was fluffed out. Her eyes heavy with sleep. She was breathing like a beaten runner.

'Think, Jim,' she gasped. 'Quick. We'll have to tell her something.'

I had grabbed up my trousers and was struggling into them. My mind was in a whirl. What was there to say? How make respectable sense out of the circumstances in which we had been discovered?

'You talk to her, Molly. I can't think of anything to say.'

There was a discreet knock at the door.

'May I come in?'

Molly's lips mouthed a silent epithet.

'Yes, darling,' she called.

Babs sidled into the room and remained standing at the door, one hand swinging off the door knob.

A long silence ensued. Molly's lips opened and closed. Soundlessly. In desperation, I said:

'Look here, Babs, it's not what you think at all.'

She stared at me, a sly grin on her face.

'No,' I continued. 'It's just that ... I happened to ... I thought I would ... I thought I'd make sure that Molly hadn't ... hadn't slept in ...'

Oh, what was the use of trying to fake up an explanation when Babs's keen eyes were already taking note of shoes, socks, shirt, tie, jacket, littered about the floor. Still—

'She's a heavy sleeper, you know,' I blundered on. 'I thought perhaps—'

Suddenly Molly cut in:

'Why make a secret of it, Jim? It's bound to leak out sometime.'

I gazed at her in amazement.

'M-M-M-M-Make a secret?' I stuttered.

Eyes gone soft and mushy, as I'd seen them so many times in the grey light of morning when I kissed her before creeping back to my own room, she turned to Babs.

'He's terribly shy,' she explained. 'Doesn't want anyone to know about it.'

'In the name of God, Molly, are you gone—'

She interposed:

'I told you, Jim. It's something we just can't keep to ourselves.'

Babs was listening, open mouthed.

'Come here, Jim,' Molly commanded. She extended one arm full length, beckoning me with a finger. Like a stoat-seduced rabbit, I shambled forward, allowing her to grasp my hand. She leaned across the bed towards Babs.

'*You're* the first to be told,' she said, softly, confidentially.

She dragged me a step nearer. Waited till Babs, agog with excitement, had moved to the bedside. Announced triumphantly:

'We're engaged.'

I flopped down on the bed. My mind a blank. All my thought processes atrophied. Without interest I watched them hug each other. Heard them babbling:

'Oh, how wonderful.'

'Isn't it great?'

'When is it to be?'

'It's not settled yet.'

'Where will you go for your honeymoon?'

'We haven't decided.'

At last Babs made for the door. Molly called after her:

'Remember, darling, you're to keep it to yourself.'

Over her shoulder, Babs hissed:

'I won't tell a soul.'

I listened to the footsteps running down the stairs. To the sound of a door opening. And slamming shut. Dry-mouthed, I croaked:

'I suppose you know where she's gone?'

'Of course I do. To tell her mother.'

Molly was sitting up very straight. Quite composed. Cheerful even, if I could believe the crinkle under her eyes that was always the prelude to a grin.

'You bloody idiot!' I exploded. 'What the hell possessed you? Look at the ridiculous situation you've created.'

'It's surely better than the situation we were found in?' She gazed at me blandly, eyebrows raised in inquiry.

'I'm damned if I see how you have improved matters by giving out that we are engaged.'

'You don't?'

'No. That Babs one is going to blurt the whole thing out to her mother. And what Mrs Mullen will say when she learns we were practically caught in bed together, is not hard to guess. We will probably both be chucked out of the digs. It will be the talk of the village for weeks.' I groaned. 'My God, what a bloody balls up.'

Molly was studying the finger-nails of her left hand.

'Babs will be so excited with her news,' she said, 'that she won't bother with the details. After all, it *is* a bit of an occasion. The two boarders suddenly deciding to get engaged. After ignoring each other studiously for the last six months. Maybe it was too cute we were entirely.'

'To hell with casting up. It will get you no place. Better for you to figure out what we'll say when Mrs Mullen gets to hear—'

'And what if she does?' Casually she polished her nails on the soft wool of her bed jacket.

'My God, are you gone clean cuckoo?'

Molly looked up.

'You've got a lot to learn, Jim,' she said. 'Don't you know that engaged couples are allowed certain ... certain liberties? People are more indulgent towards them than they would be towards ordinary couples. Mrs Mullen, when she finds out we are engaged, will not question our conduct. At most, she may hint at discretion. But that is all. The prospect of a fully-fledged romance breaking out right under her nose will be too much for her. You'll see I'm right.'

'You mean you're going to go through with this engagement business?'

'We have no other choice.'

'But people will get to hear of it. They'll be asking questions. What are we going to say?'

'That we intend getting married, stupid. What else can we say? Now, clear out of here until I get dressed. I am late enough as it is.'

I gathered up my clothes from the floor and went back to my own room. As I was dressing, I tried to figure out what should be my attitude to this grisly situation. A polite but evasive acknowledgement that the rumour was true? A jaunty nonchalance as though it were not to be taken too seriously? A grim resignation to the unavoidable?

Molly was right about Mrs Mullen. At lunch time she bustled around making a fuss over the pair of us, anxious to know if the soup was hot and the beef tender enough, if Molly had had a busy day in the Post Office and I a tiring round of Insurance calls, if we would care for a second helping of stewed apples and prefer biscuits to a nice slice of cake. When she brought in the coffee, she stood looking down at us, her brown spaniel eyes misted with emotion.

'I suppose,' she said, 'you'll not be here for tea tonight?'

Molly looked at her in astonishment.

'What makes you say that?'

Mrs Mullen stooped down, her sallow features creased in a conspiratorial smile.

'You'll be having a bit of a celebration somewhere, surely to goodness.'

She moved to the door. Wheeled around. Whispered:

'And don't do what I wouldn't do.'

The door closed on her throaty chuckle.

'Did you hear that?' said Molly. 'Isn't she the bad-minded article?'

'Though she's right about the celebration,' she added. 'We'll have to act the part of an engaged couple from now on.'

'Maybe,' I said. 'But we can do that nice and quiet. No celebrations.'

'All right, honey. No celebrations.'

But there were celebrations. When I got back from work, Dick – Mrs Mullen's husband – was lounging against the bar door, waiting for me.

'The sound man himself!' he shouted, as soon as I got out of the car.

'Hello, Dick.'

'I hear you've done the bould thing.' He held out his hand. 'Well, it had to come some time.' Vigorously he shook my hand. 'It'll take the nyah off you, if it does nothing else.'

I did not like the sound of this talk. God knows what he would come out with next.

'It is supposed to be unofficial,' I said. 'We were only going to tell a few friends.'

He gave a great shout of laughter.

'God send you sense. The Missus spent her whole day chatting the neighbours. By this time there's not a dog on the street but doesn't know of it.'

He pushed open the door.

'Come on in,' he said. 'This calls for a Papal blessing.'

He poured out two bumpers of whiskey. Held his glass aloft.

'Happy days, Jim! That you may never regret it.' In one swig he emptied the glass. 'There'll be no more outings with the boys. You're spancelled from now on.'

'Aw, it'll not be as bad as that, will it?'

'Sparing up for the big day, you'll be. So busy putting them on their edges that you'll give all your friends the go by.'

'Not a chance of that, Dick.' I didn't like the turn the conversation was taking. Finishing my drink, I said:

'A small similarity.'

When the drinks were filled, he leaned his elbows on the counter and rubbed his unshaven chin.

'I was just thinking,' he said, 'that maybe we should have a little party tonight. The Sergeant, Joe Harris, just a few of the boys. It's an occasion for a jar or two, wouldn't you say?'

'Before you go on the dry,' he added, baring his yellow fangs in a smile.

There was little use arguing the point. It was apparent that all he wanted was an excuse for a night's carousing. Besides, I had a strong suspicion that he knew all about the goings on of this morning. Maybe a good deal more. It would pay to keep in with him.

'I suppose it would be in order,' I said.

We finished our drinks and I went down to the dining-room for tea.

Molly was delighted at the idea of an engagement party.

'But look here,' I said. 'I thought we were to keep the whole thing as quiet as possible. This party will broadcast it. And give it the appearance of a real ... of an official engagement.'

'I had nothing to do with the arranging of a party. It was yourself and Dick Mullen.'

'Didn't I tell you I couldn't refuse. I was walked into it.'

'Then why blame me?'

'Nobody's blaming you.' I was properly nettled. 'It's just that you're ... you're making a skit out of this ridiculous affair ... taking it too ... a bit too lightly.'

With finicky precision, she aligned the knife and fork on her empty plate. Pushed it away. Dabbed at her lips with her napkin.

'You're mistaken, Jim,' she said. 'I'm not taking it too lightly at all.' Thrusting out her flattened left hand, palm downwards, she brandished it under my nose. 'There!'

Only then did I notice the three-stone ring on her third finger.

'Wh-Wh-What are you doing with that yoke?' I demanded.

She held up her hand towards the naked bulb overhead, wriggling her fingers, so that the diamonds sparkled in the light.

'Nice, isn't it? It was my mother's, God be good to her. Until you get me a proper one, it will have to do.'

Suddenly she pointed an accusing finger.

'If you could just see yourself, Jim. Sitting there so dour and desperate and woebegone. Like a condemned man.'

Leaning over, she ruffled my hair.

'Cheer up, sour puss. I'm not the hangman. Just your fiancée. The little girl you asked to marry you this morning. Remember?'

She began to laugh, a wry stifled laugh at first, but soon she had her head back crowing with half hysterical laughter. Against my will, I joined in and soon the pair of us were hooting and screeching and spluttering with helpless laughter.

Mrs Mullen poked her head round the dining-room door, an indulgent smile on her face.

'Isn't it well for you?' she said, as she backed out, closing the door softly behind her.

Molly wiped the tears from her eyes.

'Didn't I tell you, Jim,' she gasped, 'that the romance of the situation ... would be too much for her ... she is probably taking credit ... for bringing the two of us together.'

'An odd sort of a matchmaker, if you ask me.'

Again we laughed, this time contented happy laughter. And why not? Weren't we leagued together against the world of meddlers, a vast conspiracy of busybodies intent on our destruction? Our only hope of survival was the bond that coupled us.

I reached over and patted her hand.

'Do you know what it is? We might very well turn out to be a creditable enough combination.'

Her face lit up, eyes glittering from unshed tears, quivering lips clogged with unspoken words. At that moment it was borne in on me that she was heartbreakingly beautiful.

'I wish,' she said, at last. 'Oh, I wish—'

'Yes?' I prompted.

'That was the nicest thing you ever said to me,' she finished, but I knew it was not what she had been about to say.

Tea finished, we sat on either side of the fire, our eyes locking as we glanced up occasionally from our reading. Talk was unnecessary as was the need even to touch each other. After all, what was the urgency? Ahead of us there was time enough and to spare for all that had to be done and said. When Dick shouted in to me to come down to the bar, I obeyed reluctantly.

The sergeant and Joe Harris, cashier in the local bank, were already there.

'Well, here he is,' said the Sergeant, putting down his glass. 'So you're taking the big step.' He shook me vehemently by the hand. Put his lips to my ear. Whispered: 'A grand wee girl. You're making no mistake there.'

Joe Harris, his bald head already sweating, lumbered across.

'Congratulations,' he boomed, his swarthy simian face unsmiling.

'Isn't he the right villain, Joe?' the Sergeant said. 'He wiped *your* eye about proper. Doing a steady line on the QT and not letting on to a sinner. Oh, he's worth the watching, all right.'

'Large whiskies, Boss,' ordered Joe.

Drinks in hand, we waited whilst he held the glass to his nose. Sniffed eagerly, like an impatient terrier. Lifted the glass perfunctorily in my direction.

'Luck!' he grunted and gulched back the whiskey greedily, holding the inverted glass to his lips till the last drop was gone. Smacking his lips noisily, he replaced the glass on the counter.

'Aaaaaaaaaaah!' he sighed.

We stayed there drinking – the Sergeant and I, bottled stout, Joe Harris, whiskey – until closing time when we all moved down to the sitting-room where Molly and Mrs Mullen were awaiting us.

Joe, by this time nicely thank you, insisted that the ladies join us in large whiskies.

'Settles the stomach,' he said.

I tried to warn Molly to refuse but she was too excited to pay heed. Face flushed, eyes sparkling, she took the glass from the tray of drinks and raised it aloft.

'Your very good health, Mr Harris,' she said.

She drank, making an involuntary gesture of loathing at the first sip.

'Aaaaaaaaaah!' Joe banged his empty tumbler on the table.

Molly laughed.

'It's well somebody enjoys the stuff,' she said.

Joe smacked together his out-thrust lips.

'You can't whack it, Ma'am,' he said. 'The real Ally Dooley.'

The rounds of drink began to come up middling quick. The Sergeant and I went back to Guinness, Dick and Joe stuck to the whiskey, the ladies turned to gin and tonic. Soon we were all talking at the same time, leaning forward to shout across the room at each other. Groups formed and dissolved as people with a weighty message to deliver found themselves forced to act as audience. Patriots held forth, politicians explained, news mongers enlighted.

'What I say is—'

'What he actually said was—'

'What they're all saying is—'

Molly was sticking it out well. Waving her arms about a little too much, perhaps. But that was all. When the chance occurred, I would catch her eye and signal encouragement. The way she smiled back, a contented, trusting, completely defenceless smile, made me square my shoulders, push out my chest and sink whatever was left in my glass.

At the first lull in the pandemonium, the Sergeant called out:

'What about our charming hostess giving us a song?'

'Oh no, Sergeant,' Mrs Mullen demurred. 'Don't ask me. I'm out of practice. Haven't sung a note since God knows when.'

Overborne by the insistent clamour, she at length consented and took her seat at the battered out piano.

'What shall I sing?' she mused, rippling out a few preliminary chords. She struck the bass of the keyboard twice in a decisive manner. 'I know,' she said, over her shoulder. 'I'll sing you something from "Il Trovatore".'

She played the few opening bars with the melodramatic action of a trotting pony, lifting each hand high in the air, wrist curved down and holding it poised threateningly for a moment before slamming the spreadeagled fingers down on the keyboard. I had heard her sing the song a dozen times but was still flabbergasted at her interpretation. As long as the melody remained in the low register, she gabbled out the meaningless Italian words with a reckless, and indecent haste, battering out a *TUM-tum-tum, TUM-tum-tum,* accompaniment on the piano. Only when the high notes were reached did she get a proper chance – as she phrased it herself – to display any brio.

Striking a chord on the bass and treble, her hands extended to either side, she bent over the keyboard, shook her head violently as she gnawed and worried at the precursory note and then, like a terrier throwing a rat in the air, hurled its mangled remains at the ceiling. At last with back-flung head and mouth stretched wide, she attacked the high note.

It was an appalling sound, a hoarse rasping screech, rendered more agonizing by the piteous quaver in the voice. Sustained until there was no breath left in her lungs and accompanied by a vibratory barrage from the outstretched fingers of both hands, it set the ornaments on the mantelpiece jingling.

Clutching my empty glass, I stared into its depths and tried to arrange my features into an expression of stunned appreciation. I noticed that Molly was holding her bowed head in one hand and that the Sergeant was gaping into space with a curious stricken look on his face. When Mrs Mullen, panting triumphantly, brought her solo to an end with a series of chords executed with crossed hands, I found my forehead beaded with sweat.

We clapped and applauded and begged for more. Dick, his lips drawn back in a wolfish smile, said:

'You're in great voice tonight, Bridie.'

But she was adamant.

'That will be all for now. Maybe later on. When the rest of you have all done your party pieces.'

So Dick recited 'The Green Eye of the Little Yellow God' and I belted out 'The Irish Rover' and Molly sang in a pleasant contralto 'The Snowy Breasted Pearl' and the drinks kept coming up for further orders.

By this time we were all getting a bit mouldy, but poor bloody Joe was properly fluthered. He was crouched down in an armchair, his face knotted up in a scowl of bewilderment, his gaze fixed, as far as I could make out, on Molly's crossed legs. He kept blinking away the sleep and his mouth continually opened and closed in what could only be abortive speech. But his drinking arm was still working, though when he swallowed back his whiskey there was now a despairing note in his usual:

'Aaaaaaaaaaah!'

We were all surprised when, without taking his eyes off Molly's legs, he burst out, in a thick Kerry accent:

'Ach, doze old songs! Dey're a t'ousand years old. Is dere notting better to sing than dat?'

In one quick glance, the Sergeant had the situation sized up.

'I'll tell you what I'll do, Joe,' he said. 'I'll sing you a wee love song.'

He went over to the piano and whispered in Mrs Mullen's ear. She strummed the opening bars of 'Annie Rooney'. The Sergeant sang:

'She's . . . my . . . sweet . . . heart . . . I'm . . . her . . . beau
She's . . . my . . . Molly . . . I'm . . . her . . . Joe.

He stopped, as if searching for the words, whilst Joe struggled to his feet. Eyes closed, feet sprawled apart, clenched fists held up, he roared:

'Soon . . . we'll . . . marry . . . wah-wah . . . wah-wah
Wah . . . wah-wah—'

The bellowing ceased. Swaying on his feet, mouth open, brows drawn down in a scowl, you could see him trying to rake up the words. At last he gave up.

'Can't remember,' he muttered.

The Sergeant took up the melody again:

'Soon . . . we'll . . . marry . . . never . . . to part
Pretty . . . little . . . Molly . . . is my . . . sweet . . . heart.'

Waving his arms wildly aloft, Joe shouted:

'Again!'

And we all started to sing:

'She's . . . my . . . sweet . . . heart . . . I'm . . . her . . . beau
She's . . . my . . . Molly . . . I'm . . . her . . . Joe.'

On weaving legs, Joe went staggering across to where Molly sat on the sofa. As she made to get up, he clutched at her for support and they both reeled back amongst Mrs Mullen's hand-embroidered cushions. Nothing could be seen of Molly beneath his huge bulk except one frantically kicking leg. His arms gripped both couch and occupant, his legs were sprawled out, one on the sofa, the other on the floor, his face was buried in a cushion from which his muffled voice still bellowed:

'Wah-wah . . . wah-wah . . . Molly . . . is my . . . sweet . . .
heart.'

An elbow jogged my ribs. It was the Sergeant. A worried man by the look of it.

'Better get him up out of there, Jim, before he has her ravished. He's just about—'

Dick interrupted:

'Myself and the Sergeant will handle him. You take Molly out on the floor for a dance. That'll keep her out of harm's way.' He waved towards the piano. 'Keep playing, Bridie.'

While the two of them tugged and hauled at Joe, Mrs Mullen struck up 'Annie Rooney' again. It's a catchy air and by the time Molly was freed, I was humming away at the melody, my feet tapping out the beat on the lino.

'Come on, girl!' I said, grabbing her up.

Off we wheeled, leaning away from each other the better to gather momentum.

'That was a whirlwind courtship,' Molly gasped. Her face was flushed, her hair tossed.

'Aye, Joe's manners aren't the best when he's mad a-horsing.'

We bounced off the sideboard.

'Don't blame Joe. It wasn't his fault.'

'Begod, the Sergeant thought he was going to lepp on you.'

We crashed into the table.

'If the Sergeant hadn't started teasing Joe, it would never have happened.'

'Teasing Joe?'

'Yes. Changing the words of the song.'

She flung back her head and sang to the music:

'She's . . . my . . . Molly . . . I'm . . . her . . . Joe.'

Her foot caught in the fender and she staggered forward. Only that I had a firm grip of her, she would have fallen.

'Sorry,' I said.

It was borne in on me that Molly, who only rarely took a drink, was half tiddley. Somehow or other, this endeared her to me. As though she were in need of protection. And the support of an older brother.

'Let's take it easy,' I said. 'I'm getting winded.'

We slowed down till we were merely shuffling and swaying to the beat of the music. Molly took up the melody again:

'Soon . . . we'll . . . marry . . . never . . . to part.'

She squeezed my hand.

'Wouldn't that be nice, honey?' she said.

'Uh-huh.'

'You don't sound too enthusiastic.'

I whirled her round a few times, barking my left shin against the leg of a chair.

'Joe seems to have quieted down,' I said, slackening once more to a shuffle. 'The notion must have gone off him.'

'Never mind Joe. It's yourself we're talking about.'

Softly I hummed the catchy air:

'Daah . . . Deeh . . . Daah . . . Deeh—'

'Give over, Sly-boots. You're engaged. Remember?'

'Of course.'

'Well, do you like it?'

'Sure.'

She clutched me with both arms, crushing herself frantically against me.

'Is that any better?'

I tried to push her away but she only clung the closer.

'Go easy,' I begged. 'They're all watching us.'

'Relax, Jim. This is what they want to see. Come on!'

Swinging to the music, she sang:

'She's . . . my . . . sweet . . . heart.'

Lured to the tingle of warm breath on my neck, entrapped by the tang of heady sweat and hungry flesh, beaten and overwhelmed by the accusing eyes, clouded surely with love, I buried my face in her hair and sang:

'Soon . . . we'll . . . marry . . . never . . . to part
Pretty . . . little . . . Molly . . . is my . . . sweet . . . heart.'

Soon the others joined in, with Joe's discordant bellowing dominating the rest, until at length Dick shouted:

'That'll do, Bridie.'

Once more the company fragmented, with the ladies exchanging whispered confidences on the sofa, the Sergeant, Dick, and myself sitting round the table arguing politics, and Joe, slumped down in the armchair, chin sunk on chest, arms dangling between outspread legs, snoring and grunting in a drunken stupor.

Drinks were still coming up at rapid intervals. I tried to persuade Dick to leave Molly out of the round, but he only jeered at me.

'It's early on you're getting to act like a married man.'

He, too, was beginning to show signs of wear and tear. His tread was heavy and deliberate. He handled the glasses with exaggerated caution. He blinked continuously in the effort to steady his unfocused vision.

The Sergeant and I still stuck to Guinness. It was in powerful order and neither of us had any difficulty keeping the drinks from piling up as they are very apt to do at the tail end of an evening. In fact my thirst seemed to increase with every tumbler I sank. I had the glass up, ready to dive into a fresh one, when I heard Molly call:

'Jim!'

I looked round. Harris was half-kneeling, half-squatting, on the floor beside Molly. He was sprawled across her lap. She seemed to be put to the pin of her collar thrusting away the hands clumsily pawing at her legs. He was muttering hoarsely:

'De people in dis town talk too much. Dey all know too much about deir neighbour's business. We'd need to go away. For a holiday. Somewhere like Scarrrr-borr-ough. *Dat's* de place. Nobody bodders about you dere.'

'Stop it! Please!' Molly begged.

'It's a grand place, Scarrrr-borr-ough. Dere's cinemas. Dere's t'eatres. And dere's dance halls. And grand swanky hotels dat would house an army.'

'Will you behave yourself, Mr Harris!' she pleaded.

'D'you know what it is,' said the Sergeant. 'I'd nearly go to yon place for my summer holidays, he makes it sound so good.'

'He's making a hames of the party,' grumbled Dick. 'We'd better break it up before there's trouble.'

'A fine healthy place too, Scarrrr-borr-ough. De sea air is like a tonic. You could put up your hand and *squeeeeeeze* the salt water out of it.'

Molly screamed.

'Take your filthy groping hands off me!'

She struggled to her feet. Stood swaying uncertainly.

'Jim,' she said. 'Will you look after me?'

'She's tired out, poor thing,' said Mrs Mullen. 'Better get her to bed, Jim.'

I went to her.

'What about the hen roost, honey?' I said, putting an arm round her.

'All right.'

At the door she turned.

'It was a lovely party. Thanks a lot,' she hesitated. 'Everybody.'

'He's a horrible man, that Joe Harris,' she said, as I helped her up the stairs. 'Did you see the disgusting antics of him?'

She missed her footing on a stair and stumbled forward. I just grabbed her in time.

'Take it easy, darling,' I said.

'It's all very well for you to say that, Jim. You didn't hear the ... the ... the outrageous suggestion he came out with?'

'No, dear.' We were nearly at the top of the stairs.

'He wants me to go with him for a holiday, to some evil low-down haunt. He's a nasty old man, that's what he is.'

'I dunno. He's just a poor sod who has fallen for you.'

'It's sweet of you to put it like that, Jim.' She stumbled to a halt as we reached her door. 'But then you've been very sweet all evening.' She wound her arms round my neck. 'You should have heard Mrs Mullen. She couldn't stop talking about you. Such a nice boy. Easy to see he's a gentleman. It's lucky the girl that gets him. So quiet and well behaved. She doesn't know you the way I do, you blackguard.' She drew my head down and whispered: 'Aren't you glad now? Glad you decided to get engaged, I mean?'

'Of course,' I conceded, giving her an encouraging hug.

'We belong to each other now, don't we? There's no one else in the whole world that matters. Only the pair of us. Isn't that right?'

'Uh-huh.'

'Sure?' she insisted.

'Sure I'm sure.'

Impatiently I grasped her, lining with urgent hands her body against my own. I kissed her, lips smashing on teeth till the taste of blood was in my mouth. Groaning with desire, I buried my face in her hair, her neck, her rudely exposed breast whilst the blood pounded madly in my ears.

Struggling fiercely, she broke away from my arms.

'Now-now, Jim,' she panted. 'Behave yourself.'

She backed away from me, hurriedly putting to rights her disordered clothing.

'You're every bit as bad as Joe Harris.' Her outstretched hands groped behind her for the door handle.

'Molly,' I whispered, edging closer. 'Will I wait till they're all gone to bed or will I slip in now?'

'You'll go straight to your own room this minute, that's what you'll do. Like a good boy.'

'So you mean . . . you're not—'

'I'm not. I'm locking my door tonight.'

I tried to gather her once more into my arms but she pushed me firmly away.

'No, darling. You're not going to get round me that way.' She kissed her finger-tips and put them against my lips. 'Good-night, love. Happy dreams.'

I grabbed her hand.

'But why?' I begged.

'We're engaged. That's the why.'

'I don't see why that should make any difference?'

'Don't you? It means no more to you than that?'

'You said yourself that engaged couples were allowed liberties that . . . that . . . other couples don't get.'

'Not that sort of liberty. Where would you finish starting off like that?' She pulled her hand away.

'You mean that from now on we're to go round together like a couple of craw-thumping penitents?'

'I do. And stop shouting at me.'

'I'M . . . NOT . . . SHOUTING,' I hissed. 'I'm merely trying to din into you that we're too far gone in our ways to make a change now.'

'Speak for yourself. I've none of your old-fashioned habits.'

'My God!' I was flabbergasted. 'Would you listen to her! And she every bloody bit as bad as myself.'

'Now you're swearing. And wagging your head like a school-teacher. You're losing your temper, as usual.'

I took a deap breath.

'No wonder,' I said. 'Making out that I'm the culprit. And you leaving the door ajar any night you wanted nookey.'

She took a step towards me. Her cheeks were blotched, her

brows gathered in an ugly frown, her lips a thin resentful line.

'No gentleman would make a remark like that.'

'It's true enough though, isn't it?'

'You're hateful.'

'There were times you were eager enough for my company when, God knows, I'd have been better off in my own bed getting a proper night's sleep.'

'Oh!' she gasped. 'You've gone too far this time.'

'Well, if it means the end of this ridiculous sham we've been carrying on, so much the better.'

'It isn't ridiculous. And it is no sham. And it's about time I broke it off, the way you are behaving.'

'I like that. Making out that you're breaking it off.'

'Of course I am.'

'Are you codding yourself, girl? Don't you know damned well that there was never anything there in the first place for you to break off?'

'There was! There was! THERE WAS!'

'Keep your voice down. There's no need to screech.'

'I'm not screeching. I'm just not letting you away with that last crack.'

'You mean you've forgotten already that this phoney engagement was rigged up because you were discovered in bed with the cock lodger?'

'How dare you say such things?' she screamed, slapping me full force across the face.

My reaction was immediate. I let her have it. In the double – *Smack. Smack* – on each cheek, watching her face jerk to either side as my right hand swept back and forth across her face.

While you could count three we stood, horrified, staring dumbly at each other. She was panting heavily, her whole body rocked with agitation. Her face was blanched except where palm and knuckles had inflamed her cheeks. Her eyes glittered with tears.

'Look, Molly,' I began.

'You brute!' she burst out. 'You cruel, callous brute. Never did I think you would turn out to be so mean and bitter and treacherous.'

She buried her face in her hands and wailed:

'Oooooooooooooooh! Oh, what am I to do? I'm shamed and disgraced. Oooooooooooooh!'

Rocking her body to and fro, she sobbed and cried.

Hesitantly I reached out. Patted her shoulder. Before I could say a word, she brushed away my hand.

'Take your filthy paws off me!' she screamed. 'I want nothing more to do with you. I'm finished with you. D'you hear? Finished with you. For good.'

Once more she broke into a frenzy of weeping. Crying out, between sobs and moans, in a rush of broken speech:

'What am I to do . . . never hold up my head again . . . it's a disgrace that can't be lived down . . . leading me on like that . . . letting me tell everybody . . . even having a party to celebrate . . . what am I to say to people . . . Ooooooooooooooh.'

As, bewildered and distraught, I strove for words of comfort, I heard from the well of the stairs, a dry, throat-clearing, apologetic cough.

'Hush!' I whispered, but Molly, sobbing and lamenting, paid no heed.

Appalled and panic-stricken, I would have fled to my own room but I knew it was imperative that the eavesdropper be identified. There would be no peace of mind for either of us unless this was known.

On rubber legs, I tiptoed the few steps to the banisters, the creaking of the floor boards muffled by a wild outburst of weeping from Molly. Cautiously I peeped over.

Below me, huddled on the stairs, was a group of figures, their upturned faces floating in the gloom of the stair well like phosphorescent masks. Silently they stared at me. The Sergeant, Mrs Mullen, Joe Harris, Babs. And a few steps above the rest, Dick.

For an agonizing moment I was impaled by their impassive stares. Then Dick's head bent further back.

'Are you all right up there?' he inquired politely.

William Trevor

THE BALLROOM OF ROMANCE

On Sundays, or on Mondays if he couldn't make it and often he couldn't, Sunday being his busy day, Canon O'Connell arrived at the farm in order to hold a private service with Bridie's father, who couldn't get about any more, having had a leg amputated after gangrene had set in. They'd had a pony and cart then and Bridie's mother had been alive: it hadn't been difficult for the two of them to help her father on to the cart in order to make the journey to Mass. But two years later the pony had gone lame and eventually had to be destroyed; not long after that her mother had died. 'Don't worry about it at all,' Canon O'Connell had said, referring to the difficulty of transporting her father to Mass. 'I'll slip up by the week, Bridie.'

The milk lorry called daily for the single churn of milk, Mr Driscoll delivered groceries and meal in his van, and took away the eggs that Bridie had collected during the week. Since Canon O'Connell had made his offer, in 1953, Bridget's father hadn't left the farm.

Apart from Mass on Sundays and her weekly visits to a wayside dance-hall Bridie went shopping once every month, cycling to the town early on a Friday afternoon. She bought things for herself, material for a dress, knitting wool, stockings, a newspaper, and paper-backed Wild West novels for her father. She talked in the shops to some of the girls she'd been at school with, girls who had married shop-assistants or shop-keepers, or had become assistants themselves. Most of them had families of their own by now. 'You're lucky to be peaceful in the hills,' they said to Bridie, 'instead of stuck in a hole like this.' They had a tired look, most of them, from pregnancies and their efforts to organize and control their large families.

As she cycled back to the hills on a Friday Bridie often felt that they truly envied her her life, and she found it surprising that they should do so. If it hadn't been for her father she'd have wanted to work in the town also, in the tinned meat factory maybe, or in a shop. The town had a cinema called the Electric, and a fish-and-chip shop where people met at night, eating chips out of newspaper on the pavement outside. In the evenings, sitting in the farmhouse with her father, she often thought about the town, imagining the shop-windows lit up to display their goods and the sweet-shops still open so that people could purchase chocolates or fruit to take with them to the Electric cinema. But the town was eleven miles away, which was too far to cycle, there and back, for an evening's entertainment.

'It's a terrible thing for you, girl,' her father used to say, genuinely troubled, 'tied up to a one-legged man.' He would sigh heavily, hobbling back from the fields, where he managed as best he could. 'If your mother hadn't died,' he'd say, not finishing the sentence.

If her mother hadn't died her mother could have looked after him and the scant acres he owned, her mother could somehow have lifted the milk-churn on to the collection platform and attended to the few hens and the cows. 'I'd be dead without the girl to assist me,' she'd heard her father saying to Canon O'Connell, and Canon O'Connell replied that he was certainly lucky to have her.

'Amn't I as happy here as anywhere?' she'd say herself, but her father knew she was pretending and was saddened because the weight of circumstances had so harshly interfered with her life.

Although her father still called her a girl, Bridie was thirty-six. She was tall and strong; the skin of her fingers and her palms was stained, and harsh to touch. The labour they'd experienced had found its way into them, as though juices had come out of vegetation and pigment out of soil: since childhood she'd torn away the rough scotch grass that grew each spring among her father's mangolds and sugar beet; since childhood she'd harvested potatoes in August, her hands daily rooting in the ground she loosened and turned. Wind had toughened the flesh of her face, sun had browned it; her neck and nose were lean, her lips touched with early wrinkles.

But on Saturday nights Bridie forgot the scotch grass and the soil. In different dresses she cycled to the dance-hall, encouraged to make the journey by her father. 'Doesn't it do you good, girl?' he'd say, as though he imagined she begrudged herself the pleasure. 'Why wouldn't you enjoy yourself?' She'd cook him his tea and then he'd settle down with the wireless, or maybe a Wild West novel. In time, while still she danced, he'd stoke the fire up and hobble his way upstairs to bed.

The dance-hall, owned by Mr Justin Dwyer, was miles from anywhere, a lone building by the roadside with treeless boglands all around and a gravel expanse in front of it. On pink, pebbled cement its title was painted in an azure blue that matched the depth of the background shade yet stood out well, unfussily proclaiming *The Ballroom of Romance.* Above these letters four coloured bulbs – in red, green, orange and mauve – were lit at appropriate times, an indication that the evening rendezvous was open for business. Only the façade of the building was pink, the other walls being a more ordinary grey. And inside, except for pink swing-doors, everything was blue.

On Saturday nights Mr Justin Dwyer, a small, thin man, unlocked the metal grid that protected his property and drew it back, creating an open mouth from which music would later pour. He helped his wife to carry crates of lemonade and packets of biscuits from their car, and then took up a position in the tiny vestibule between the drawn-back grid and the pink swing-doors. He sat at a card-table, with money and tickets spread out before him. He'd made a fortune, people said: he owned other ballrooms also.

People came on bicycles or in old motor-cars, country people like Bridie from remote hill farms and villages. People who did not often see other people met there, girls and boys, men and women. They paid Mr Dwyer and passed into his dance-hall, where shadows were cast on pale-blue walls and light from a crystal bowl was dim. The band, known as the Romantic Jazz Band, was composed of clarinet, drums and piano. The drummer sometimes sang.

Bridie had been going to the dance-hall since first she left the Presentation Nuns, before her mother's death. She didn't mind the journey, which was seven miles there and seven back: she'd travelled as far every day to the Presentation Nuns on the same bicycle, which had once been the property of her mother, an old Rudge purchased originally in 1936. On Sundays she cycled six miles to Mass, but she never minded either: she'd grown quite used to all that.

'How're you, Bridie?' inquired Mr Justin Dwyer when she arrived in a new scarlet dress one autumn evening in 1971. She said she was all right and in reply to Mr Dwyer's second query she said that her father was all right also. 'I'll go up one of these days,' promised Mr Dwyer, which was a promise he'd been making for twenty years.

She paid the entrance fee and passed through the pink swing-doors. The Romantic Jazz Band was playing a familiar melody of the past, *The Destiny Waltz*. In spite of the band's title, jazz was not ever played in the ballroom: Mr Dwyer did not personally care for that kind of music, nor had he cared for various dance movements that had come and gone over the years. Jiving, rock and roll, twisting, and other such variations had all been resisted by Mr Dwyer, who believed that a ballroom should be, as much as possible, a dignified place. The Romantic Jazz Band consisted of Mr Maloney, Mr Swanton, and Dano Ryan on drums. They were three middle-aged men who drove out from the town in Mr Maloney's car, amateur performers who were employed otherwise by the tinned-meat factory, the Electricity Supply Board, and the County Council.

'How're you, Bridie?' inquired Dano Ryan as she passed him on her way to the cloakroom. He was idle for a moment with his drums, *The Destiny Waltz* not calling for much attention from him.

'I'm all right, Dano,' she said. 'Are you fit yourself? Are the eyes better?' The week before he'd told her that he'd developed a watering of the eyes that must have been some kind of cold or other. He'd woken up with it in the morning and it had persisted until the afternoon: it was a new experience, he'd told her, adding that he'd never had a day's illness or discomfort in his life.

'I think I need glasses,' he said now, and as she passed into the cloakroom she imagined him in glasses, repairing the roads, as he was employed to do by the County Council. You hardly ever saw a road-mender with glasses, she reflected, and she wondered if all the dust that was inherent in his work had perhaps affected his eyes.

'How're you, Bridie?' a girl called Eenie Mackie said in the cloakroom, a girl who'd left the Presentation Nuns only a year ago.

'That's a lovely dress, Eenie,' Bridie said. 'Is it nylon, that?'

'Tricel actually. Drip-dry.'

Bridie took off her coat and hung it on a hook. There was a small wash-basin in the cloakroom above which hung a discoloured oval mirror. Used tissues and pieces of cotton-wool, cigarette-butts and matches covered the concrete floor. Lengths of green-painted timber partitioned off a lavatory in a corner.

'Jeez, you're looking great, Bridie,' Madge Dowding remarked, waiting for her turn at the mirror. She moved towards it as she spoke, taking off a pair of spectacles before endeavouring to apply make up to the lashes of her eyes. She stared myopically into the oval mirror, humming while the other girls became restive.

'Will you hurry up, for God's sake!' shouted Eenie Mackie. 'We're standing here all night, Madge.'

Madge Dowding was the only one who was older than Bridie. She was thirty-nine, although often she said she was younger. The girls sniggered about that, saying that Madge Dowding should accept her condition – her age and her squint and her poor complexion – and not make herself ridiculous going out after men. What man would be bothered with the like of her anyway? Madge Dowding would do better to give herself over to do Saturday-night work for the Legion of Mary: wasn't Canon O'Connell always looking for aid?

'Is that fellow there?' she asked now, moving away from the mirror. 'The guy with the long arms. Did anyone see him outside?'

'He's dancing with Cat Bolger,' one of the girls replied. 'She has herself glued to him.'

'Lover boy,' remarked Patty Byrne, and everyone laughed because the person referred to was hardly a boy any more, being over fifty it was said, a bachelor who came only occasionally to the dance-hall.

Madge Dowding left the cloakroom rapidly, not bothering to pretend she wasn't anxious about the conjunction of Cat Bolger and the man with the long arms. Two sharp spots of red had come into her cheeks, and when she stumbled in her haste the girls in the cloakroom laughed. A younger girl would have pretended to be casual.

Bridie chatted, waiting for the mirror. Some girls, not wishing to be delayed, used the mirrors of their compacts. Then in twos and threes, occasionally singly, they left the cloakroom and took their places on upright wooden chairs at one end of the dance-hall, waiting to be asked to dance. Mr Maloney, Mr Swanton and Dano Ryan played *Harvest Moon* and *I Wonder Who's Kissing Her Now* and *I'll be Around*.

Bridie danced. Her father would be falling asleep by the fire; the wireless, tuned in to Radio Eireann, would be murmuring in the background. Already he'd have listened to *Faith and Order* and *Spot the Talent*. His Wild West novel, *Three Rode Fast* by Jake Matall, would have dropped from his single knee on to the flagged floor. He would wake with a jerk as he did every night and, forgetting what night it was, might be surprised not to see her, for usually she was sitting there at the table, mending clothes or washing eggs. 'Is it time for the News?' he'd automatically say.

Dust and cigarette smoke formed a haze beneath the

crystal bowl, feet thudded, girls shrieked and laughed, some of them dancing together for want of a male partner. The music was loud, the musicians had taken off their jackets. Vigorously they played a number of tunes from *State Fair* and then, more romantically, *Just One of Those Things*. The tempo increased for a Paul Jones, after which Bridie found herself with a youth who told her he was saving up to emigrate, the nation in his opinion being finished. 'I'm up in the hills with the uncle,' he said, 'labouring fourteen hours a day. Is it any life for a young fellow?' She knew his uncle, a hill-farmer whose stony acres were separated from her father's by one other farm only. 'He has me gutted with work,' the youth told her. 'Is there sense in it at all, Bridie?'

At ten o'clock there was a stir, occasioned by the arrival of three middle-aged bachelors who'd cycled over from Carey's public house. They shouted and whistled, greeting other people across the dancing area. They smelt of stout and sweat and whiskey.

Every Saturday at just this time they arrived, and, having sold them their tickets, Mr Dwyer folded up his card-table and locked the tin box that held the evening's takings: his ballroom was complete.

'How're you, Bridie?' one of the bachelors, known as Bowser Egan, inquired. Another one, Tim Daly, asked Patty Byrne how she was. 'Will we take the floor?' Eyes Horgan suggested to Madge Dowding, already pressing the front of his navy-blue suit against the net of her dress. Bridie danced with Bowser Egan, who said she was looking great.

The bachelors would never marry, the girls of the dance-hall considered: they were wedded already, to stout and whiskey and laziness, to three old mothers somewhere up in the hills. The man with the long arms didn't drink but he was the same in all other ways: had the same look of a bachelor, a quality in his face.

'Great,' Bowser Egan said, feather-stepping in an inaccurate and inebriated manner. 'You're a great little dancer, Bridie.'

'Will you lay off that!' cried Madge Dowding, her voice

shrill above the sound of the music. Eyes Horgan had slipped two fingers into the back of her dress and was now pretending they'd got there by accident. He smiled blearily, his huge red face streaming with perspiration, the eyes which gave him his nickname protuberant and bloodshot.

'Watch your step with that one,' Bowser Egan called out, laughing so that spittle sprayed on to Bridie's face. Eenie Mackie, who was also dancing near the incident, laughed also and winked at Bridie. Dano Ryan left his drums and sang. 'Oh, how I miss your gentle kiss,' he crooned, 'and long to hold you tight.'

Nobody knew the name of the man with the long arms. The only words he'd ever been known to speak in the Ballroom of Romance were the words that formed his invitation to dance. He was a shy man who stood alone when he wasn't performing on the dance-floor. He rode away on his bicycle afterwards, not saying good night to anyone.

'Cat had your man leppin' tonight,' Tim Daly remarked to Patty Byrne, for the liveliness that Cat Bolger had introduced into foxtrot and waltz was noticeable.

'I think of you only,' sang Dano Ryan. 'Only wishing, wishing you were by my side.'

Dano Ryan would have done, Bridie often thought, because he was a different kind of bachelor: he had a lonely look about him, as if he'd become tired of being on his own. Every week she thought he would have done, and during the week her mind regularly returned to that thought. Dano Ryan would have done because she felt he wouldn't mind coming to live in the farmhouse while her one-legged father was still about the place. Three could live as cheaply as two where Dano Ryan was concerned because giving up the wages he earned as a road-worker would be balanced by the saving made on what he paid for lodgings. Once, at the end of an evening, she'd pretended that there was a puncture in the back wheel of her bicycle and he'd concerned himself with it while Mr Maloney and Mr Swanton waited for him in Mr Maloney's car. He'd blown the tyre up with the car pump and had said he thought it would hold.

It was well known in the dance-hall that she fancied her chances with Dano Ryan. But it was well known also that Dano Ryan had got into a set way of life and had remained in it for quite some years. He lodged with a widow called Mrs Griffin and Mrs Griffin's mentally affected son, in a cottage on the outskirts of the town. He was said to be good to the affected child, buying him sweets and taking him out for rides on the cross-bar of his bicycle. He gave an hour or two of his time every week to the Church of Our Lady Queen of Heaven, and he was loyal to Mr Dwyer. He performed in the two other rural dance-halls that Mr Dwyer owned, rejecting advances from the town's more sophisticated dance-hall, even though it was more conveniently situated for him and the fee was more substantial than that paid by Mr Dwyer. But Mr Dwyer had discovered Dano Ryan and Dano had not forgotten it, just as Mr Maloney and Mr Swanton had not forgotten their discovery by Mr Dwyer either.

'Would we take a lemonade?' Bowser Egan suggested. 'And a packet of biscuits, Bridie?'

No alcoholic liquor was ever served in the Ballroom of Romance, the premises not being licensed for this added stimulant. Mr Dwyer in fact had never sought a licence for any of his premises, knowing that romance and alcohol were difficult commodities to mix, especially in a dignified ballroom. Behind where the girls sat on the wooden chairs Mr Dwyer's wife, a small stout woman, served the bottles of lemonade, with straws, and the biscuits and the crisps. She talked busily while doing so, mainly about the turkeys she kept. She'd once told Bridie that she thought of them as children.

'Thanks,' Bridie said, and Bowser Egan led her to the trestle table. Soon it would be the intermission: soon the three members of the band would cross the floor also for refreshment. She thought up questions to ask Dano Ryan.

When first she'd danced in the Ballroom of Romance, when she was just sixteen, Dano Ryan had been there also, four years older than she was, playing the drums for Mr Maloney as he played them now. She'd hardly noticed him then because of his not being one of the dancers: he was part of the ballroom's scenery, like the trestle table and the lemonade bottles, and Mrs Dwyer and Mr Dwyer. The youths who'd danced with her then in their Saturday-night blue suits had later disappeared into the town, or to Dublin or Britain, leaving behind them those who became the middle-aged bachelors of the hills. There'd been a boy called Patrick Grady whom she had loved in those days. Week after week she'd ridden away from the Ballroom of Romance with the image of his face in her mind, a thin face, pale beneath black hair. It had been different, dancing with Patrick Grady, and she'd felt that he found it different dancing with her, although he'd never said so. At night she'd dreamed of him and in the daytime too, while she helped her mother in the kitchen or her father with the cows. Week by week she'd returned to the ballroom, smiling on its pink façade and dancing then in the arms of Patrick Grady. Often they'd stood together drinking lemonade, not saying anything, not knowing what to say. She knew he loved her, and she believed then that he would lead her one day from the dim, romantic ballroom, from its blueness and its pinkness and its crystal bowl of light and its music. She believed he would lead her into sunshine, to the town and the Church of Our Lady Queen of Heaven, to marriage and smiling faces. But someone else had got Patrick Grady, a girl from the town who'd never danced in the wayside ballroom. She'd scooped up Patrick Grady when he didn't have a chance.

Bridie had wept, hearing that. By night she'd lain in her bed in the farmhouse, quietly crying, the tears rolling into her hair and making the pillow damp. When she woke in the early morning the thought was still naggingly with her, and it remained with her by day, replacing her daytime dreams of happiness. Someone told her later on that he'd crossed to Britain, to Wolverhampton, with the girl he'd married, and she imagined him there, in a place she wasn't able properly to visualize, labouring in a factory, his children being born and acquiring the accent of the area. The Ballroom of Romance wasn't the same without him, and when no one else stood out for her particularly over the years and when no one offered her marriage, she found herself wondering about Dano Ryan. If you couldn't have love, the next best thing was surely a decent man.

Bowser Egan hardly fell into that category, nor did Tim Daly. And it was plain to everyone that Cat Bolger and Madge Dowding were wasting their time over the man with long arms. Madge Dowding was already a figure of fun in the ballroom, the way she ran after the bachelors; Cat Bolger would end up the same if she wasn't careful. One way or another it wasn't difficult to be a figure of fun in the ballroom, and you didn't have to be as old as Madge Dowding: a girl who'd just left the Presentation Nuns had once asked Eyes Horgan what he had in his trouser pocket and he told her it was a penknife. She'd repeated this afterwards in the cloakroom, how she'd requested Eyes Horgan not to dance so close to her because his penknife was sticking into her. 'Jeez, aren't you the right baby!' Patty Byrne had shouted delightedly; everyone had laughed, knowing that Eyes Horgan only came to the ballroom for stuff like that. He was no use to any girl.

'Two lemonades, Mrs Dwyer,' Bowser Egan said, 'and two packets of Kerry Creams. Is Kerry Creams all right, Bridie?'

She nodded, smiling. Kerry Creams would be fine, she said.

'Well, Bridie, isn't that the great outfit you have!' Mrs Dwyer remarked. 'Doesn't the red suit her, Bowser?'

By the swing-doors stood Mr Dwyer, smoking a cigarette that he held cupped in his left hand. His small eyes noted all developments. He had been aware of Madge Dowding's anxiety when Eyes Horgan had inserted two fingers into the back opening of her dress. He had looked away, not caring for the incident, but had it developed further he would have spoken to Eyes Horgan, as he had on other occasions. Some of the younger lads didn't know any better and would dance very close to their partners, who generally were too embarrassed to do anything about it, being young themselves. But that, in Mr Dwyer's opinion, was a different kettle of fish altogether because they were decent young lads who'd in no time at all be doing a steady line with a girl and would end up as he had himself with Mrs Dwyer, in the same house with her, sleeping in a bed with her, firmly married. It was the middle-aged bachelors who required the watching: they came down from the hills like mountain goats, released from their mammies and from the smell of animals and soil. Mr Dwyer continued to watch Eyes Horgan, wondering how drunk he was.

Dano Ryan's song came to an end, Mr Swanton laid down his clarinet, Mr Maloney rose from the piano. Dano Ryan wiped sweat from his face and the three men slowly moved towards Mrs Dwyer's trestle table.

'Jeez, you have powerful legs,' Eyes Horgan whispered to Madge Dowding, but Madge Dowding's attention was on the man with the long arms, who had left Cat Bolger's side and was proceeding in the direction of the men's lavatory. He never took refreshments. She moved, herself, towards the men's lavatory, to take up a position outside it, but Eyes Horgan followed her. 'Would you take a lemonade, Madge?' he asked. He had a small bottle of whiskey on him, he added in a whisper: if they went into a corner they could add a drop of it to the lemonade. She didn't drink spirits, she reminded him, and he went away.

'Excuse me a minute,' Bowser Egan said, putting down his bottle of lemonade. He crossed the floor to the lavatory. He too, Bridie knew, would have a small bottle of whiskey on him. She watched while Dano Ryan, listening to a story Mr Maloney was telling, paused in the centre of the ballroom, his head bent to hear what was being said. He was a big man, heavily made, with black hair that was slightly touched with grey, and big hands. He laughed when Mr Maloney came to the end of his story and then bent his head again, in order to listen to a story told by Mr Swanton.

'Are you on your own, Bridie?' Cat Bolger asked, and Bridie said she was waiting for Bowser Egan. 'I think I'll have a lemonade,' Cat Bolger said.

Younger boys and girls stood with their arms still around one another, queueing up for refreshments. Boys who hadn't danced at all, being nervous because they didn't know any steps, stood in groups, smoking and making jokes. Girls who hadn't been danced with yet talked to one another, their eyes wandering. Some of them sucked at straws in lemonade bottles.

Bridie, still watching Dano Ryan, imagined him wearing the glasses he'd referred to, sitting in the farmhouse kitchen, reading one of her father's Wild West novels. She imagined the three of them eating a meal she'd prepared, fried eggs and rashers and fried potato-cakes and tea and bread and butter and jam, brown bread and soda and shop bread. She imagined Dano Ryan leaving the kitchen in the morning to go out to the fields in order to weed the mangolds, and her father hobbling off behind him, and the two men working together. She saw hay being cut, Dano Ryan with the scythe that she'd learned to use herself, her father using a rake as best he could. She saw herself, because of the extra help, being able to attend to things in the farmhouse, things she'd never had time for because of the cows and the hens and the fields. There were bedroom curtains that needed repairing where the net had ripped, and wallpaper that had become loose and needed to be stuck up with flour paste. The scullery required whitewashing.

The night he'd blown up the tyre of her bicycle she'd thought he was going to kiss her. He'd crouched on the ground in the darkness with his ear to the tyre, listening for escaping air. When he could hear none he'd straightened up and said he thought she'd be all right on the bicycle. His face had been quite close to hers and she'd smiled at him. At that moment, unfortunately, Mr Maloney had blown an impatient blast on the horn of his motor-car.

Often she'd been kissed by Bowser Egan, on the nights when he insisted on riding part of the way home with her. They had to dismount in order to push their bicycles up a hill and the first time he'd accompanied her he'd contrived to fall against her, steadying himself by putting a hand on her shoulder. The next thing she was aware of was the moist quality of his lips and the sound of his bicycle as it clattered noisily on the road. He'd suggested then, regaining his breath, that they should go into a field.

That was nine years ago. In the intervening passage of time she'd been kissed as well, in similar circumstances, by Eyes Horgan and Tim Daly. She'd gone into fields with them and permitted them to put their arms about her while heavily they breathed. At one time or another she had imagined marriage with one or other of them, seeing them in the farmhouse with her father, even though the fantasies were unlikely.

Bridie stood with Cat Bolger, knowing that it would be some time before Bowser Egan came out of the lavatory. Mr Maloney, Mr Swanton and Dano Ryan approached, Mr Maloney insisting that he would fetch three bottles of lemonade from the trestle table.

'You sang the last one beautifully,' Bridie said to Dano Ryan. 'Isn't it a beautiful song?'

Mr Swanton said it was the finest song ever written, and Cat Bolger said she preferred *Danny Boy*, which in her opinion was the finest song ever written.

'Take a suck of that,' said Mr Maloney, handing Dano Ryan and Mr Swanton bottles of lemonade. 'How's Bridie tonight? Is your father well, Bridie?'

Her father was all right, she said.

'I hear they're starting a cement factory,' said Mr Maloney. 'Did anyone hear talk of that? They're after striking some commodity in the earth that makes good cement. Ten feet down, over at Kilmalough.'

'It'll bring employment,' said Mr Swanton. 'It's employment that's necessary in this area.'

'Canon O'Connell was on about it,' Mr Maloney said. 'There's Yankee money involved.'

'Will the Yanks come over?' inquired Cat Bolger. 'Will they run it themselves, Mr Maloney?'

Mr Maloney, intent on his lemonade, didn't hear the questions and Cat Bolger didn't repeat them.

'There's stuff called Optrex,' Bridie said quietly to Dano Ryan, 'that my father took the time he had a cold in his eyes. Maybe Optrex would settle the watering, Dano.'

'Ah sure, it doesn't worry me that much–'

'It's terrible, anything wrong with the eyes. You wouldn't want to take a chance. You'd get Optrex in a chemist, Dano, and a little bowl with it so that you can bathe the eyes.'

Her father's eyes had become red-rimmed and unsightly to look at. She'd gone into Riordan's Medical Hall in the town and had explained what the trouble was, and Mr Riordan had recommended Optrex. She told this to Dano Ryan, adding that her father had had no trouble with his eyes since. Dano Ryan nodded.

'Did you hear that, Mrs Dwyer?' Mr Maloney called out. 'A cement factory for Kilmalough.'

Mrs Dwyer wagged her head, placing empty bottles in a crate. She'd heard references to the cement factory, she said: it was the best news for a long time.

'Kilmalough'd never know itself,' her husband commented, joining her in her task with the empty lemonade bottles.

' 'Twill bring prosperity certainly,' said Mr Swanton. 'I was saying just there, Justin, that employment's what's necessary.'

'Sure, won't the Yanks–' began Cat Bolger, but Mr Maloney interrupted her.

'The Yanks'll be in at the top, Cat, or maybe not here at all – maybe only inserting money into it. It'll be local labour entirely.'

'You'll not marry a Yank, Cat,' said Mr Swanton, loudly laughing. 'You can't catch those fellows.'

'Haven't you plenty of homemade bachelors?' suggested Mr Maloney. He laughed also, throwing away the straw he was sucking through and tipping the bottle into his mouth. Cat Bolger told him to get on with himself. She moved towards the men's lavatory and took up a position outside it, not speaking to Madge Dowding, who was still standing there.

'Keep a watch on Eyes Horgan,' Mrs Dwyer warned her husband, which was advice she gave him at this time every Saturday night, knowing that Eyes Horgan was drinking in the lavatory. When he was drunk, Eyes Horgan was the most difficult of the bachelors.

'I have a drop of it left, Dano,' Bridie said quietly. 'I could bring it over on Saturday. The eye stuff.'

'Ah, don't worry yourself, Bridie—'

'No trouble at all. Honestly now—'

'Mrs Griffin has me fixed up for a test with Dr Cready. The old eyes are no worry: only when I'm reading the paper or at the pictures. Mrs Griffin says I'm only straining them due to lack of glasses.'

He looked away while he said that, and she knew at once that Mrs Griffin was arranging to marry him. She felt it instinctively: Mrs Griffin was going to marry him because she was afraid that if he moved away from her cottage, to get married to someone else, she'd find it hard to replace him with another lodger who'd be good to her affected son. He'd become a father to Mrs Griffin's affected son, to whom already he was kind. It was a natural outcome, for Mrs Griffin had all the chances, seeing him every night and morning and not having to make do with weekly encounters in a ballroom.

She thought of Patrick Grady, seeing in her mind his pale, thin face. She might be the mother of four of his children now, or seven or eight maybe. She might be living in Wolverhampton, going out to the pictures in the evenings, instead of looking after a one-legged man. If the weight of circumstances hadn't intervened she wouldn't be standing in a wayside ballroom, mourning the marriage of a roadmender she didn't love. For a moment she thought she might cry, standing there thinking of Patrick Grady in Wolverhampton. In her life, on the farm and in the house, there was no place for tears. Tears were a luxury, like flowers would be in the fields where the mangolds grew, or fresh whitewash in the scullery. It wouldn't have been fair ever to have wept in the kitchen while her father sat listening to *Spot the*

Talent: her father had more right to weep, having lost a leg. He suffered in a greater way, yet he remained kind and concerned for her.

In the Ballroom of Romance she felt behind her eyes the tears that it would have been improper to release in the presence of her father. She wanted to let them go, to feel them streaming on her cheeks, to receive the sympathy of Dano Ryan and of everyone else. She wanted them all to listen to her while she told them about Patrick Grady who was now in Wolverhampton and about the death of her mother and her own life since. She wanted Dano Ryan to put his arm around her so that she could lean her head against it. She wanted him to look at her in his decent way and to stroke with his road-mender's finger the backs of her hands. She might wake in a bed with him and imagine for a moment that he was Patrick Grady. She might bathe his eyes and pretend.

'Back to business,' said Mr Maloney, leading his band across the floor to their instruments.

'Tell your father I was asking for him,' Dano Ryan said. She smiled and she promised, as though nothing had happened, that she would tell her father that.

She danced with Tim Daly and then again with the youth who'd said he intended to emigrate. She saw Madge Dowding moving swiftly towards the man with the long arms as he came out of the lavatory, moving faster than Cat Bolger. Eyes Horgan approached Cat Bolger. Dancing with her, he spoke earnestly, attempting to persuade her to permit him to ride part of the way home with her. He was unaware of the jealousy that was coming from her as she watched Madge Dowding holding close to her the man with the long arms while they performed a quickstep. Cat Bolger was in her thirties also.

'Get away out of that,' said Bowser Egan, cutting in on the youth who was dancing with Bridie. 'Go home to your mammy, boy.' He took her into his arms, saying again that she was looking great tonight. 'Did your hear about the cement factory?' he said. 'Isn't it great for Kilmalough?'

She agreed. She said what Mr Swanton and Mr Maloney

had said: that the cement factory would bring employment to the neighbourhood.

'Will I ride home with you a bit, Bridie?' Bowser Egan suggested, and she pretended not to hear him. 'Aren't you my girl, Bridie, and always have been?' he said, a statement that made no sense at all.

His voice went on whispering at her, saying he would marry her tomorrow only his mother wouldn't permit another woman in the house. She knew what it was like herself, he reminded her, having a parent to look after: you couldn't leave them to rot, you had to honour your father and your mother.

She danced to *The Bells Are Ringing*, moving her legs in time with Bowser Egan's while over his shoulder she watched Dano Ryan softly striking one of his smaller drums. Mrs Griffin had got him even though she was nearly fifty, with no looks at all, a lumpish woman with lumpish legs and arms. Mrs Griffin had got him just as the girl had got Patrick Grady.

The music ceased, Bowser Egan held her hard against him, trying to touch her face with his. Around them, people whistled and clapped: the evening had come to an end. She walked away from Bowser Egan, knowing that not ever again would she dance in the Ballroom of Romance. She'd been a figure of fun, trying to promote a relationship with a middle-aged County Council labourer, as ridiculous as Madge Dowding dancing on beyond her time.

'I'm waiting outside for you, Cat,' Eyes Horgan called out, lighting a cigarette as he made for the swing-doors.

Already the man with the long arms – made long, so they said, from carrying rocks off his land – had left the ballroom. Others were moving briskly. Mr Dwyer was tidying the chairs.

In the cloakroom the girls put on their coats and said they'd see one another at Mass the next day. Madge Dowding hurried. 'Are you OK, Bridie?' Patty Byrne asked and Bridie said she was. She smiled at little Patty Byrne, wondering if a day would come for the younger girl also, if one day she'd decide that she was a figure of fun in a wayside ballroom.

'Goodnight so,' Bridie said, leaving the cloakroom, and the girls who were still chatting there wished her goodnight. Outside the cloakroom she paused for a moment. Mr Dwyer was still tidying the chairs, picking up empty lemonade bottles from the floor, setting the chairs in a neat row. His wife was sweeping the floor. 'Goodnight, Bridie,' Mr Dwyer said. 'Goodnight, Bridie,' his wife said.

Extra lights had been switched on so that the Dwyers could see what they were doing. In the glare the blue walls of the ballroom seemed tatty, marked with hair-oil where men had leaned against them, inscribed with names and initials and hearts with arrows through them. The crystal bowl gave out a light that was ineffective in the glare; the bowl was broken here and there, which wasn't noticeable when the other lights weren't on.

'Goodnight so,' Bridie said to the Dwyers. She passed through the swing-doors and descended the three concrete steps on the gravel expanse in front of the ballroom. People were gathered on the gravel, talking in groups, standing with their bicycles. She saw Madge Dowding going off with Tim Daly. A youth rode away with a girl on the cross-bar of his bicycle. The engines of motor-cars started.

'Goodnight, Bridie,' Dano Ryan said.

'Goodnight, Dano,' she said.

She walked across the gravel towards her bicycle, hearing Mr Maloney, somewhere behind her, repeating that no matter how you looked at it the cement factory would be a great thing for Kilmalough. She heard the bang of a car-door and knew it was Mr Swanton banging the door of Mr Maloney's car because he always gave it the same loud bang. Two other doors banged as she reached her bicycle and then the engine started up and the headlights went on. She touched the two tyres of the bicycle to make certain she hadn't a puncture. The wheels of Mr Maloney's car traversed the gravel and were silent when they reached the road.

'Goodnight, Bridie,' someone called, and she replied, pushing her bicycle towards the road.

'Will I ride a little way with you?' Bowser Egan asked.

They rode together and when they arrived at the hill for which it was necessary to dismount she looked back and saw in the distance the four coloured bulbs that decorated the façade of the Ballroom of Romance. As she watched the lights went out, and she imagined Mr Dwyer pulling the metal grid across the front of his property and locking the two padlocks that secured it. His wife would be waiting with the evening's takings, sitting in the front of their car.

'D'you know what it is, Bridie,' said Bowser Egan, 'you were never looking better than tonight.' He took from a pocket of his suit the small bottle of whiskey he had. He uncorked it and drank some and then handed it to her. She took it and drank. 'Sure, why wouldn't you?' he said, surprised to see her drinking because she never had in his company before. It was an unpleasant taste, she considered, a taste she'd experienced only twice before, when she'd taken whiskey as a remedy for toothache. 'What harm would it do you?' Bowser Egan said as she raised the bottle again to her lips. He reached out a hand for it, though, suddenly concerned lest she should consume a greater share than he wished her to.

She watched him drinking more expertly than she had. He would always be drinking, she thought. He'd be lazy and useless, sitting in the kitchen with the *Irish Press*. He'd waste money buying a second-hand motor-car in order to drive into the town to go to the public houses on fair-days.

'She's shook these days,' he said, referring to his mother. 'She'll hardly last two years, I'm thinking.' He threw the empty whiskey bottle into the ditch and lit a cigarette. They pushed their bicycles. He said:

'When she goes, Bridie, I'll sell the bloody place up. I'll sell the pigs and the whole damn one-and-twopence worth.' He paused in order to raise the cigarette to his lips. He drew in smoke and exhaled it. 'With the cash that I'll get I could improve some place else, Bridie.'

They reached a gate on the left-hand side of the road and automatically they pushed their bicycles towards it and leaned them against it. He climbed over the gate into the field and she climbed after him. 'Will we sit down here, Bridie?' he said offering the suggestion as one that had just occurred to him, as though they'd entered the field for some other purpose.

'We could improve a place like your own one,' he said, putting his right arm around her shoulders. 'Have you a kiss in you, Bridie?' He kissed her, exerting pressure with his teeth. When his mother died he would sell his farm and spend the money in the town. After that he would think of getting married because he'd have nowhere to go, because he'd want a fire to sit at and a woman to cook food for him. He kissed her again, his lips hot, the sweat on his cheeks sticking to her. 'God, you're great at kissing, ' he said.

She rose, saying it was time to go, and they climbed over the gate again. 'There's nothing like a Saturday,' he said. 'Goodnight to you so, Bridie.'

He mounted his bicycle and rode down the hill, and she pushed hers to the top and then mounted it also. She rode through the night as on Saturday nights for years she had ridden and never would ride again because she'd reached a certain age. She would wait now and in time Bowser Egan would seek her out because his mother would have died. Her father would probably have died also by then. She would marry Bowser Egan because it would be lonesome being by herself in the farmhouse.

Julia O'Faolain

A POT OF SOOTHING HERBS

I'd like to make this brief, but I doubt if I shall. Like my friends, I talk a great deal. *Why* is probably going to become clear from this letter. (Is it a letter? That too may become clear.) The depressing thing about our talk is that it is not about activity. It is about talk. I'm told the Irish were always that way – given to word-games since the sixth century. It is typical of us too to say 'the Irish' instead of 'I': a way of running for tribal camouflage. I am trying to be honest here, but I can't discard our usual rituals. In a way, that would be more dishonest. It would mean trying to talk like someone else: like some of my friends, sheep in monkeys' clothing, who chatter cynically all day in pubs, imitating the tuneful recusancy of a Brendan Behan while knowing damn' well all the while that they'd tar and feather anyone who seriously threatened the comfortable values of the Irish Republican Middle Classes. Not that anyone is likely to. We're a modest, solid little oligarchy. The bloodshot eyes of our drunks are the pinkest things about us. So we can be smug. And in a way we are. And in a way we aren't. The collective memory ripples in our sky like a damp, nostalgic flag. A red flag. Our parents didn't work their way up selling underwear or sweat out their fantasy for scholarships. They fought – they meant to fight – a social revolution. Even now, they can still find a frondeur's rage in the dregs of their third double whiskey. Of course, you might see that happen anywhere. I've caught flickers of it in the *bien-pensant* French families with which I've stayed *au pair* – we have, you see, all the habits. I've had the traditional advantages – but with us a whole class is prone. My mother's college-day memories are of raids, curfews, and dancing in mountain farmhouses with irregular soldiers who were sometimes shot a few hours after the goodnight kiss. She once carved up an ox and served it in sandwiches to a retreating procession of civil-war rebels. She has the track of a Black and Tan bullet in her thigh and spent a brief spell in prison. My father and all my friends' fathers have the same memories. Even the nuns in school had nonconformist quirks, traces of a deviated radicalism which crept with heady irrelevance into the conventional curriculum. We've never known what to do with it. When our parents sing their old marching songs and thrill to images they won't pass on to us – scenes from those haylofts, for instance, where the young men hid and their girl couriers rested after long bicycle rides – we, with our blood pumping to their tunes, neat and shy in the deep clasp of the armchairs, finger our cocktail glasses and feel faintly silly. They mock us. 'Yerrah, ye missed it!' they say, their vowels broadening reminiscently. 'I have to pity the young today ...' They return to the Eden of memory. It is as if sex, in Ireland, were the monopoly of the over-fifties.

And why should it be? an outsider might ask. Why *do* we sit there listening to them like envious paralytics? Why has it taken me this long to get to sex if that is what I want to talk about? If I knew, I wouldn't be telling this ridiculous story. It wouldn't have happened in the first place. If I were talking now instead of writing, the rush of my breath would be noticeable, a faint bravado at having taken even such a gingerly hold on the matter. I suppose it would be clear then that I am a virgin, a twenty-one-year-old virgin, which is something I usually try to conceal from foreigners. From the Irish I couldn't – and besides it's nothing to want to conceal here. '*Mon petit capital*' (as Robert, my disappointed French beau of last June, called it) is really just that in Holy Catholic Ireland. Though it's not that I wouldn't like to disperse it secretly, feed my cake to the pigeons and have it too. But? Oh, a lot of impalpables. For one thing, I'm mechanically very ignorant. I've read *Ulysses* carefully and the *Complete Rabelais* and *Fanny Hill* and a number of other promising and disappointing books, but I don't quite know how humans make love. In the convent we didn't study biology and my mother's explanations when my brother was born were unclear. When I add that contraceptives – *whatever* they are – are unavailable in Ireland and that *three* of my mother's maids ended in the Magdalene Homes with illegitimate babies, I think I've stated the most tangible reason for my hesitation.

I imagine the girls in my group are even more ignorant than I am. Of course, if one did emancipate herself she would conceal the fact with all her might, so it's hard to tell. Maeve may have 'gone rather far' – our favourite euphemism – with her French escort in Paris last summer. I know I went further with mine than I'd been before. I would probably have trusted to his precautions and slept with him if I'd liked him better. But there's where the residual native romanticism – my grand-opera morality – hamstrings me like a mucky umbilical cord. And I abominate it!

For my degree, I chose all the periods and poets who worked with their eyes on the object: brisk Gallic *gaillards* of the sixteenth century, late Latin sensualists whose tight rhythms leave no room for droll, eighteenth-century types like N. de Lenclos or Ch. de Laclos whose *Liaisons* I've studied as a chess player studies old strategies. And then after all that and hours defending Mme de Merteuil to Maeve, who can't see that hers was the only response to a phony society like ours, I pull away from Robert when he moors the boat under a bush in the Bois – what more setting did I want anyway? – and asks: *'Eh bien, tu as envie ou pas?' 'Non,'* I said. He was the most beautiful creature I'd ever seen – casual, well-tailored, amusing. '*Menteuse*!' The boat rocked under us as he slid his hands all over me and I felt liquids racing within me, tides quivering down my spine and along the soles of my feet, and I wondered when I must stop him before he got too excited to be stopped. This is one of our great anxieties which I discuss constantly with Maeve. Can they – men – really not control themselves? I don't mean Irish men, because they don't seem to have any needs at all. Or they're queer. Aidan is queer. And I need hardly add that I don't know precisely what that means, either. I wonder how much precision matters? I mean anatomical precision. It's curious how abstract the most reputedly bawdy French writers are when you get right down to trying to understand details from them. Maybe if I'd read classics instead I'd have learned more by now. Because I can't ask anyone. I'm twenty-one and it seems ridiculous. I'll probably learn in practice if someone I like enough to satisfy my disgusting romanticism ever does try to sleep with me. I go round in a constant state of excitement. I wonder does everybody? Maeve says she doesn't, but I think she's a liar. When I'm in a crowd, on the bus, say, and something touches me – often it turns out to be a shopping basket or a dog – I get violent sensations of liquids running inside me. Everywhere: the back of my knees, my breasts. Sometimes I can hardly stand up. Then if I see Aidan it becomes almost unbearable. Usually I do see him from a bus, and often, even if it's the rush hour and I've had to queue for forty minutes to get on it, I get off and dash round the block just so that I can pass him by casually and say, 'Hullo, Aidan.' 'Hullo', he says with his furtive smile, and rushes off with his head bent. He has a long white face and has neither the poise nor the class, the looks or the taste of Robert. He's unsure of himself, bad-tempered, and with a chip on his shoulder. All that. I enjoy saying this about him. It's true, and I say it not so much to try and deceive people about my feelings for him – Maeve has probably told everyone anyway, so there wouldn't be much use – but simply because I like to talk about him. He seems tormented, and this – romanticism again – I'm afraid I enjoy. I know his torment comes from something quite ignoble like the fact that his family propably live in a slum. We've deduced this from his always insisting on being set down at Merrion Square when he gets a lift home, which is about a mile from his postal address.

It suddenly occurs to me, seeing the ingredients of my love set down on paper, that they look like the ingredients for hate, or as if I were insincere and didn't *want* sex at all and so chose to fall for a queer, or were masochistic, or reacting against my class or some such oddity. It would no doubt be easy for some dab to erect theories like this which it would be hard for me to deny. One can never prove things, anyway, which is what makes them rather dull. I only know that I am attracted where I sense tensions and dissatisfactions – I prefer the fat, panting Hamlet to Hotspur – and that it was the grace and *easiness* of Robert's approach that turned me away from him. This may seem to contradict what I said earlier about liking the eighteenth century; I would answer that one can choose one's intellectual pole star but not the way one's bowels jump.

I am usually rude to Aidan. It is the one form of intimacy open to me. I think he's aware of this. I also think he likes me and that the reason he doesn't invite me out is simply that he has no money. Though as a matter of fact he once did invite me. We met uncomfortably on the canal bridge where our bus routes cross. It was damp and we walked along the towpath while he talked allusively of Rimbaud. I don't know whether this is his technique with businessmen in pubs who like listening to a University boy, or whether it was intended as an oblique confession of queerness – though if he thought that necessary he underrates the grape-vine. He talked French the whole time, saying, *'C'est difficile, c'est difficile!'* and giving me the *vous*. Then suddenly he rushed me into Mooney's. 'Jesus! A drink!' He paid, which must make me one of the only people ever to have got a drink out of him – hardly a consoling distinction. Still, I went home feeling less miserable than someone who doesn't know Dublin might think. I'm used to Irish dates. For one thing, he had given me to understand that he was not a virgin, and I had hopes of him – and had until this past Saturday.

I wish there were someone whose advice I could ask about *that*. Not Maeve's. And priests make me sad with their good-housekeeping morality. ('Now you wouldn't,' says our PP on the subject of matrimony, 'if you were giving someone a present, want it to be chipped or cracked?') So I am writing this down and maybe I shall send it to Aidan. Why not? Or to

Robert, whom I shall probably be seeing at Easter. (Actually, I know I shall do neither, but one has to pretend if the writing is to be a vent. Besides, I might.)

Since Saturday I've been feeling like a shaken thunder-sheet. What is bad is not the hollow sensation itself but the importance I find myself attributing to it, the way the mind gets subordinated to the belly and I take my bloody blood throbs for telepathic messages: Morse tattoos from some friendly *deus ex machina* – Aidan? ha! – who is going to solve my troubles without my having to take any responsibility. This feeding on fancy must do something to the brain. (Do Irish women ever recover?) Even writing this I am ridiculously expectant. I *must* lay out the facts.

Saturday? Maeve and I went to Enda O'Hooey's. He was giving a party together with Simon FitzSimons and had asked the two of us to come early and help. We accepted. A party is a party, and I knew that Aidan was to come later. It was the usual thing. While we made sandwiches, the men talked and we giggled appropriately from time to time or said: 'You're terrible!' or: 'Don't make me laugh!' Half mechanical, half ironical. They talked about their families (Enda's was away for the weekend), pretending to deride them; boasting. Simon comes from a line of Castle-Catholics – pre-revolutionary collaborators, which gives his gentility seniority over ours – and he talked about *that*. Enda's father made his money in children's prayer books with pastel celluloid bindings. He got a monopoly from the Republican government in return for *his* father's having been hanged by the British – which is the bit of family past which Enda prefers to remember. The O'Hooeys own an enormous eighteenth-century house with a rather tarty nineteen-sixtyish bathroom on the ground floor, fitted, including the lavatory bowl, in bright baby-pink. It was while Enda was regaling us in the drawing-room with a doggerel ballad on his grandfather's death that Maeve broke this lavatory bowl. How she did I don't know, unless it was made from celluloid left over from the prayer-book bindings. Once broken, the ensuing fuss left us feeling flighty for the rest of the evening. It is not the sort of misdemeanour that a girl of our set feels comfortable about confessing to her host. If Maeve had broken a decanter or something of that sort she would have insisted on paying. We are sticklers about money. Unfortunately, we are sticklers too about taboo words, and 'lavatory' tops the list. So Maeve, who couldn't think of an acceptable euphemism, was in a fix. She stayed for a while in the bathroom drinking whiskey and laughing at herself in the mirror, then dashed into the drawing room and began hissing at me in French: *'Ecoute, Sheila, j'ai cassé le cabinet, le water, la machin, le ... enfin tu me comprends!'* This embarrassed me. I calculated quickly that (a) she would not confess; (b) Enda might suspect me of breaking the thing; (c) I might as well encourage her nervousness in the hope that this would give the men a clue as to where, eventually, to lay the blame. So I teased her, whipping her, and by the way myself, into a state of hilarious idiocy. '*N'y touchez pas*,' Maeve yelled, '*elle est brisée*', and cackled untunefully – to the obvious annoyance of Simon, who had been trying to set the atmosphere for a little mild necking before the arrival of other guests. When he tried to cuddle her, Maeve – she doesn't like him, anyway – let out a screech. 'I'm mortified!' she called, and began to hop about waving a beer-glass full of whiskey. 'Am I positively repulsive to her?' Simon asked me in earnest distress.

By the time Aidan came we were so lightheaded that, with most unnatural aplomb, I kissed him on the cheek and told him what had happened. It charmed him since he rather dislikes Enda, and our amusement cut out the need we usually feel to spar. 'Come into the kitchen,' he said. Aidan always gravitates towards kitchens. I felt promoted and physically tranquil, which often happens when I am with someone who attracts me.

We went on talking French, which was a help. It gives one a feeling of detachment. We managed to laugh a lot, too, and were warming agreeably towards each other – I had always known he liked me really, else why would I like him? A half-hour later, as we began to talk of some place to which we could go on, the back door opened, letting in a stream of cold air and a crowd of gate-crashers to interrupt us. 'Will yez look who's here – Aidan!' Red-faced from wind and drink, they arrived like pantomime demons with jovial, fake brogues and gushes of pestilential breath. 'A friendly face!' said the same crasher, although Aidan's face had actually relapsed to its driest and prissiest detachment; his furtive grin was back, stuck across it like sticking-plaster. Being queer, he has whole sets of acquaintances outside the college crowd, and he is at pains to keep each apart from the other. It occurred to me, too, that he might not like it to be thought in certain circles that he shows interest in women. 'Who's giving this bloody party anyway?' yelled the crashers, gargling their consonants, drunken and pretending to be more so. An older crowd than we, they had not bothered to bring the usual gift of liquor. Aidan appeared to be savouring a sedate interior joke. The old empty feeling had come over me. I have had such practice in controlling disappointment that I freeze it before it gets started, only recognizing it in the vacancy of my own grin. 'Any drink?' a crasher asked the absent Aidan. 'Remember what Whistler said? I drink to make my hosts seem witty?' Feeling I must be embarrassing him, I turned away from Aidan. As I did so I noticed that among the arrivals, though in her containment very much apart from them, was Claudia Rain. She is a tall, bee-blonde creature with stemlike neck and wrists and immense, painted, Byzantine eyes. One of those slightly monstrous females whose beauty is disputable but, to those who recognize it, overwhelming. She had always impressed me, though I had only seen her before across streets – the exhalations from damp lounge bars. She is a fable round town: the sort who strikes young girls' mothers as 'a common tart' and the girls themselves as a creature of daring, both gallant and *galante*. I lend her figure when I read Proust to Odette de Crécy and prefer her for peopling Yeats's poems to the fuzzy-haired photos of Maud Gonne. She manages to project an image that is both exotic and sedate. She is English but has, as they say, 'been around'. She arrived in town first with

Rory MacMourragh – who met her when he was sculpting in Vienna – and is still officially with him, although she has picked and dropped half the emancipated males of Dublin in the eighteen months since she came.

'Aidan, my dear!' She dived on him with a swish of expensively eccentric clothes. 'Your horrid little friend, the host, is threatening to throw us out. Come and restrain him. He's ringing the *gardaí.*' She said *gardaí* in Gaelic as we never would, an English concession which might be mocking or punctilious. The artificial pipe of her voice surprised me at first, but after a second I decided it was not affected, merely strange. Aidan muttered some excuse, gave me a mean, little grin, and trotted after her. He had not introduced us. I was furious. Did he think her too strong meat for me? I stood sipping my drink, staring in sulky wonder at the sottish men with whom she had arrived. What did such a splendid creature want with them? In a second or two she was back. She had begun unknotting the vast nest of hair which she wears, wound like family-sized brioche, on top of her head. Suddenly she poured it over the face of one of the sots who was sitting on a chair drinking stout – *not*, I noticed, Rory MacMourragh. The man laughed and grabbed at her. She evaded him.

'Will you look at that one?' said Maeve, who had staggered in without my noticing her, although she was easy enough to pick out with her royal blue taffeta and Coral Glow lipstick. She had become dishevelled and tarty to an extent to which I could not imagine the English girl ever being reduced.

'You *have* been drinking!' I observed. There was a bleary patina, a kind of sweaty bloom, over her make-up which was dissolving her face in a pointillist glow. 'My mirror,' I thought sourly, looking at her; 'the drunken, rat-tailed virgin.'

Maeve took no notice of my remark. She was staring sagely at Claudia. '*They* say,' she stated, 'that she's nympho!'

'Well, a damn' good thing for *them* if she is!' I snapped. 'Given what the rest of us are!'

Maeve giggled, swaying on her spike heels. 'Enda has taken down his grandfather's gun,' she confided excitedly. 'The one hanging over the mirror. He keeps threatening Aidan with it and all the crashers.'

'Are guns dangerous after three generations?' I asked. 'Not that it would be loaded.' But I was annoyed with myself for even listening to Maeve. She is like a maidservant, always trying to frighten and excite herself with stories. I stared at the gores in the English girl's tweed skirt. They limbered the flow of it until it achieved some of the swirl of a dancer's dress. She was moving off again now, supple inside it as a paper streamer.

'I've heard,' Maeve muttered, 'that Rory MacMourragh likes Aidan. They say,' she went on with typical Dublin mime of lowered voice and furtive eye which advertises to a room of twenty that you're saying something scandalous, 'that *she* has him so tormented that he's taken to the men ...' Maeve's sour breath was so close now I could feel its warmth horribly on my cheek and upper lip. 'They say,' and she dug her angular elbow into me with the rough gesture of country grandparents (it will take the convent schools a few more generations to lay *those* ghosts), 'that her mother was a kind of kept woman until the end when the father married her! *He*'s a peer, you know.'

I was beginning to feel mortally tired. Standing and the issueless excitement of earlier in the evening had left me limp. 'I'm going to see what *is* happening in front,' I announced.

'That's right,' Maeve said approvingly. 'Keep an eye on Aidan!'

'Are you coming?' I asked with distaste.

'No,' Maeve answered loudly. 'I can't face Enda!' She raised her glass at me as I left. 'I'm too mortified,' she shouted, and smiled intriguingly at the men around her.

In the front room, among the usual Dublin mixture of Georgian antiques bought by lot and Dunlopillo upholstering, Enda was still posturing with the gun. 'My grandfather shot sixteen men with this,' he said. 'Isn't that a poem by Willy Yeats?' someone inquired. Enda's mouth was drawn down, his movements heavy. 'Don't provoke me now,' he begged with ponderous politeness. 'I might feel it my duty to shoot.'

I saw Aidan standing in the listless little group of onlookers, drinking Enda's whiskey. I went into the library. Rory MacMourragh was lying on a couch. He got up.

'An apparition,' he said.

'Yes,' I agreed, 'and as brief.' I turned back.

'Do you hate this party?' he asked. 'Will you come home with me?'

'No,' I said. 'I'm waiting for Aidan.'

'Are you in love with Aidan?'

'Yes.'

'He's no good for you,' said MacMourragh – who is, I should add, disturbingly attractive with an eighteenth-century Irish face, black curls, square jaw, and a sculptor's heft.

'I suppose I know that,' I admitted.

MacMourragh caught my arm, and fixed his black eyes lengthily on mine. It's a trick I've had played on me before by men, but it always disconcerts me. His ease was of a quality different from Robert's. I imagined that I could sense reserves of controlled violence here, but this may have been suggested by stories I'd heard of his fights over Claudia. He is Anglo-Irish, of a different *pâte* to the natives. 'You're probably thinking that Claudia went off with that sot Hennessey,' Rory went on. 'And you're doing a division sum in your head. Stop it. I'm not offering you a fraction of anything. Besides, calculations are so dreary!' He was still fixing me with both eyes. I did not want to flinch, but was aware that if anyone came in we would look rather absurd, and laughed to give myself a countenance. I did not want to break away from him, either, and the tides within me which had ebbed and curdled earlier in the evening were back, hammering at my temples and impeding my usual spate of words. I tried to laugh as unconsentingly as possible. 'Come,' said Rory. I stopped laughing. We faced each other in silence for several moments. It was then that I noticed someone watching us. Aidan was slouching in the door, whiskey glass still in hand, looking ridiculously censorious. The tides turned sickeningly. 'Aidan!' Rory called easily. 'You hide your friends from each other. But you're in time to make amends! I don't know this young lady's name yet.'

'I shall *not* introduce you,' said Aidan, loping towards us. 'And I want you to keep away from this girl!' He straddled the fireplace, leaning back, surveying us down the slope of his nose. His absurdity was warming me to him until I remembered what Maeve had said about his liking Rory. Or was it Rory liking him? Which? Either way, *that* little element turned me into a piece of camouflage in the triangle, a fig-leaf, a *cache-sexe*. I sat dejectedly down in an armchair. Rage, despair, and my own fatal ignorance had me again by the groin. What an evening!

I was scarcely surprised, and anyway indifferent, when Enda came rushing in with his gun, yelling that he was giving no more parties. 'Fine thanks I get!' He had got rid of the other guests, he told us, 'before they did any more damage! They broke the bloody jakes!' he explained. 'Bogmen! God knows what they're used to. I don't know what my mother will say!' He seemed near tears.

'I wouldn't be surprised,' Rory suggested, 'if it was that sot Hennessey.'

'He's a gurrier,' stated Enda. 'Yez are all low-bred gurriers! Get out of my house!' I stood up. 'You stay here, Sheila,' Enda commanded. 'I invited you out tonight and I'm responsible to your father.'

'Oh, shut up, Enda!'

'I won't let you out of my sight,' he bullied. 'That pair of gurriers might take advantage of you. You don't know what you're up against. You're an innocent girl!'

This low cut roused me. 'I'm going,' I said. 'I'm getting out of here.' I went to look for my coat. It was the last one left in the bedroom except for Maeve's.

She herself had evidently passed out, for she was stretched across the bed, blowsier than ever, with powder spilled all down one side of her skirt. But even now she lay in a neat, convent-girl attitude, with clasped hands and crossed ankles.

When I left the bedroom the men were still threatening each other in the hall. I couldn't make out how drunk or serious they might be, so I skittered down the basement stairs and out the side door into the garden. By the time I reached the gate Aidan was with me. Then the other two appeared, and it looked as though Enda was not going to let us out. He stood with his back to the gate, waving the gun again and talking about his responsibilies.

'I'll shoot,' he threatened. 'I'll telephone your father, Sheila!'

'Enda if you do that...'

'They'll take advantage of you,' he pleaded. 'I can't stand by... Sheila, *I* asked you out this evening!'

This sad little appeal, coming after his rambunctious threats, might have moved me if he had been less drunk. But he was an unappetizing sight: mouth caked with the black lees of Guinness, sparse, pale stubble erupting on his chin, and a popped button on his chest revealing the confirmation medal underneath. Besides, I had never given Enda any reason to suppose I took him seriously. 'Don't be childish, Enda,' I said.

He lifted the gun as if to strike me. Rory snatched it. 'Steady, now, fellow, steady! Remember that old Irish hero, Cuchulain, whose weapon used to get out of control and had to be put in a pot of soothing herbs? I think that's what *we* need here.' And he planted the gun, barrel down, in one of Enda's mother's geranium pots. 'Come on, now, good chap! Let us pass.' He pushed Enda easily and gently out of the way, and the three of us went out the gate. The last I saw of Enda was through the railing. He was sitting on the ground weeping and muttering about 'insensitivity' and his grandfather.

It was rather a miserable little incident, but in an odd way it made the three of us friendlier towards each other, which was a good thing as it turned out that neither Aidan nor I had the money to take taxis back to our opposite suburbs. Rory had no money either, and Claudia had taken their car.

'You'd better spend the night in my studio,' he said. 'That seems the best solution.'

'What about Claudia?'

'She won't be back tonight!'

So we walked down Pembroke Road, Leeson Street, and the Green, singing the song about Enda's grandfather. There wasn't much for us to talk about and it hasn't a bad tune. When we got to the studio, Rory kicked over a milk bottle and began swearing, which diverted any embarrassment I might have felt. Who did seem embarrassed was Aidan. He kept whispering to me behind his hand that he was responsible for this and would never forgive himself and that I needn't be afraid. When Rory suggested that we all three get into the large and only bed. Aidan began twittering like a nun.

'Don't worry, don't worry,' he kept telling me.

'I'm *not* worried,' I said bitterly.

Rory yawned. 'I'm sleepy. I'll sleep on the outside.' He pulled off his trousers and climbed in. Aidan began pulling cushions about until he had a sort of barricade all down one side of the bed. Then he climbed in on Rory's side of this, fully dressed, and motioned me into the little furrow between the cushions and wall.

I took off my dress and climbed in in my slip. In the dark I tried to fix a couple of pin curls so that my hair wouldn't be straight as a stick in the morning. Then I lay staring at the light which was beginning to dilute the studio window and at the pattern formed by paper scraps pasted over broken panes. A rubber plant, which I remembered seeing in some of Rory's sketches of Claudia in the Grafton Gallery, complicated the design, giving it a live, animal, and foreign savour, reminding me that this was a studio: a place of freedom, alchemy, and secret intuitions. I almost expected the air to affect me as I lay there breathing it. The men had fallen silent and the only communication was when Rory passed across an egg-saucepan full of water. 'Take a swig,' he said. 'The old malt dries the throat.' Then there was more isolating silence. When Aidan's hand burrowed under the barricade towards mine, it was so obviously a fraternal grip that I couldn't presume on it. Besides, if I pressed or bit it, wouldn't he think this was from fear? And could I be sure that I wouldn't be afraid if one of them were to make a move?

In the middle of these wonderings the light snapped on. Aidan pulled the sheet over my head and the delicate, piping voice of Claudia Rain produced a four-letter word. 'To think,' she followed it up, 'that I should come home to this! You have a virgin in my bed. A tight little virgin! And I could have had a passionate night with Louie Hennessey! I left him to come home to you,' she called loudly to Rory, while Aidan's hand clamped over my mouth. 'You clod! Get that virgin out of my bed! I won't have virgins in my bed! Damn you! Unblooded virgins!'

'Put a sock in it, Claudia!' Aidan growled. Rory said nothing and I, even if Aidan hadn't got both hands, like metal hooks, on me now, was too paralysed with embarrassment to stir from under my sheet.

I could hear Claudia moving roughly around the room and lay in terror of a physical attack. 'I could have had a passionate night,' she repeated.

'Come and lie with me, then,' Rory's voice coaxed. 'Come on, sweetie!'

'I don't want *you*!' Claudia's accents were more and more cultured, British, and musical. 'I want Aidan. I want to make love with Aidan. His virgin won't mind, will she?'

'Shut *up*,' yelled Aidan. 'Can't you shut her up, Rory?'

'Come on,' said Rory, 'I'll give it to you, sweetie, let me give it to you.'

'I want Aidan. You'll never get another chance, Aidan!'

'Shut you filthy mouth, Claudia!' said Aidan, whose hands were kneading me ferociously in his rage.

'Well, make love with your virgin, then,' Claudia suggested. 'I won't have you lying there masturbating unhealthily in my bed.'

Aidan nearly throttled me in his fury. Rory apparently got hold of Claudia, because the light went out and heavings of the mattress took the place of talk. After a while even that stopped and after another while Aidan cautiously released me, even uncovering my head so that I could breathe a bit and see the window, which had grown paler, and the rubber plant, which was greyer now and more three-dimensional than before. It must have been about three or four in the morning. Astonishing, I fell asleep.

I woke up to find sun streaming across my face and that it was eleven o'clock by my watch. The others were still asleep. I crept off the bed and dressed fast and furtively. I wanted to confront them from as poised a position as possible. In the bathroom I found pots of make-up with which I constructed for myself as understated and elegant a face as their tones permitted. Then I mooched about the studio, observing the odd appeal of things whose uses had got confused. I found food tangled up in some piles of scrap iron and the skeleton of a sheep. As there didn't seem to be much else to do, I got breakfast and brought it in on a tray. Claudia had been woken up by my clatter and had, to my relief, put on a very *Harper's Bazaar* dressing-gown.

'Good morning,' she said. 'How sweet of you. Let's eat it on the bed. There are bits of plaster and junk on the table.'

We smiled at each other over cups of tea and boiled eggs and, when the men sat up, the four of us had a session as formal and sedate as any old county figures nodding their hats together in the Shelbourne Lounge. When he'd finished, Rory sprawled back on his pillow.

'Let's drive out to the country,' he suggested. 'Let's visit Crazy Shaughnessy, the bird-man in Glencree. You'll like him,' he told me, 'and I'm sure he'll like you. I'm going to do a bust of Sheila,' he told Claudia. 'She has a fine neck.' Claudia agreed.

Were they being *too* sweet? I wondered. But they seemed

spontaneous and I felt more relaxed than I ever do, almost as if I'd come to terms with my wretched state or as if its acknowledgement had in some way exorcized it. 'I'd love to,' I said. 'But I'll have to ring my parents. They'll think I spent the night with Maeve, but even so they'll be expecting me back by now.'

'The phone's broken,' Rory told me. 'But we can call in on them on our way to Glencree. Don't worry. We'll be out of here in a jiffy.'

But it was another two hours before we managed to seat ourselves in Rory's ancient and elegant car. It was a tall, black, angular affair and Claudia, in unfashionably long hobble skirt and Ferragamo shoes, emphasized its antiquity. I wondered how consciously she planned her effects. The drive was convivial. The men sang, quoted, joked. Claudia smoked and I was happy in a way I never had been before and can't explain. It was as if their ease and freedom were communicable and everything was now going to be very simple for me. I was still careless as the wind when we turned in our drive and I saw my parents in their Sunday clothes, standing on the steps with their missals in their hands. 'Wait a second,' I told the others, 'I'll just tell them I'm not lunching and be back.'

My mother's outraged abuse was like a foreign language to me at first. I didn't understand. When I did I turned back to the others – I was still sufficiently attuned to them to know I needn't put a face on things – and asked them to go. 'I can't come,' I said. As they drove off my mother's words and sentiments began to assume impact.

'Consorting,' I heard her say, 'consorting with . . . bringing to the house . . . a filthy little whore like that! And where did you spend the night? Maeve's mother rang up. She's beside herself. Maeve hasn't been home all night. And you can imagine how we felt! Where is you self respect? Your values? . . .' And on and on.

I screamed at her, which was stupid as I like her a lot and she may be honest. I'm not sure. I don't, I realize, understand her at all, but she *does* get hurt. I think of the wild youth she had and the erotic books she enjoys and has let me read and I am utterly confused. Because of course I prefer not to think of my parents as consciously hypocritical. And, worst of all, I can feel the comfortable depression of my familiar groove ready to receive me again, and as nothing *actual* – goddamn it and damn me for being as vulgarly physical as they are – happened last night, maybe I am back where I began. Maybe nothing snapped – or mentally ever will. Maybe I am as unfree as ever. Maybe too I have ruined myself with Rory and Claudia and maybe Rory and Claudia are a mirage and the next time I see them she will strike *me* as a 'common little tart'? Or perhaps all this is irrelevant and I am just suffering from blood-pressure or something – though, my God, I am physically and mentally in a state and this bloody letter is doing me no good at all . . .

Fred Johnston

FARETHEEWELL

Abby crossed her legs for the second time and pulled in on the cigarette as if it was some satisfaction to do so; I looked casually over her shoulder and saw my own face in the café mirror, and the sight of it embarrassed me. The sun was soft-brilliant, kissing now and then from behind secret little clouds the glasses in front of us on the red-formica table, round like a bathing-pool. I saw reflections and distortions there, even as we spoke, and could not help thinking of them, like flies, buzzing around my eyes.

Smoothly, and without saying anything, but smiling like a younger girl would, she unfastened her jacket-top, and slid the cigarette into the ash-tray; I looked over at her, and smiled too. The sun peeped in again, and the reflections and distortions went away. In that moment she spoke, and I moved, elbows before me on the table, closer to hear her. She sniffled.

'So,' she began; then she stopped, as if she expected me to continue in the vacuum.

I said: 'So? So, we find ourselves here, an' it's almost time for you to be gone.'

Abby grew morose, and fingered the ash-tray.

'I want you to know that I appreciate you comin' down with me, knowin' how I'd have hated to meet my parents on my own.' She smiled absurdly, and smoked again. The little veil of tension left us.

'No trouble, luv. Margaret is baby-sitting, or some damn thing! She knew you were leavin' but I guess she just couldn't get away; she would've liked to.'

'Would she? I wouldn't have thought so.'

I leaned back in my seat and watched an elderly man approach the café counter, and slide lumbering into position before it.

'She knew you well, and she knew how *we* stood. Have no fear; she would've liked to say goodbye.'

'Oh, God!'

Abby stopped smoking; she threw her butt on to the floor, where it reeled and spluttered and died fizzing at our feet. The man at the counter was chesty, and his voice gurgled around the room like the sound of a car-exhaust in the walling-in of night. Abby, her eyes now as empty and as lost as a child's, now as full and as wild as those of a young girl not turned seventeen – Abby still slipped a smile between her teeth, and where her eyelids met there were drains of salt and water, which made me think of the sea so close to us, and the boat she would soon step on to.

Rain pittered like stones against the window: then the sunshine pushed glass out on to the street outside, so that you had to hold your hand over your eyes to look out to it. Abby was facing the street, and she squinted against the glare, and almost remarked something about it.

'Want another coffee, a sandwich? Have a sandwich. You'll be glad of it on the boat.'

She accidentally, but not unconsciously, kicked her travelling-bags with her feet.

'I'll most likely be sick all the way over, sea-sick.'

'Best way to avoid it is a full stomach.' I watched her eyes, but they did not move from the floor.

'Who told you that?' She was not questioning me, rather she was inviting conversation: a gap faced us which required filling; for soon, too soon we both knew, we would talk no longer.

'I heard it so long ago I can't remember where or from who,' I answered, half-correcting myself with a grin. I saw my reflection again, and was repulsed behind my empty cup of tea. I hadn't known Abby long, just long enough for a friendship to have arisen, and an understanding deeper than that which emotions of love presume: rather it was easy for myself and Abby to speak openly to each other about ourselves, and we would not feel ashamed to say what we felt, in the way that at times I was ashamed to tell my own girl, Margaret, all in its entirety that I felt, or was at times capable of feeling. With Abby O'Neill there was no compulsion to be 'committed': we knew each other well, and that was that. She had often told me that given the chance she would join her brother in Birmingham and here she was, near the big boats at Dun Laoghaire, and her parents would arrive soon, and she didn't agree at all with them, and at times she blamed them for her going. She would've gone anyway, such is the force of that 'thing' which eats inside us, which makes us leave our homes and families and all that provides unearned shelter and effortless life: it was greater and stronger than Abby, than any love she might ever have had for her parents, and it had her here with me now, in the café in Dun Laoghaire.

I ate the remains of a ham sandwich, and crumbs fell on the floor, and on to my lap: I brushed them hastily and not fully away, turning at the sound of an approaching car to look to the doorway: but Abby relaxed me with a sighing noise, and I found myself gazing at her as one does at something one has never seen before.

'It's not Peter,' she said innocently, 'if it was him, he'd shout to us.'

What she said was absurd: Peter was driving her parents down to meet her; he would not have shouted to her in front of her parents, no more than I would have done so. Her parents, from what I knew of them – and that was not much – were conservative to the point of being possessive of their only daughter; four sons, and all away from home. Now Abby was going, and for them I felt just a tinkling of grief. Abby kicked her bags again, and I looked up. From the first time we'd met at a party thrown by herfriend – Margaret had been with me then, as busy as a bee around me – she had effused mixtures and sentiments I could not touch with my own: she would have been a marvellous nurse, a kind person, though taken a little at times to Vodka or Gin and Tonic, especially when among girl-friends. As it was, she was a sewer, and sewing was considered a good thing by her mother, and she now had to sew her way through life in Birmingham, and I thought and believed that she was about to attempt the impossible. I looked at my watch, and she asked me the time, again for conversation's sake.

'Ten t' three.' She lapsed into a coma of gazing at windows, and the café was one great window, steamed up here and there: someone turned a radio on, and it uttered sparse and incoherent phrases like '... down in the town ...'

Abby heard another vehicle drawing up, and I missed her heavy glancing at the doorway and found myself being pulled into the radio-noise.

'... never seen a gal like ...'

'Freddy?'

'... someone tol' me so, yeh ...'

'What? (ev'rybody says yu IS MAAAH BAABY!): sorry, luv. Was miles away.'

Abby took the apology, and continued.

'I will write to you, and to Peter, and I won't write to my parents! No. Not to them. I won't even tell them where I'm staying.'

I said bluntly, and with much sarcasm, 'You'll be staying with your brother.' She drew up her legs against my own, and a tingle of touched excitement ran down my spine and buried itself in the chair behind me: I looked at her eyes, and they were again the eyes of a child who, overcome with guilt, had returned from street-wandering to its parents. I smiled at my thoughts, and my ears pricked automatically to the whine of a Mini drawing alongside the kerb outside: I stood up before Abby, partially blocking her view of the door, and her eyes and hands and shoulders moved shallowly over her travelling bags. I said I'd carry them for her, then Peter was standing before me, not smiling at all, blazer-buttons breaking the blue-tinted serge of his jacket and his shirt-cuffs brilliantly white. 'I have a few things for you,' he said as if she were alone.

We walked one behind the other into the street and up to the car; at first, on seeing the parents sitting judge-like in the back seats, I was afraid, then silent-struck and almost ashamed. I was being stupid, I thought, but still I thought I would be left to walk or take a bus, as surely there was no room in the Mini for all of us. Abby sat in the front, and with a certain apathy Peter showed me into the back seats beside the parents, who, on seeing and recognizing me, smiled weak smiles, and the father offered me a cigarette which I declined in case it should seem like I was taking advantage. Peter got in and we drove away from the café: I glanced back at it, and the blue exhaust smoke was like octopus-ink, shielding our escape beneath rocks.

Mrs O'Neill asked me politely how I was, and having answered as best and as quietly – for Abby's sake – as I could, I returned her question. Oh, she was alright, and so was the 'oulfella,' and she laughed at him, but he did not move. I knew what she was trying to do, and I pitied her: no laughing could hide the emotion which, at every glance to her daughter in the front of the car, loomed like light behind her feverish-grey eyes, and at times she put her hand on her husband's, and at times he withdrew it, and we thus drove through the streets of Dun Laoghaire until the black backs of the big boats threw themselves before us down a little entry; Peter slowed the car up a little, and we relaxed, myself visibly.

'I'll give you these few things, a dress and a costume I had put together for you during the week,' said Peter as we leaned out into the stiffer, salted air. Abby glanced furtively at him as he bent himself into the boot and withdrew beside Mr O'Neill, holding clothes on his arms. Abby said 'Thank you, Peter, very much,' and 'You shouldn't have done a thing like this,' and Peter was content to wink at me and her together, and take two cases from inside the car again: I in turn took one from him. There was a whistling sound, then a groan as if from chains crossing cement, and people moved before and around us like ants surrounding the mating-pair, surrounding the symbolic ones. Now we saw the crowds, saw the hull of the boat, saw the name *Ulidian*, and I remarked to Abby, who now for an instant was at my side, that it referred to a man of Ulster, and wasn't that where I came from, and wasn't life funny? Peter walked stiffly erect behind the father, and the mother walked Chinese-fashion behind Peter. We stopped amongst others at a part of the quayside which was directly beneath the hull of the *Ulidian*, and which was shadow-cast by it; sea-birds, and two crows, fighting for food in the footsteps of Columbus. Abby fastened her jacket and pulled a neck-scarf tightly around her throat: the breeze which now sprung up was like all breezes which accompany a parting, low, cold, and bitter-sweet with distant sounds you cannot hear well, but are a part of, forever. The bags were put to the ground and Abby suddenly silently burst forth, like a great rushing of water and threw her arms about her father and mother at the same time, and her mother said 'Write t'us, write t'us.' Over and over they embraced, leaving myself and Peter embarrassedly staring backs-to-them into the hulks of other vessels, down and up the quay, to his car, to other notches of little spongy crowds, to the birds, to the slipped lines of small sailing-boats, to the tarry ropes, to the earth-held little shops and the cafés and longer, nameless buildings: back in eternal-drawn circle of eyes to the girl we knew and loved, both of us, for the rebel she had become, as we thought ourselves *all* rebels, and the parents she was now embracing still, as sobbingly and as well as she could without also embracing their feet, or the very ground. My throat ached, and in a panic I thought I would never have my turn to say goodbye to her; she let her parents go free, looked at myself and Peter, smiled wetly, and approached us. Her hands embraced my arms: I felt embarrassed and very shy.

''Bye, Fred. I'll write to you an' say how things go. Tell Margaret I was askin' for her; invite me to the wedding.'

I smiled and said my goodbyes: I kissed her cheek, and she began to sob again. I let her go, and Peter took her. I walked back to the car, and the ground mottled under heavy rain, and it was with one hand over my head that I opened the front door of Peter's car in the alley-way and sat myself down to wait for him and Mr and Mrs O'Neill: I did not want to stand in the rain and wave to Abby; I did not want to see her weep, for against the rain her tears would be as nothing at all. Margaret would ask me all about it, what it had been like, and maybe in her own way, she would be slightly, erratically sarcastic too. I watched a plastic Saint Christopher swing, hanged, from the rear-view mirrors. I watched the rain hit the windows and bounce shattered. In a while Peter came into view round a corner, and I opened the driver's door, looking over him down the alley until I saw the O'Neills, arms over each other like wounded soldiers, limping along behind him.

Kate Cruise-O'Brien

HENRY DIED

Henry died.

University students are rarely able to cope with universals and death is the most embarrassing universal. I was shocked, and I was embarrassed.

I was sitting on the steps of the college chapel eating apples in the sun and watching people emerge from the front gate into the enclosed cobbled front square. I was counting smiles as opposed to stumbles. Some people who emerged from the dark hall, hopefully called gate, stumbled, some smiled. I was sure it was significant and was trying to make up my mind why. Then I saw my most recent boyfriend smilingly stumble out of the front gate and picked up my newspaper. I dislike watching people approaching from a long distance or I dislike acknowledging their approach from a long distance. A greeting smile wanes somewhat after five minutes and yet one cannot cease smiling. It seems impolite. My concern over this was superfluous as he immediately crossed the square in the opposite direction. Having ascertained this, I returned to my newspaper. Then I saw Henry's picture. It was familiar to me. Peter, his best friend, had taken it the term before. There was Henry with his long pointed nose, his myopic eyes concealed by round rimless glasses and his curly hair surmounting a heading on the front page of one of Dublin's less restrained evening papers: 'TCD student takes own life.'

There is a rhyme:

'Mary's the one who never liked angel stories,
But Mary's the one who has died.'

I always thought it was inept. It is easier to mourn the gay than it is to mourn the morose. One can write inept rhymes, one can remember their funniness with a suitable catch of the breath. The morose, who do not become life, become death even less. One should not even say that they 'were somehow marked out for death'. Though one does say it. The morose are usually morose through the disparity between their expectations and their reality. They are glum because life is mistreating them and they are misjudged. This however is supposed to be a comment on poor Henry who had taken his own life and it could be said that Henry had been marked out for death. He had, after all, marked death out for himself. He must have contemplated it. He achieved it, I read, with gas and sleeping pills. He had sealed up his windows and door with 'Fixit – the self-adhesive that really sticks', locked the door, taken six sleeping pills and turned on the gas. 'He died holding a letter from his fiancée, Miss Jennifer Carter, terminating their engagement.'

Miss Jennifer Carter at that moment jumped across into the sun from the dark hallway of Front Gate. She yelled at me across the busy quiet square, 'Sarah, you bitch, I've been searching for you everywhere.' I smiled and waved as she bounced across the intervening space. I was never embarrassed by Jennifer's approach. We always smiled and waved and shouted in ironic acknowledgement of the difficulty of that situation, and of our enjoyment of our exhibitionism.

She reached me and grasped my shoulder. She was giggling and breathless. 'I'm pissed, don't be cross, Sarah, it's such fun.' She always apologized for what she hoped I would be shocked by. She liked to regard me as her strict mentor from time to time. It added interest to two mild glasses of shandy.

I handed her the paper. She read the column, handed the paper back to me and sat down beside me. She picked up an apple and began to eat it in large bites, munching and swallowing it quickly.

'I've known that, Sarah. They rang. Henry's parents rang last night and told me.'

'Well why didn't you tell me?' She fiddled with a corner of her eyelash (false) and looked across the square.

'Because I didn't know what to say, I don't know how to deal with this.'

'You don't have to say anything, not to me, anyway, but when you do, don't pretend it was your fault or that you have to feel guilty. All right, you're sorry. You were engaged to him. You once thought you were in love with him and you'll have to see people blaming you because you discovered you weren't. You might make that easier for yourself if you rushed around saying it was your fault and that you felt guilty. People would pity you. It would be bad for you, though, and untrue. You might get to believe it, and no one, no one is responsible for taking their own lives but themselves. Don't dramatize it, Jenny, it's a supreme situation for self-dramatization and you mustn't do it because this time self-dramatization is dangerous.'

She had watched me carefully throughout this speech. 'You're dramatizing, you're acting the wise friend, the knowing confidante. And I don't know why you're so defensive about my guilt.' And then she grasped my wrist and began to laugh, hiccupping pieces of half-chewed apple out of her mouth. She coughed then and choked, and I withdrew her grasp from my wrist and thumped her back until she stopped choking. She looked at me again.

'I could have cried then, laughter to tears, but I won't, I promise. Let's go away from here.' And so we went.

Despite my homily, I began to realize the next morning why Jennifer hadn't told me until she had to. I did not at all know how to deal with this situation and I was very tempted to pretend it had not happened. But I had gone out with Henry's best friend the term before and I loved Jennifer. Since I could not pretend with them, I could not pretend with anyone, for acting over something as large as this would have to be an uninterrupted business.

Jennifer I saw, when I arrived in the coffee bar, was definitely dressed for a part, which I noted commenced with everyone else's knowledge of Henry's death, not with her own. She was wearing a very dashing black floppy hat, with a veil which half-covered her face, a brown and white checked coat, and a black dress.

I looked at her as I sat down on the bench beside her. She was smoking a cigarette with difficulty because of the veil, and also because her fingers were shaking.

'Why are you wearing that thing?' I asked, nodding at the hat.

'Isn't it gorgeous! I think I look mysterious and dangerous.' She lifted the veil a little and peered out at me.

'And a little, little bit tragic?'

'No,' I said.

'No, I didn't think so either, really.' She opened her handbag and took out a pair of dark glasses. She then lifted the veil and put them on and lowered it again.

'More mysterious, more dangerous, Sarah?'

'Yes,' I said. Then I paused. 'Jennifer, what did you say to Henry's parents?'

'Oh, I was quite terse really, you know, "yes, no, how, when?" '

'Were they nice about it?'

'Well,' she said, or drawled with consideration. She is accurate and careful in her assessment of behaviour. 'It was his mother, and she was really very nice to me. And it was a bit difficult for her because I was so terse. So she said I should come to the funeral, which is tomorrow, and then she said something at the end like "You mustn't blame yourself, my dear, and you must let your feelings go, have a good cry." The main idea was that underneath my tough exterior there was a heart of pure molten gold, that I was pretending not to care when I did really.'

'Do you?'

'I don't care,' she said. 'I didn't depend on him any more, and if someone is dead, and one doesn't see them dying, and one didn't depend on them, how can one care?'

She took off her glasses and I saw that the skin around her eyes was puckered and red. Above her eyes she wore her usual rather strange make-up. Wispy black lines were drawn out in a radius from a black socket line. From her eyes to her eyebrows her skin was painted a light blue-white. The veins of her eyelids showed through the paint.

'Have you been crying?'

'A bit, but it's more or less acting to myself really, and worry because I'm frightened of meeting people.'

'You mustn't, love. The people who matter will know you well enough not to blame you.'

'Do you really think they shouldn't blame me?' It was a question I didn't want to answer.

'Are you coming to this lecture?' I asked. She pulled her long hair. Her hair was inclined to be very wavy and grew unevenly. It was one of her permanent and irregular attractions, for it stood out around her head like a jagged brown and yellow cloud in blurring bars of colour. Jennifer put a yellow end of hair in her mouth and sucked it. 'No,' she said, out of the other side of her mouth.

'Will you be all right?' We allowed ourselves to look after each other, for although we were aware of the occasional excess of our concern, or because of our awareness of it, we were never embarrassed by our own sentimentality. It was like talking to oneself to cheer oneself up.

'Yes, love,' she put a hand on my shoulder. 'Run along, Sarah, and I'll be a big brave girl, big certainly.' She giggled. She was tall with very big bones, but not fat. Her figure was a constant source of worry to her and again, as in the case of her hair, in not conforming to the skeleton standard of conventional beauty, it held an attraction of its own.

I went out of the coffee bar and walked along a line of low Elizabethan rubrics towards my lecture, which was in an ugly, but not obtrusive building in the square behind. As I turned the corner I saw Peter coming towards me. Peter and I together had formed, for a short while, a foil for Henry and Jennifer. Or, as Jennifer said, 'I got you and Peter together, love, to mitigate the boredom, the ghastly, intolerable boredom.'

'Sarah, I want to talk to you,' said Peter.

'Yes, I'm going to a lecture, but I don't have to go. I think we should talk. I mean—' I stumbled on the cobbles and, as Peter put out a hand to help me, I bent my head. I am incapable of exchanging looks with men I care for.

'Come for a walk,' said Peter. 'Around College Park.' We walked into College Park, where young men in track suits were training by running slowly around the periphery of the shorn grass. We both sat down on a bench and, for a time, sat still. Peter watched the runners and I watched the trees which grew around the sides of the park. They were large elms. The sun shone through them, dappling the long grass at the side of the track. I could see two friends of mine lying side by side, their heads against the bole of a tree. The man was tickling the girl's neck with a twig.

'How does Jenny feel now?' asked Peter. He turned his head towards me. I thought that I had forgotten how big his nose was and his chin.

'How do you mean "How does she feel"?' The young man had abandoned his twig and now gently eased his arm under the girl's neck.

'About Henry.' The girl settled her head against the man's shoulder and I could see her two white feet, twisting.

'Sorry, but not guilty. She shouldn't, you know, feel guilty. Henry never tried to help himself whenever she broke it off. He just ran around after her and asked for more.'

'You are a bitch, Sarah. I mean that.' Peter bent over towards me. His eyes, which were big and blue, opened widely. The muscles at one side of his nose contracted and the corresponding side of his mouth lifted. He achieved a sneer. He had large features, big eyes, a large crooked nose and a long chin. His cheeks were fleshless. Until I met Peter I never believed that there was such a thing as a gaunt face. His was gaunt. When he smiled his face did not relax, it tautened, and the skin around his eyes wrinkled. His whole face was used in his smile, and when he sneered now I felt a little sick.

'I liked Henry, he did Jenny good, he made her grow up a

lot.' I lied, and then was afraid that Peter knew that I was lying and would despise me for betraying the integrity of my own feelings, and then I thought that I was not betraying my integrity, for my first feeling was of wanting Peter. I knew that was a lie, for if I had to change myself to please Peter, wanting Peter was an illusion, but I knew I wanted Peter. These thoughts made themselves felt in an unhappy confusion which resolved itself in uneasiness and a sudden desire to cry and run away, to go home and wait until Henry had been forgotten.

'Yes, Henry did help Jenny, and he really loved her. She just used him. She kept the engagement going until Trinity Ball because she wanted a partner, and she kept herself amused in the meanwhile by having constant rows with him. I went through it, Sarah. I sat up with him each night after their constant quarrels. And I know what he felt like because I've been through that too.' As he spoke, he lowered his voice. I suppose he thought that I would be moved. But I was too much at his emotional mercy to pity him now for his past and vague sufferings. Also because I felt *I* was to be pitied I was sure *his* self-pity was insincere. I did not, of course, say this to him. Because I act so constantly I hate catching other people out in their little acts.

'You don't know what Jennifer felt like.'

'Why don't you tell me?'

'She acts, you know. The quarrels weren't real to her, they just alleviated the boredom.'

'Boredom?' asked Peter. His face seemed to fall away from his eyes now and he swept his hair back from his face dramatically, but ineffectually.

'Is that all it meant to her?'

'No, it isn't at all all it meant to her. It was just extra.'

'Extra?' He was really quite funny with his one-word interjections. Peter truly has an expression that represents to me all the things that I associate with the word quizzical. He can look attractive, questioning and amused all at the same time. I feel then like a young and intelligent child who has been so clever that her schoolmaster almost loves her. The expression was there now and, in response, I was clever.

'She loved his love, you see. It was the one thing in Henry she felt above all others, and by quarrelling she could see it working.'

'There were, eh' – the 'eh' sounded silly – 'other ways of seeing love work?' I was disappointed in him and I deteriorated. Back to amateur Freud, the bane of my young life, when I couldn't be ill without my clever elder sister telling me that it was only my unconscious.

'She didn't trust those ways.' I felt uncomfortable. I couldn't say sex. Not to somebody I'd been to bed with.

'She felt that those ways were the only reason Henry wanted her, and she kept on having to remind him they weren't.'

'That's nonsense.'

'I know,' I said, and was pleased that Peter should think it was nonsense. I like people knowing I'm being trite when I am being trite.

'Well, if you know, don't try and justify her. She just wanted to manipulate Henry, and she did, out of existence. A great power game.' I felt very shaky. Peter said the last sentence with a pause after each word and I felt a terrible impulse to giggle, and once I started to giggle I knew that I would be unable to stop. I decided to pretend to cry instead and curiously, once I let the hiccupping motion which was in my stomach out, I was crying.

'Don't do that, Sarah.' He patted my shoulder from behind. Not caressingly. Just trying to stop me. 'Don't get yourself torn up by this, don't make yourself believe that Jennifer was justified and then get upset because you can't convince yourself, and you can't feel sorry for Jennifer and Harry at once.' Peter saying Harry made me cry again. Because of the late-night coffee sessions they had together, their camaraderie, their being funny together. At last I did feel sorry and, more than that, unhappy, that Henry was dead.

'Don't, Sarah, I can't leave you like this. Here.' He gave me a large, dirty handkerchief and I mopped my face with it. I refrained from blowing my nose, though I wanted to. 'Look, if you face the fact that your defence is useless to Jenny and you, you'll be a lot better off. The most important thing now is that Henry is dead and he died because Jennifer was too occupied with her frivolities to see that his feelings for her were entirely serious. That must have been terrible. Feeling so much and never getting a response that wasn't calculated, for effect.'

I blew my nose. I decided that it was, after all, childlike and endearing to blow the nose. 'I know that, Peter.'

'Well, don't defend her then.'

'It is nothing to do with defending her. Jennifer acts. That's Jennifer. It was a terrible accident.'

'All right, she acts, but she should have gone somewhere else to act. She should have seen that Henry wasn't acting. It was not seeing that's unforgivable, and if she refuses to see her guilt that's even more unforgivable.' I was pulling a button on my coat, and as I tightened my hand the thread broke and it fell to the ground. Peter picked it up and give it to me.

'Didn't you see that, Sarah?'

'Yes, I suppose I did.' I had, of course. It is easier not to realize something one does not want to realize alone. When someone one respects realizes it for one it is unhappily inescapable. Now I had been forced to face her guilt, which was considerable, and appalling to me because she did not seem to have recognized it at all. I had tried to avoid thinking about her guilt because I did not want to be separate from her. To disapprove of her without her approval.

We got up to go by common, but mute consent. We had nothing else to say to each other and I needed to see Jennifer.

As we approached the coffee bar I saw Jennifer peering out of the window. Her hat had slipped back on her head and the veil of the hat was now covering, not her eyes, but her hair. I did not tell Peter I could see her, although I knew he had seen her and though I knew he knew I had seen her.

'Thank you for the walk,' I said. I wouldn't have said that

if I could have thought of anything else to say, or if I could have borne silence. Silence was embarrassing between us now. We were neither companionable nor uninterested.

'What are you thanking me for?' asked Peter.

'For nothing, obviously, if you can ask that.'

'How do you mean "if you can ask that"?' Now that Henry was dead, the only subject on which we could talk with any ease at all was his death. Every other subject would be affected by that fact. Because any other subject would be an escape from the embarrassment of Henry's death, which was much less embarrassing than the escape. At least that was what I felt Peter felt. What I knew was that the escape was from the sudden absence of intimacy between us, which left us with no knowledge of how to deal with each other. I felt regret for this, but I wanted the ending to be over.

Jennifer came out of the coffee bar. Her veil was back over her eyes.

'I must go, Sarah. I'll see you sometime.' The sometime meant he wouldn't see me. Then he looked at Jennifer as she came up and smiled, or grinned. For the smile was concentrated towards one end of his mouth and his nose wrinkled.

'What a hat, Jennifer, are you by any chance Miss Garbo wanting to be alone?'

'I vant to be alowne,' said Jennifer.

Peter laughed, waved and left us. I both admired and despised him for his manner with Jennifer. I admired him because I hate scenes and I dislike coolness, and I despised him because he ought to have addressed his complaints about Jennifer to Jennifer. I knew that in the same situation I would have behaved in the same way. Unfortunately for me, I always hope that my men will have greater integrity than I have myself. Integrity is a quality that I admire because I find it so hard to possess it. I would rather be liked than to sit in judgement because I would rather be protected than be the protector.

'Let's go to the park,' said Jennifer. She grabbed my arm and I clung to it.

'Thank God for you, Jenny.'

She lowered her glasses and looked at me. 'Was it that bad?'

'Worse.'

'Is it over?'

'I can't think of any way it wouldn't be.'

The park was empty now. The lovers had gone and whitish clouds had come over the sun. They were low clouds, for one of them raked the top of the trees and began to look like mist, fading from cloud to thick air to air.

'What did Peter say?'

'Nothing much.'

'Did he say anything about me?' A small piece of cloudy mist seemed to be caught in a branch of the tree. The two ends of it moved slowly apart and together, embracing the branch and then letting it go.

'I'm not going to the funeral.'

'Why not?'

'Because there'll be all those people knowing it was my fault.'

'Knowing?'

'You know it was, don't you, Sarah? I've been thinking about it. I know it was my fault because I've enough knowledge of psychology to know that that's why I'm afraid of people thinking it was. But I don't know it for any other reason. I mean I don't feel guilty.'

I was released from blaming Jennifer because as soon as she knew it was her fault, I didn't have to know for her. It was a shared, not a separating motion. But I still didn't see what the trouble was.

She sat on the grass, which was moist, for the mist was gradually thickening and dampening. She dug little holes in the grass with her bare fingers. 'Sarah,' she said, and her voice was very high, 'I don't feel anything at all. I know everything and I don't feel anything, and I know everything because I've been informed. I do really want to feel something.'

And a line came into my head:

'Oh God, I believe. Help Thou my unbelief.'

John McGahern

MY LOVE, MY UMBRELLA

It was the rain, the constant weather of this city, made my love inseparable from the umbrella, a black umbrella, white stitching on the seams of the imitation leather over the handle, the metal point bent where it was caught in Mooney's grating as we raced for the last bus to the garage out of Abbey Street. The band was playing when we met; Blanchardstown Fife and Drum. They were playing *Some day he'll come along/The man I love/And he'll be big and strong/The man I love* at the back of the public lavatory on Burgh Quay, facing a few persons on the pavement in front of the Scotch House; it was the afternoon of a Sunday.

'It is strange, the band,' I said; her face flinched away, and in the same movement back, turned to see who'd spoken. Her skin under the black hair had the glow of health and youth and the solidity at the bones of the hips gave promise of a rich seedbed.

'It's strange,' she answered, and I was anxious for her body.

The conductor stood on a wooden box, continually breaking off his conducting to engage in some running argument with a small grey man by his side, but whether he waved his stick jerkedly or was bent in argument seemed to make no difference to the players. They turned their pages. The music plodded on, *Some day he'll come along/The man I love/And he'll be big and strong/The man I love.* At every interval they looked towards the clock, Mooney's clock across the river.

'They're watching the clock,' I said.

'Why?' her face turned again.

'They'll only play till the opening hour.'

I too anxiously watched the clock. I was afraid she'd go when the band stopped. Lights came on inside the Scotch House. The music hurried. A white-aproned barman, a jangle of keys into the quickened music, began to unlock the folding shutters and with a resounding clash drew them back. As the tune ended the conductor signalled to the band that they could put away their instruments, got down from his box, and started to tap the small grey man on the shoulder with the baton as he began to argue in earnest. The band came across the road towards the lighted globes inside the Scotch House, where already many of their audience waited impatiently on the slow pulling of the pints. The small grey man carried the conductor's box as they passed together in.

'It is what we said would happen.'

'Yes.'

The small family cars were making their careful way home across the bridge after their Sunday outings to their cold ham and tomato and lettuce, the wind blowing from the mouth of the river, gulls screeching above the stink of its low tide, as I forced the inanities towards an invitation.

'Would you come with me for a drink?'

'Why?' She blushed as she looked me full in the face.

'Why not?'

'I said I'd be back for tea.'

'We can have sandwiches.'

'But why do you want me to?'

'I'd like very much if you come. Will you come?'

'All right I'll come but I don't know why.'

It was how we began, the wind blowing from the mouth of the river while the Blanchardstown Fife and Drum downed their first thirstquencher in the Scotch House.

They'd nothing but beef left in Mooney's after the weekend. We had stout with our beef sandwiches. Soon, in the drowsiness of the stout, we did little but watch the others drinking. I pointed out a poet to her, I recognized him from his pictures in the paper. His shirt was open-necked inside a gaberdine coat and he wore a hat with a small feather in its band. She asked me if I liked poetry.

'When I was younger,' I said. 'Do you?'

'Not very much.'

She asked me if I could hear what the poet was saying to the four men at his table who continually plied him with whiskey. I hadn't heard. Now we both listened. He was saying he loved the blossoms of Kerr Pinks more than roses, a man could only love what he knew well, and it was the quality of the love mattered and not the accident. The whole table said they'd drink to that, but he glared at them as if slighted, and as if to avoid the glare they called for a round of doubles. While the drinks were coming from the bar the poet turned aside and took a canister from his pocket. The inside of the lid was coated with a white powder which he quickly licked clean. She thought it was baking soda, her father in the country took baking soda for his stomach. We had more stout and we noticed, while each new round was coming, the poet turned away from the table to lick clean the fresh coat of soda on the inside of the canister lid.

That was the way our first evening went. People who came into the pub were dripping with rain and we stayed until they'd draped the towels over the pump handles and called 'Time' in the hope the weather would clear, but it did not.

The beat of rain was so fierce when we came out that the street was a dance of glass shapes, and they reminded me of the shape of the circle of blackened spikes on the brass candleshrine which hold the penny candles before the altar.

'Does it remind you of the candlespikes?' I asked.

'Yes, now that you mention it.'

Perhaps the rain, the rain will wash away the poorness of our attempts at speech, our bodies will draw closer, closer than our speech, I hoped, as she returned on the throat my kiss in the bus, and that we'd draw closer to a meal of each other's flesh; and from the bus, under the beat of rain on the umbrella, we walked beyond Fairview church.

'Will I be able to come in?' I asked.

'It would cause trouble.'

'You have your own room?'

'The man who owns the house watches. He would make trouble.'

Behind the church is a dead end overhung with old trees, and the street lights do not reach far as the wall at its end, a grey orchard wall with some ivy.

'Can we stay here a short time then?'

I hung upon the silence, afraid she'd use the rain as excuse, and breathed when she said, 'Not for long, it is late.'

We moved under the umbrella out of the street light, fumbling for certain footing between the tree roots.

'Will you hold the umbrella?'

She took the imitation leather with the white stitching in her hands.

Our lips moved on the saliva of our mouths as I slowly undid the coat button. I tried to control the trembling so as not to tear the small white buttons of the blouse. Coat, blouse, brassière as names of places on a road. I globed the warm soft breasts in hands. I leaned across the cold metal above the imitation leather she held in her hands to take the small nipples gently in teeth, the steady beat on the umbrella broken by irregular splashes from the branches.

Will she let me? I was afraid as I lifted the woollen skirt; and slowly I moved hands up the soft insides of the thighs, and instead of the 'No' I feared and waited for, the handle became a hard pressure as she pressed on my lips.

I could no longer control the trembling as I felt the sheen of the knickers, I drew them down to her knees, and parted the lips to touch the juices. She hung on my lips. She twitched as the fingers went deeper. She was a virgin.

A memory of the cow pumping on the rubbered arm of the inseminator as the thick juice falls free and he injects the semen with the glass plunger came with a desire to hurt. 'It hurts,' the cold metal touched my face, the rain duller on the sodden cloth by now.

'I won't hurt you,' I said, and pumped low between her thighs, lifting high the coat and skirts so that the seed fell free into the mud and rain, and after resting on each other's mouth I replaced the clothes.

Under the umbrella, one foot asleep, we walked past the small iron railings of the gardens towards her room, and at the gate I left her with, 'Where will we meet again?'

We would meet at eight against the radiators inside the Metropole.

We met against those silver radiators three evenings every week for long. We went to cinemas or sat in pubs, it was the course of our love, and as it always rained we made love under the umbrella beneath the same trees in the same way. They say the continuance of sexuality is due to the penis having no memory, and mine each evening spilt its seed into the mud and decomposing leaves as if it was always for the first time.

Sometimes we told each other stories.

The story she told that most interested me had some cruelty, which is possibly why I found it exciting.

She'd grown up on a small farm. The neighbouring farm was owned by a Pat Moran who lived on it alone after the death of his mother. As a child she used to look for nests of hens that were laying wild on his farm and he used to bring her chocolates or oranges from the fairs. As she grew, feeling the power of her body, she began to provoke him, until one evening on her way to the well through his fields, where he was pruning a whitethorn hedge with a billhook, she lay in the soft grass and showed him so much of her body beneath the clothes that he dropped the billhook and seized her. She struggled loose and shouted as she ran, 'I'll tell my Daddy, you pig.' She was far too afraid to tell her father, but it was as if a wall came down between her and Pat Moran who soon afterwards sold his farm and went to England though he'd never known any other life but that of a small farmer.

She'd grown excited in the telling and asked me what I thought of the story. I said that I thought life was often that way. She then, her face flushed, asked me if I had any stories in my life. I said I did, but there was a story that I read in the evening paper that had interested me, since it had indirectly got to do with us.

It had been a report of a prosecution. In the rush hour at Bank station in London two city gents had lost tempers in the queue and had assaulted each other with umbrellas. They had inflicted severe injuries with the umbrellas. The question before the judge: was it a case of common assault or, much more seriously, assault with dangerous weapon with intent to wound? In view of the extent of the injuries inflicted it had not been an easy decision, but he eventually found for common assault, since he didn't want the thousands of peaceable citizens who used their umbrellas properly to feel that when they travelled to and from work they were carrying dangerous weapons. He fined and bound both gentlemen to the peace, warned them severely as to their future conduct, but he did not impose a prison sentence, as he'd be forced to do if he'd found the umbrella to be a dangerous weapon.

'What do you think of the story?'

'I think it's pretty silly. Let's go home,' she said though it was an hour from the closing hour, raising the umbrella as soon as we reached the street. It was raining as usual.

'Why did you tell that silly story about the umbrellas?' she asked on the bus.

'Why did you tell the story of the farmer?'

'They were different,' she said.

'Yes. They were different,' I agreed. For some reason she resented the story.

In the rain we made love again, she the more fierce, and after the seed had spilled she said, 'Wait,' and moving on a dying penis, under the unsteady umbrella in her hands, she trembled towards an inarticulate cry of pleasure, and as we walked into the street lamp I asked, we had so fallen into the habit of each other, 'Would you think we should ever get married?' 'Kiss me,' she leaned across the steel between us. 'Do you think we ever should?' I repeated. 'What would it mean to you?' she asked.

What I had were longings or fears rather than any meanings. To go with her on the train to Thurles on a Friday evening in summer, and walk the three miles to her house from the station. To be woken the next morning by the sheepdog barking the postman to the door and have tea and brown bread and butter in a kitchen with the cool of brown flagstones and full of the smell of recent baking.

Or fear of a housing estate in Clontarf, escape to the Yacht Sunday mornings to read the papers in peace over pints, come home dazed in the midday light of the sea front with a peace offering of sweets to the Sunday roast. Afterwards in the drowse of food and drink to be woken by, 'You promised to take us out for the day, Daddy,' until you backed the hire-purchased Volkswagen out the gateway and drove to Howth and stared out at the sea through the gathering condensation on the semicircles the wipers made on the windshield, and quelled quarrels and cries of the bored children in the back seat.

I decided not to tell her either of these pictures as they might seem foolish to her.

'We'd have to save if we were to think about it,' I heard her voice.

'We don't save very much, do we?'

'At the rate the money goes in the pubs we might as well throw our hat at it. Why did you ask?'

'Because,' it was not easy to answer then, when I had to think, 'I like being with you.'

'Why, why,' she asked, 'did you tell that stupid story about the umbrellas?'

'It happened, didn't it? And we never make love without an umbrella. It reminded me of your body.'

'Such rubbish,' she said angrily. 'The sea and sand and hot beach at night, needing only a single sheet, that'd make some sense, but an umbrella?'

It was the approach of summer and it was the false confidence it brings that undid me. It rained less. A bright moonlit night I asked her to hold the umbrella.

'For what?'

She was so fierce that I pretended it'd been a joke.

'I don't see much of a joke standing like a fool holding an umbrella to the blessed moonlight,' she said and we made love awkwardly, the umbrella lying in the dry leaves; but I was angry that she wouldn't fall in with my wish, and another night when she asked, 'Where are you going on your holidays?' I lied that I didn't know. 'I'll go home if I haven't enough money. And you?' I asked. She didn't answer. I saw she resented that I'd made no effort to include her in the holiday. 'Sun and sand and sea,' I thought maliciously and decided to break free from her. Summer was coming, and the world full of possibilities. I would be tied to no stake. I did not lead her under the trees behind the church, but left after kissing her lightly, 'Goodnight.' Instead of arranging to meet as usual at the radiators I said, 'I'll ring you during the week.' Her look of anger and hatred elated me. 'Ring if you want,' she said as she angrily closed the door.

I was so clownishly elated that I threw the umbrella high in the air and laughing loudly caught it coming down, and there was the exhilaration of staying free those first days, but it soon palled. In the empty room trying to read, while the trains went by at the end of the garden with its two apple trees and one pear, I began to realize I'd fallen more into the habit of her than I'd known. Not wanting to have to see the umbrella I put it behind the wardrobe, but it seemed to be more present than ever there; and often the longing for her lips, her body, grew close to sickness, and eventually dragged me to the telephone, though I wouldn't admit it was weakness, it was no more than a whim.

'I didn't expect to hear from you after this time,' were her first words.

'I was ill.'

She was ominously silent as if she knew it for the lie that it was.

'I wondered if we could meet?'

'If you want,' she answered. 'When?'

'What about tonight?'

'I cannot but tomorrow night is all right.'

'At eight then at the radiators?'

'Say at Wynn's Hotel instead.'

The imagination, quickened by distance and uncertainty, found it hard to wait till the seven of the next day, but when the bus drew in at seven, and she was already waiting, the mind slipped back to its original complacency.

'Where'd you like to go?'

'Some place quiet. Where we can talk,' she said.

Crossing the bridge and past where the band had played the first day we met, the Liffey was still in the summer evening.

'I missed you a great deal,' I tried to draw close, her hands were white gloved.

'What was your sickness?'

'Some kind of flu.'

She was hard and separate as she walked. It was one of the new lounge bars she picked as quiet, with piped music and red cushions. The bar was empty, the barman polishing glasses. He brought the Guinness and sweet sherry to the table.

'What did you want to say?' I asked when the barman had returned to polishing the glasses.

'That I've thought about it and that our going out is a waste of time. It's a waste of your time and mine.'

It was as if a bandage had been torn from an open wound.

'But why?'

'It will come to nothing.'

'You've got someone else then?'

'That's got nothing to do with it.'

'But why then?'

'I don't love you.'

'But we've had many happy evenings together.'

'Yes, but it's not enough.'

'I thought that after a time we would get married,' I would grovel on the earth or anything to keep her then. Little by little my life had fallen into her keeping, it was only in the loss I had come to know it, life without her the pain of the loss of my own life without the oblivion the dead have, all longing changed to die out of my own life on her lips, on her thighs, since it was only in her it lived.

'It wouldn't work,' she said and sure of her power. 'All those wasted evenings under that old umbrella. And that moonlit night you tried to get me to hold it up like some eejit. What did you take me for?'

'I meant no harm and couldn't we try to make a new start?'

'No. There should be something magical about getting married and we know too much about each other. There's nothing more to discover.'

'You mean with our bodies?'

'Yes.'

She moved to go and I was desperate.

'Will you have one more drink?'

'No, I don't really want.'

'Can we not meet just once more?'

'No,' she rose to go. 'It'd only uselessly prolong it and come to the same thing in the end.'

'Are you so sure? If there was just one more chance?'

'No. And there's no need for you to see me to the bus. You can finish your drink.'

'I don't want,' and followed her through the swing door.

At the stop in front of the Bank of Ireland I tried one last time, 'Can I not see you home this last night?'

'No, it's easier this way.'

'You're meeting someone else then?'

'No. And it's beside the point.'

It was clean as a knife. I watched her climb on the bus, fumble in her handbag, take the fare from a small purse, open her hand to the conductor as the bus turned the corner. I watched to see if she'd look back, if she'd give any sign, but she did not; all my love and life had gone and I had to wait till it was gone to know it.

I then realized I'd left the umbrella in the pub, and started to return slowly for it. I went through the swing door, took the umbrella from where it leaned against the red cushion, raised it and said, 'Just left this behind,' to the barman's silent inquiry, as if the performance of each small act would numb the pain.

I got to no southern sea or city that summer. The body I'd tried to escape from became my only thought. In the late evening after pub-close, I'd stop in terror at the thought of what hands were fondling her body, and would if I had power have made all casual sex a capital offence. On the street I'd see a coat or dress she used to wear, especially a cheap blue dress with white dots, and zipped at the back, that was fashionable that summer, and with beating heart would push through the crowds till I was level with the face that wore the dress but the face was never her face.

I often rang her, pleading, and she consented to see me for one lunch hour when I said I was desperate. We walked aimlessly through streets of the lunch hour, and I'd to hold back tears as I thanked her for her kindness, though when she'd given me all her evenings and body I'd hardly noticed. The same night after pub-close I went – driven by the urge that brings people back to the rooms where they once lived and no longer live, or to sleep in the same sheets and bed of their close dead the night after they're taken from the house – and stood out of the street lamps under the trees where so often we had stood, in the hope that some meaning of my life or love would come, but only the night hardened about the growing absurdity of a man standing under an umbrella beneath the drip from the green leaves of the trees.

Through my love it was the experience of my own future death I was passing through, for the life of the desperate equals the anxiety of death, and before time had replaced all its bandages I found relief in movement, in getting on buses and riding to the terminus; and one day at Killester I heard the conductor say to the driver as they sat downstairs through their ten-minute rest, 'Jasus this country is going to the dogs entirely. There's a gent up there who looks normal enough who must umpteen times this last year have come out here to nowhere and back,' and as I listened I felt as a patient after a long illness when the doctor says, 'You can start getting up tomorrow,' and I gripped the black umbrella with an almost fierce determination to be as I was before, unknowingly happy under the trees, and the umbrella, in the wet evenings that are the normal weather of this city.

Ita Daly

VIRGINIBUS PUERISQUE

Rome is best approached by road and best of all approached from the North, Liza felt. Your starting out point should be Florence. Leave Florence and journey down the Autostrada Del Sol. You will whizz along the smooth efficient highway, so much at odds with the countryside beyond. You will leave behind the soft voluptuousness of Tuscany and savour the approaching thrift of the Umbrian landscape. And thus you will be prepared gradually for the city itself. For Rome.

That was how Liza had first seen Rome. But this time as she stood in Rome's international airport and looked around at its smart anonymity, she could feel only dullness. She waited behind Stephen in the queue for the Customs and wondered if it was because of their comparative newness that airports were always so characterless. She was uneasy and apprehensive, because she realized, guiltily, that what she had been looking forward to about her honeymoon was the fact that it was being spent in Rome. There would be no first-night raptures of course. June, honeymoon. Whimsically she wondered about this kind of lyricism. She found it appealing though she realized that to her its appeal could only be academic. 'Here I am in Rome,' she thought, 'with a new husband, new suitcases and new underwear, and I never felt so silly in my life.' Did she look as silly as she felt? She caught a glimpse of herself in a mirror opposite. The large picture-hat was regular honeymoon gear in Dublin. Like the honeymoon itself, it was felt that one was not decently wedded without it. Oh well, stop moaning girl. Enjoy it. Play the game. Where's the much-lauded sense of humour? Coyly she looked at the Customs official, and when she caught his glance, modestly she lowered her eyes. She wished she could have managed a blush. He laughed, delighted with this obvious bride, who behaved in such a seemly, almost latin manner. Stephen smiled too, pleased that his bride was being admired.

Stephen Hero she called him. She looked at him now, appraising him. She had a predilection for handsome men, and Stephen looked very handsome today. He had an air of distinction about him, a fine dry intelligence emanating from him which somehow diluted his physical handsomeness, preventing it from becoming brash. All this and beddable too. Liza pulled herself up, displeased with herself. One ought not to analyze thus a new husband, with such a mixture of off-handed wryness. Well, never mind. Maybe tonight they would make love in a frescoed room, overlooking a cool courtyard, dusty and quiet, while Rome throbbed outside. She felt her excitement grow.

They boarded the airport bus. The heat was oppressive and she welcomed it, wallowed in its heaviness. Her smart linen suit was limp and stained with perspiration at the armpits. Her hair was sticky and she knew that no number of cool showers or glasses of icy lemonade would revive her. She would grow more and more limp until finally her very nerves would become blunt and her mind like her body would accept and submit. Rome had the ability to sap one's being like no other city she knew – to leave one drained, void, so satisfyingly empty.

Rome, the slattern, spread herself in front of them. Her appalling monuments, her decaying churches, her vulgar fountains were revealed mercilessly in the brilliant sunshine. She laughed back, careless of her appearance, frank, friendly, generous. Thank God they hadn't chosen Florence, Liza thought, prim and classical, full of echoes of John Milton and his puritan breed. Stephen Hero sat looking out the window. He held her hand and Liza realized that only Stephen Hero could hold one's hand in such heat, with no suggestion of clamminess. Again she marvelled at her own good taste, in men as in suitcases: Stephen Hero and brown pig-skin suitcases – only the nicest of sensibilities could achieve such a combination. 'Roma, I love you.' Liza mouthed the words.

She had begun to recognize some of the streets now as they crossed over the Ponte Sixto. The buildings had a grey, still quality. The leaves of the trees that lined the Tiber were dust laden and ready to fall off under their weight. The water of the river was sluggish and oily. Liza looked with affection. Absurd to feel this affection for a city that one had only visited once for a fortnight, four years ago. She felt the need to explain, to herself as much as to Stephen.

'Oh, Stephen', she said, 'I'm so happy to be in Rome. And you are *so* kind to agree to our coming here when you know how much it means to me. It was my first taste of Europe you know, of being away from home. Jonny and I spent a fortnight here. We hadn't a penny. We stayed in the youth hostel up on the Via Caligula. And we walked miles every day to our lunch ...'

'I know, darling,' Stephen said gently, 'you have told me before, you know'.

'Oh, L'm sorry, I'm being such a bore ...'

'You know you can never bore me.'

She felt a rush of affection for him. He was so honest about his love for her.

'It was such a special holiday.'

Liza could almost feel again the texture of the happiness she had experienced four years ago. 'Jonny and I, well, you know how close we have always been. I suppose it was because there were only the two of us. My father gave me the money to mind – he knew Jonny – and every morning after breakfast we'd see how many lira we could afford to spend that day. And we learned the Italian for ice-cream – *gelati,* and where is – *dove e,* and thank you – *grazie.* I wore jeans for the whole fortnight. I brought them with me again – I'm going to change when we get to the hotel.'

Their room was indeed beautiful. Shuttered against the sunlight, gold strips of brightness lightened the green of the carpet. Below, from a great distance, came the hum of the Roman traffic. The bed was huge and ornate, and over it, in the middle of the ceiling, was a group of cherubs, their rounded cheeks cracked with age. As Liza stood under the shower in the adjoining bathroom, she had the absurd feeling that she could recognize a familiar quality in the Roman water as it fell on her back. In the youth hostel, there had been one shower in the women's quarters – the rest were out of order. Jonny had wanted her to use the fountains – 'Go on, don't be so illogical. It's water going to waste.' He had been great at getting lifts too, Jonny, and he had encouraged her mild flirtations with the drivers, highly amused that anyone should want to flirt with his sister. He was proud of her though. Said she shared the family distinction. 'My soror,' he would roar at the drivers, eccentrically convinced that all Italians must speak Latin as well as Italian.

Liza returned to the bedroom and took out her jeans. She fitted them on, but they would not close over her hips. Two years of love-making had broadened those hips. They were virgin hips the last time she was in Rome. Boyish. Smart, economical. She felt a stab of nostalgia – for what? For the freedom of being a virgin in Rome, with her brother, when her future was so unknown and uncertain as to be full of magic.

Stephen came from the shower and threw the towel on the floor. She looked at him with interest and detachment. Stephen's body was compact and vibrant. The ripple of the muscles under the milky skin had always reminded her of Michelangelo's 'David'. In fact, now that she came to think of it, the first time she had seen Stephen on the beach at Carraroe, he had been christened 'David' by Jonny. The family had taken a cottage there that year and Jonny and herself were walking down the little road to the shore. He was sulking because she had refused to give him half-a-crown he wanted for his morning pint. Suddenly he nudged her, his sulky face brightening. 'Hey,' he said, 'look over there – a real live "David".' He had pronounced it in the Italian way, as they had learned to do in Florence the year before. They had both been bored by Tuscan perfection, but still she had wanted to stay on, going back day after day to gaze at the marble perfection in the hallway of the Academia. He had grown impatient with her, 'Art my eye; it's sex, my girl, that's what it is, nothing more. And it's all right for you, but I'm left with nothing but those cow-eyed madonnas.'

He pointed out Stephen on the beach that day in Carraroe. 'Now you can recoup some of those lost lira. Off and wiggle your hips at him. He might take you out for a jar and then you could lend me the half dollar.'

Well, she had wiggled them. But that had been four years ago.

'Fatty, who are you trying to fool?' Stephen came over and put his hands on Liza's hips. 'Take them off,' he whispered, beginning to pull them down. She moved away gently, controlling her irritation. Stephen didn't usually mis-time things so badly. Energetically she began to unpack. 'Come on, darling, get dressed. We'll have an early dinner, and then an early night.' She tried to put warmth into her voice as she said it. As she got dressed she became conscious of her own ambivalence. What was wrong with her? Why the hell was she feeling like this? She realized that she had been narked with Stephen since they arrived at the airport. He was, somehow, an intrusion. Ironic thought, that, on your honeymoon. She smiled.

'I'll tell you what,' she turned towards him, taking his hand. 'Could we eat at Mario's, you know, the place I told you about. It's not very far away, and I'd really love to.'

Stephen never sulked. With grace and tolerance he indulged her, straightening a new olive tie with precision and kissing her with the friendliness and lack of warmth that he realized the moment demanded.

They left the hotel arm-in-arm and in the softening light walked the quarter of a mile to Mario's. It didn't seem to have changed at all in the last four years. It was still dark and small and surprisingly cool. Wine from Orvieto lay in barrels behind the bar. The smell of garlic mixed with cooking tomatoes. The bread lying in the baskets was coarse and wholesome. The clients were mostly family parties, slightly shabby, with one or two groups of students.

'You like it, Stephen?' Now that she had been pleased, Liza wanted Stephen to share her enthusiasm. The meal was solid and heavy as she remembered them, soup and pasta, chicken and salad. The salad dressing, like the water of the shower, had a familiar tang. They drank the harsh wine of Orvieto and grew gay and closer than they had been all day. The wine, red and thick, sent currents of ease and satisfaction coursing through their bodies. The enervating effect created an intimacy between them, as their two bodies sank in lassitude together. 'Let's have another glass of wine, and then go back. Remember, I said an early night'. This time Liza had no difficulty putting warmth into her voice. She was greatly relieved that her strange reluctance of the afternoon had disappeared. Now she wanted desperately, and suddenly, to go to bed with her husband. Her face grew red with passion, blood rushing to it as she looked at him across the table. His eyes met hers and locked, then broke away again. It was a glance of animal awareness, subtle yet blatant, a glance that could not be misinterpreted. Liza realized with amazement and delight that even after marriage the ritual of courtship must always be renewed before each new onslaught.

So involved had they become, one with another, that their consciousness had shrunk, and included now only the table, with its little pool of light encircling the two of them. Suddenly their island became an isthmus, as a street band, of the type one sees so often in Rome, entered the restaurant and made its way in a straggling line towards the couple, picking out tourists with ease. The accordions were insistent and discordant. Liza looked up, annoyance on her face. But could it be? Was it possible after four years? Enrico! The monkey face was an ancient and nut-like as ever; the tiny body still supported the huge accordion, as by a miracle. On one occasion she and Jonny had spent a whole night with Enrico. They had ended up in a dirty little trattoria behind the Forum, with Enrico producing half-a-dozen conceited Italian boys as possible suitors for Liza, and lamenting the fact, with laudable insincerity, that he, alas, was too old.

'Enrico, Enrico, you remember me? Liza, *Irlandesa*?' Enrico had obviously no idea who she was, but he gallantly took off his hat, swept a bow and said, 'Of course ... of course, *bella, pui bella.*' He kissed her hand, and began to play, a sentimental Sicilian tune. Stephen ordered more wine, they sat together, they talked. For hours they talked, the ridiculous, extravagant Roman bonhomie, false and seductive, replacing the limitations of words.

As they strolled back to the hotel, Liza was a little unsteady on her feet. Stephen took her arm, guided her. In the lobby she stopped. 'You go on up, Stephen, I'm going to phone Jonny.'

'Darling, are you crazy, it's one o'clock in the morning. They'll all be in bed.'

'No, I'm going to phone him, I must.'

'Really Liza, this is absurd, come on now ...'

'Oh please, Stephen,' she repeated to him.

'Well alright,' he sighed, 'I'll wait for you here.'

'No,' her voice was sharp. 'Leave me alone. Go up to bed, I told you I'd be up afterwards.' She noticed that Stephen looked surprised and hurt. His back seemed somehow vulnerable as he walked towards the stairs.

It took an age to get through to Dublin. The hotel porter who was helping her and the Roman operator seemed to chatter endlessly, laughing and joking. But Liza did not mind. She sat and savoured the Roman night. She remembered. How delighted Jonny would be that she had met Enrico again. The Dublin operator sounded cheerful. And finally she heard her own phone ring. It rang for a long time.

'I'm sorry, Rome, no reply.'

'Keep trying, please, just for another while.'

It rang out again, and then a cross voice said, 'Yes, who is it?'

She didn't wait for the Dublin operator. 'Jonny, it's me, Liza.'

'Liza, my God, what's wrong? Are you alright? Has something happened to Stephen?' His voice was no longer sleepy, but anxious as he fired the quick succession of questions.

'Don't be silly, Jonny, everything's fine, I'm in Rome. Rome, Jonny. And guess who I met tonight? Enrico!'

'Enrico who? For God's sake, Liza, shut up and stop wasting time. What *is* the matter?'

'I told you, nothing. I just wanted to ring to tell you that I met Enrico tonight. You remember the man who played the accordion in that restaurant, Mario's. I thought you'd be interested. You know . . .'

'Good God, Liza, have you gone mad? Ringing me at this hour of the night about nothing. Where's Stephen?'

'Upstairs waiting for me in our room.'

'Well, go to bed yourself, for goodness sake. Do you hear me Liza?' His voice was stern and uninterested.

'Yes, Jonny. *Buona séra*.'

Quietly she put down the phone.

'*Grazie*,' she said to the night porter, gave him the money and sat once more in the lobby.

She sat and thought. She sat for a long time. A calmness settled on her as she examined her position. So she wasn't nineteen any more and her jeans didn't fit. She felt sad, but it was a pleasant nostalgic sadness. Life, she supposed, would be lived as a woman from now on. Perhaps it had always been so. It was hard to say. But one had certain consolations, had achieved certain realizations. For a short time, she had been mistress of her flesh. For a short time, she had come into her own. Once, when she was nineteen and a virgin in Rome. With a brother and no money and tight blue jeans.

Sean O'Faolain

A DEAD CERT

Whenever Jenny Rosse came up to Dublin, for a shopping spree, or a couple of days with the Ward Union Hunt, or to go to the Opera, or to visit some of her widespread brood of relations in or around the city, or to do anything at all just to break the monotony of what she would then mockingly call 'my life in the provinces', the one person she never failed to ring was Oweny Flynn; and no matter how busy Oweny was in the courts or in his law chambers he would drop everything to have a lunch or a dinner with her. They had been close friends ever since he and Billy Rosse – both of them then at The King's Inns – had met her together twelve or thirteen years ago after a yacht race at The Royal Saint George. Indeed, they used to be such a close trio that, before she finally married Billy and buried herself in Cork, their friends were always laying bets on which of the two she would choose, and the most popular version of what happened in the end was that she let them draw cards for her. 'The first man,' she had cried gaily, 'to draw the ace of hearts!' According to this account the last card in the pack was Billy's, and before he turned it she fainted. As she was far from being a fainter this caused a great deal of wicked speculation about which man she had always realized she wanted. On the other hand one of her rivals said that she had faked the whole thing to get him.

This Saturday afternoon in October she and Oweny had finished a long, gossipy lunch at the Shelbourne, where she always stayed whenever she came up to Dublin. ('I hate to be tied to my blooming relatives!') They were sipping their coffee and brandy in two deep, saddleback armchairs, the old flowery chintzy kind that the Shelbourne always provided. The lounge was empty and, as always after wine, Oweny had begun to flirt mildly with her, going back over the old days, telling her, to her evident satisfaction, how lonely it is to be a bachelor of thirty-seven ('My life trickling away into the shadows of memory!'), and what a fool he had been to let such a marvellous lump of a girl slip through his fingers, when, all of a sudden, she leaned forward, and tapped the back of his hand like a dog pawing for still more attention.

'Oweny!' she said. 'I sometimes wish my husband would die for a week.'

For a second he stared at her in astonishment. Then, in a brotherly kind of voice, he said, 'Jenny! I hope there's nothing wrong between you and Billy?'

She tossed her red head at the very idea.

'I'm as much in love with Billy as ever I was! Billy is the perfect husband. I wouldn't change him for worlds.'

'So I should have hoped,' Oweny said, dutifully, if a bit stuffily. 'I mean, of all the women in the world you must be one of the luckiest and happiest that ever lived. Married to a successful barrister. Two splendid children. How old is Peter now? Eight? And Anna must be ten. There's a girl who is going to be a breaker of men's hearts and an engine of delight. Like,' he added, remembering his role, 'her beautiful mother. And you have that lovely house at Silverspring. With that marvellous view down the Lee . . .'

'You can't live on scenery!' she interposed tartly. 'And there's a wind on that river that'd cool a tomcat!'

'A car of your own. A nanny for the kids. Holidays abroad every year. No troubles or trials that I ever heard of. And,' again remembering his duty, 'if I may say so, every time we meet, you look younger, and,' he plunged daringly, 'more desirable than ever. So, for God's sake, Jenny Rosse, what the hell on earth are you talking about?'

She turned her head to look out pensively at the yellowing sun glittering above the last, trembling, fretted leaves of the trees in the Green, while he gravely watched her, admiring the way its light brought out the copper gold of her hair, licked the flat tip of her cocked nose and shone on her freckled cheek that had always reminded him of peaches and cream, and 'No,' he thought, 'not a pretty woman, not pretty-pretty, anyway I never did care for that kind of prettiness, she is too strong for that, too much vigour. I'm sure she has poor old Billy bossed out of his life!' And he remembered how she used to sail her water-wag closer to the wind than any fellow in the yacht club, and how she used to curse like a trooper if she slammed one into the net, always hating to lose a game, especially to any man, until it might have been only last night that he had felt that aching hole in his belly when he knew that he had lost her for ever. She turned her head to him and smiled wickedly.

'Yes,' she half agreed. 'Everything you say is true but ...'

'But what?' he asked curiously, and sank back into the trough of his armchair to receive her reply.

Her smile vanished.

'Oweny! You know exactly how old I am. I had my thirty-fourth birthday party last week. By the way, I was very cross with you that you didn't come down for it. It was a marvellous party. All Cork was at it. I felt like the Queen of Sheba. It went on until about three in the morning. I enjoyed every single minute of it. But, the next day, I got the shock of my life! I was sitting at my dressing-table brushing my hair.' She stopped dramatically, and pointed her finger tragically at him as if his face were her mirror. 'When I looked out the window at a big, red, grain boat steaming slowly down the river, out to sea, I stopped brushing, I looked at myself, there and then I said, "Jenny Rosse! You are in your thirty-fifth year. And you've never had a lover!" And I realized that I never could have a lover, not without hurting Billy, unless he obliged me by dying for a week.'

For fully five seconds Oweny laughed and laughed.

'Wait,' he choked, 'until the lads at the club hear this one!'

The next second he was sitting straight up in his armchair.

'Jenny,' he said stiffly, 'would you mind telling me why exactly you chose to tell this to me?'

'Aren't you interested?' she asked innocently.

'Isn't it just a tiny little bit unfair?'

'But Billy would never know he'd been dead for a week. At most he'd just think he'd lost his memory or something. Don't you suppose that's what Lazarus thought? Oh! I see what you mean. Well, I suppose yes, I'd have betrayed Billy. That's true enough, isn't it?'

'I am not thinking of your good husband. I am thinking of the other unfortunate fellow when this week would be out!'

'What other fellow? Are you trying to suggest that I've been up to something underhand?'

'I mean,' he pressed on, quite angry now, 'that I refuse to believe that you are mentally incapable of realizing that if you ever did let any other man fall in love with you for even five minutes, not to speak of a whole week, you would be sentencing him to utter misery for the rest of his life.'

'Oh, come off it!' she huffed. 'You always did take things in High C. Why are you so bloody romantic? It was just an idea. I expect lots of women have it only they don't admit it. One little, measly wild oat? It's probably something I should have done before I got married, but,' she grinned happily, 'I was too busy then having a good time. "In the morning sow thy seed and in the evening withhold not thine hand." Ecclesiastes. I learned that at Alexandra College. Shows you how innocent I was – I never knew what it really meant until I got married. Of course, you men are different. You think of nothing else.'

He winced.

'If you mean me,' he said sourly, 'you know damned well that I never wanted any woman but you.'

When she laid her hand on his he knew that they both understood why she had said that about Billy dying for a week. When he snatched his hand away and she gathered up her gloves with all the airs of a woman at the end of her patience with a muff, and strode ahead of him to glare at the levelling sun outside the hotel, he began to wonder if he really had understood, and he began to wonder if he had upset her with all that silly talk about old times. But a side-glance caught a look in her eyes that was much more mocking than hurt and at once his anger returned. She had been doing much more than flirting. Had she just wanted to challenge him? Close-hauling? Whatever she was doing she had manoeuvred him into a ridiculous position. Then he thought, 'Now, she will drive to Cork tonight and I will never be certain what she really meant.' While he boggled she started talking brightly about her holiday plans for the winter. A cover-up? She said she was going to Gstaad for the skiing next month with a couple of Cork friends.

'Billy doesn't ski, so he won't come. We need another man. Would you like to join us? They are nice people. Jim Chandler and his wife. About our age. You'd enjoy them.'

He said huffily that he was too damned busy; and she might not know it but some people in the world have to earn their living; anyway, he was saving up for two weeks' sailing in the North Sea in June; at which he saw that he had now genuinely hurt her. ('Dammit, if we really were lovers this would be our first quarrel!') He forced a smile.

'Is this goodbye, Jenny? You did say at lunch that you were going to drive home this evening? Shan't I see you again?'

She looked calculatingly at the sun now shivering coldly behind the far leaves.

'I hate going home. I mean so soon. I hate driving alone in the dark. I think I'll just go to bed after dinner and get up bright and early on Sunday morning before the traffic. I'll be back at Silverspring in time for lunch.'

'If you are doing nothing tonight why don't you let me take you to dinner at the Yacht Club?'

She hesitated. Cogitating the long road home?

'Do come, Jenny! They'd all love to see you. It will be like old times. You remember the Saturday night crowds?'

She spoke without enthusiasm.

'So be it. Let's do that.'

She presented her freckled cheek for his parting kiss. In

frank admiration he watched her buttocks swaying provocatively around the corner of Kildare Street.

Several times during the afternoon, back in his office, he found himself straying from his work to her equivocal words. Could there, after all, be something wrong between herself and Billy? Could she be growing tired of him? It could happen, and easily: a decent chap, fair enough company, silent, a bit slow, not brilliant even at his own job, successful only because of his father's name and connexions, never any good at all at sport. He could easily see her flying down the Eggli at half a mile a minute, the snow powder leaping from her skis when she would be doing a Christy. But not Billy: he would be down by the railway station paddling around like a duck among the beginners – and he remembered what a hopeless sheep he had always been with the girls, who nevertheless seemed to flock around him all the time, perhaps (it was the only explanation he ever found for it) because he was the sort of shy, fumbling kind of fellow that awakens the maternal instinct in girls. At which he saw her, not as a girl in white shorts dashing on the tennis courts, but as the splendidly mature woman who had turned his face into her mirror by crying along her pointing finger, 'You are in your thirty-fifth year!'

How agile, he wondered, would she now be on the ski-slopes? He rose and stood for a long time by his window, glaring down at the Saturday evening blankness of Nassau Street, and the deserted playing fields of Trinity College, and the small lights of the buses moving through the blueing dusk, until he shivered at the cold creeping through the pane, and felt the tilt of time and the failing year, and in excitement understood her sudden lust.

As always on Saturday nights, once the autumn came and the sailing finished, the lounge and the bar of the club were a cascade of noise and, if he had been alone, he would at once have added his bubble of chatter to it. He stood proudly beside the finest woman in the crowd, covertly watching her smiling around her, awaiting attention from her rout, (What was that great line? *Diana's foresters, gentlemen of the shades, minions of the moon?*) until, suddenly, alerted and disturbed, he found her eyes turning from the inattentive mob to look out unsmilingly to where the lighthouse on the pier's end was writing slow circles on the dusty water of the harbour. He said, 'Jenny, you are not listening to me?' and was bewildered when she whispered, 'But I don't know a single one of these young people!' He pointed out the commodore, whom she should have remembered from the old days. She peered and said, 'Not *that* old man?' He said, 'How could you have forgotten?' The 'old man' had not forgotten as he found when he went to the bar to refresh their drinks.

'Isn't that Jenny Rosse you have there?' he asked Oweny. 'She's putting on weight, bedad! Ah, she did well for herself.'

'How do you mean?' Oweny asked, a bit shortly.

'Come off it. Didn't she marry one of the finest practices in Cork! Handsome is as handsome does, my boy! She backed a dead cert.'

It washed off his back. Jealous old bastard! As he handed her the glass she asked idly, 'Who is that strong looking girl in blue, she is as brown as if she has been sailing all summer?' He looked.

'One of the young set. I think she's George Whitaker's daughter.'

'That nice looking chap in the black tie? He looks the way Billy used to look. Who is he?'

'Saturday nights!' he said impatiently. 'You know the way they bring the whole family, it gives their wives a rest from the cooking.'

It was a relief to lead her into the dining-room and to find her mood suddenly change to complete happiness.

'So this,' she laughed, 'is where it all began. And look! The same old paintings. They haven't changed a thing.'

The wine helped, and now safely islanded in their corner, even the families baying cheerfully at one another from table to table, though she got on his nerves by dawdling so long over the coffee, even asking for a second pot, that the maids had cleared every table but theirs, before she revealed her mood by saying:– 'Oweny! Please let's go somewhere else for our nightcap.'

'But where?' he said irritably. 'Some scruffy pub?'

'Or your flat?' she suggested, and his hopes beamed like a water lily. They shrivelled when she stepped out ahead of him into the cold night air, looked up at the three-quarter moon, and then at the Town Hall clock, and said, 'What a stunning night! Oweny, I've changed my mind. Just give me a good strong coffee and I'll drive home right away.'

'So,' he said miserably, 'we squabbled at lunch, and our dinner was a flop.'

She protested that it had been a marvellous dinner; and wasn't it grand the way nothing had been changed, 'They even still have that old picture of the Duke of Windsor when he was a boy in the navy.' He gave up. He had lost the set. All the way into town she only spoke once.

'We had good times,' she said. 'I could do it all over again.'

'And I suppose change nothing?' he growled.

Her answer was pleasing, but inconclusive – 'Who knows?'

If only he could have her in the witness box, under oath, for fifteen minutes!

In his kitchenette, helping him to make the coffee, she became so full of good spirits (because, he understood dourly, she was about to take off for home) that he thrust an arm about her waist, assaulted her cheek with a kiss as loud as a champagne cork, and said fervently (he had nothing to lose now), 'And I thinking how marvellous it would be if we could be in bed together all night!' She laughed mockingly, handed him the coffee pot, a woman long accustomed to the grappling hook, and led the way with the cups back into his living-room. They sat on the small sofa before his coffee table.

'And I'll tell you another thing, Jenny!' he said, 'If I had this flat twelve years ago it might very easily have happened that you would have become my one true love! You would have changed and crowned my whole life.'

Had she heard him? She had let her head roll back on the carved moulding of the sofa and was looking out past him at the moon. Quickly he kissed her mouth. Unstirring she looked back into his eyes, whispered, 'I should not have let you do that,' returned her eyes to the moon, and whispered, 'Or should I?'

'Jenny!' he coaxed. 'Close your eyes, and let's pretend we really are back twelve years ago.'

Her eyelids sank. He kissed her again, very softly, felt her hand creep to his shoulder and impress his kiss, felt her lips fall apart, her hand fall weakly away, desire climb into his throat, and then, he heard her softly moan the disenchanting name. He drew back, rose, and looked helplessly down at her until she opened her eyes, stared uncomprehendingly around her, and looked up at him in startled recognition.

'So,' he said bitterly, 'he did not die even for one minute.'

She laughed wryly, and lightly, and stoically, a woman who would never take anything in a high key, except a five-barred gate or a double-ditch.

'Whenever I dream of having a lover I always find myself at the last moment in my husband's arms.'

She jumped up, snatched her coat and turned furiously on him.

'Why the hell, for God's sake, don't you go away and get married?'

'To have me dreaming about you? Is that what you really want?'

'To put us both out of pain!'

They glared hatefully at one another.

'Please drive me to the Shelbourne. I want to get on the road right away.'

They drove to the Green without a word, she got out, slammed the car door behind her and raced into the hotel. He whirled, drove hell for leather back to the club, killed the end of the night with the last few gossipers, drank far too much and lay awake for hours staring sideways from his pillow over the grey, frosting roofs and countless yellow chimney pots of Dublin.

Past twelve. In her yellow sports Triumph she would tear across the Curragh at seventy and along the two straight stretches before and after Monasterevan. By now she has long since passed through Port Laoise and Abbey-leix where only a few lighted upper storey windows still resisted sleep. From that, for hour after hour, south and south, every village street and small town she passes will be fast asleep, every roadside cottage, every hedge, field and tree, and the whole, widespread moonblanched country pouring past her headlights until she herself gradually becomes hedge, tree, field, greenness and fleeting moon. Hedges, arched branches underlit by her headlights, old demesne walls, a closed garage, a grey church, a lifeless gate-lodge, all motionless until the black rock and ruin of Cashel comes slowly wheeling about the moon. A street lamp falling on a black window makes it still more black. Cars parked beside a kerb huddle from the cold. In Cahir the boarded windows of the old granaries are blind with age, its dull square empty. Her wheeling lights flash the vacant eyes of the hotel, leap the humpbacked bridge, fleck the side of the Norman castle. She is doing seventy again on the level, windy uplands of the Galtee mountains, heedless of the sleep-wrapt plain that slopes for miles and miles away to her left.

Why is she stopping? To rest, to look, to listen? He can see nothing for her to see but a scatter of mushroom farmhouses on the plain, hear nothing but one sleepless dog as far away as the lofty moon. He lights his bedside lamp. Turned half past two. He puts out his light and there are her kangaroo lights, leaping, climbing, dropping, winding, slowing now because of the twisting strain on her arms. She does not see the sleeping streets of Fermoy; only the white signpost marking the remaining miles to Cork. Her red tail-lights disappear and reappear before him every time she winds and unwinds, down to the sleeping estuary of the low-tide Lee, not so much a river as lough, cold, grey, turbulent and empty. He tears after her as she rolls smoothly westward beside its shining slobland. Before them low, bruised clouds hung over her lighted city, silently awaiting the silent morning.

She brakes to turn in between her white gates, her wheels spit back the gravel, she zooms upward to her house and halts under its staring windows. She switches off the engine, struggles out, stretches her arms high above her head with a long, shivering, happy, outpouring groan, and then, breathing back a long breath, she holds her breasts up to her windows. There is not a sound but the metal of her engine creaking as it cools, and a cold, small wind whispering up from the river. She laughs to see their cat flow like black water around the corner of the house. She leans into the car, blows three long, triumphant horn blasts, and before two windows can light up over her head she has disappeared indoors as smoothly as her cat. And that, at last, it is the end of sleep, where, behind windows gone dark again, she spreads herself for love.

From the Liffey or the Lee neither of them hears the morning seagulls. He wakes unrefreshed to the sounds of late church bells. She half opens her eyes to the flickering light of the river on her ceiling, rolls over on her belly, and stretching out her legs behind her like a satisfied cat dozes off again. He stares for a long time at his ceiling hardly hearing the noise of the buses going by. It is cold. His mind is clear and cold. I know now what she wants. But does she? Let her lie. For a while longer.

She called me a romantic and she has her own fantasy. She has what she wanted, wants what she cannot have, is not satisfied with what she has got. I have known her for over twelve years and never known her at all. The most adorable woman I ever met. And a slut. If she had married me would she be dreaming now of him? Who was it said faithful women are always pondering on their fidelity, never on their husbands'? Die for a week? He chuckled at her joke. Joke? Or gamble? Or a dead cert? If I could make him die for a week it might be a hell of a long week for her. Should I write to her? I could telephone.

Hello, Jenny! It's me. I just wanted to be sure you got back safely the other night. Why wouldn't I worry? About anyone as precious as you? Those frosty roads. Of course it was, darling, a lovely meeting, and we must do it again. No, nothing changes. That's a dead cert. Oh, and Jenny! I nearly forgot. About that skiing bit next month in Gstaad. Can I change my mind? I'd love to join you. May I? Splendid! Oh, no! Not for that long. Say . . . Just for a week?

He could see her hanging up the receiver very slowly.